BLENDING OUT

BLENDING OUT

PRIYANKA BAGRODIA

NEW DEGREE PRESS

BLENDING OUT

ISBN   978-1-63676-832-8   *Paperback*

        978-1-63730-210-1   *Kindle Ebook*

        978-1-63730-276-7   *Ebook*

To my family,
my friends,
and the many wonderful people who saw me
when I couldn't see myself.

"I thought how unpleasant it is to be locked out;
and I thought how it is worse, perhaps, to be
locked in."

VIRGINIA WOOLF

CONTENTS

AUTHOR'S NOTE

———

I don't know if anyone's life plan goes as expected. Maybe it does for a select few, but it's safe to say mine has not exactly panned out as I thought it would. I am twenty-six, and yet, I am currently writing this novel from my childhood bedroom with my vast collection of Beanie Babies rooting me on as I type away.

Whenever someone asked twelve-year-old me what I wanted to be when I grew up, I'd always respond that I wanted to be successful. This answer was simultaneously brilliant and really dumb. Brilliant, because in theory, there was no way I could fail to achieve success if I were the one defining success, and dumb because the concept of success is obviously very nebulous; so, given a personality type like mine, every time someone would look down on me or look through me, I'd tell myself, "Still a long way to go." Unfortunately, it got to a point where I was having anxiety attacks because of the pressure I put on myself. I realized that either my mindset had to change or I had to get knee pads to make tucking my head between my knees more comfortable.

One day, when I was feeling quite blue, I came across an old journal of mine from the sixth grade. In it, I'd written an adaptation of William Blake's *The Tyger* poem. It centered on dragons and was completely ridiculous, but I loved it. I loved how twelve-year-old me was trying to process some feelings of vulnerability even then and had instinctively turned to writing as an outlet. I decided to start writing again, and as my journal entries multiplied in number, I gained ever-increasing clarity about myself and realized I was consistently discussing the same themes again and again. Over the last year, I have happily become comfortable enough with myself that I would like to share that journey with you, the reader.

I decided to make this work into one of fiction to create enough distance between me and the protagonist and give myself the breathing room to honestly discuss certain underlying concepts important to me. Although some things are dramatized and other things are just not true, this book at its core seeks to address the manner I used to give up parts of myself just to fit in. In the following pages, I discuss parts of my identity I love now but caused me a lot of inner turmoil over the years because I just felt off and like I didn't belong. If you've ever felt that internal struggle and discontent, I hope you'll find something to relate to in this book. If nothing else, I hope you'll enjoy Ryley's journey.

PART I

SEPTEMBER

———

CHAPTER 1

SEPTEMBER 2008

———

Ryley galloped into the kitchen, having smelled the mouth-watering combination of frying onion, oil, and spice wafting into her room. The aroma had effectively jarred her out of her bout of melancholia, induced by thoughts of what the day would hold. They had a giant shopping trip planned mainly because Ryley's mom had decided Ryley's current collection of clothing did not befit a tenth grader. Ryley would have preferred to skip the mall and instead do any number of things: play baseball—badly—with her brother Harrison in their backyard, read a book, or just hole up in her room and play one of her angsty bands on loop, appropriating the singer's heartbreak for herself. She was a girl of simple pleasures.

Nonetheless, Ryley made a good-faith effort to bury her resentment as she walked by her mother in the kitchen, shooting her a nice enough attempt at a smile. Her mother instinctively smiled back, but the smile transformed into a light grimace upon seeing Ryley's red capri pants and her white shirt with owls and a caption that said *love hoo you are*. She then very obviously looked Ryley up and down, immediately making her disapproval known in the downturn of her lips and the furrow of her delicate brow. Ryley ignored her, pretending obliviousness even as a little pool of uncertainty formed in her belly, causing her to tug at the shirt slightly riding up on her lanky frame. She had spent fifteen minutes deciding on the outfit and was a huge fan of owls. They reminded her of the owls that would sit outside her room at night as she lay in bed reading or daydreaming; sometimes, they'd hoot back and forth at each other past midnight.

"Are you sure you want to wear that to the mall?" her mom finally asked, never one to beat around the bush for long.

Ryley simply said, "Yeah," not bothering to defend her outfit choice. She knew the other teens at her prep school were moving on to nice sweaters and plain, flattering shirts, but she liked the owls.

Ryley's mom, still standing at the stove to char bread for them, provided no further response, so Ryley quickly and silently took her place by Harrison at the kitchen table. She then rapidly dug into the *poha* her mom had laid out for her. Ryley was almost proud of how quickly she scarfed down the mix of yellow, flattened rice, tomatoes, potatoes, and onions, all flavored with an intricate assortment of spices. In truth, the only thing at which she was remotely athletic was how fast she could tuck away food. Harrison, sitting to her right at the antique oak table, unsurprisingly made the easy, lazy joke that she ate as much as a teenage boy on a football team. She ignored him. Their father too kept his silence as he ate, reading the newspaper with an intensity and thoroughness in keeping with his position as an executive in finance.

Ryley looked back over at her mom, still cooking, even as the rest of the family began to eat. She chafed and startled inside, her heartbeat picking up, as she got a glimpse of a future that felt more real to her now. She'd seen the same dynamic in other Indian homes, and because her parents' Indian friends had recently begun asking her if she had a boyfriend, the idea of being made to be the nurturer, the caretaker, no longer felt as foreign and only reserved for actual grown-ups.

Eventually, her mother joined them, placing the bread down with a sigh and Ryley immediately hopped up, perhaps wanting to punish, absurdly, her mother for the role she played in all this. If her mother continued to perpetuate this gendered dynamic, she wouldn't get Ryley's company; however, before Ryley could complete her huff-off in style, her mother spoke again. "Ryley, please change. You look childish. Also, don't forget we need to stop at Claire's to get your ears pierced. I want you to be able to wear earrings at your cousin's wedding next month."

Ryley took several deep breaths in an attempt to control herself, but her anger rose too fast. It was the sort of tidal anger that welled up only when she felt powerless and trapped. She didn't like earrings and disliked jewelry in general. She'd let the holes in her ears close on purpose—her earlobes would turn red and irritated whenever she wore earrings as her body rejected the metal. Her mom had needed to badger her for an entire week before she'd agreed to get them re-pierced, so her poor ears could play unwilling host to the heavy ornate Indian earrings necessary for a wedding.

Everything was a show, and as long as she could remember, her parents had walked a fine tightrope, showing that even though they'd fully acclimated to America, they still valued and embraced their Indian heritage. There was Indian Mama and Papa Agarwal with their *salvar kamiz* and *saris*, boisterous Hindi, enjoyment of Indian songs and Bollywood, and emphasis on the proper hierarchy of a family; then there was American Mama and Papa Agarwal with their designer clothes, muted accents, and adoption of stiffness and aplomb, her dad emphasizing that he went to Wharton and was an executive at Merrill Lynch.

Ryley didn't see how they thought she could walk that same tightrope. She saw all the holes. Getting her ears pierced to wear Indian earrings for one day wouldn't make her any more connected to their (her?) Indian heritage. Even if she wore the boring prep school clothes her mom forced upon her, talking about visiting India with her mostly white classmates would ruin the thin veneer of protection afforded by any French designer shirt. She'd rather stay in Los Angeles or go to some place in Europe, like the rest of her cohort. An Indian going back to India was not cool, not like it would have been if she were white, if she could talk about it all with a comfortable sense of foreign wonder.

Ryley spent a good thirty seconds in a sort of test sulk in the aftermath of her mother's offhand, careless directive, but the grievances she'd been stockpiling in her head overwhelmed her. She took savage joy in finally breaking free and shedding the accommodating, easygoing skin starting to suffocate her.

"What business do you have telling me how to dress when you have more Indian clothes than American clothes? When people can't understand your accent half the time? When it's clear to everyone that you still don't belong here? That you'll only ever be just a transplant, an immigrant?" She let condescension color her voice as she called her mother an *immigrant*.

Her dad looked like he was going to explode with his heavy black eyebrows drawing close together over his dark brown eyes, even as his wide mouth, usually only smiling at her, contorted into an *O* as he drew in a breath to bellow at her. Her mother jumped in though, placing a calming hand on her father's arm even as she ordered Ryley to "get in the car." Ryley stayed frozen, waiting to see what would happen. Her mother always had a retort at the ready; she'd never been silent. Finally, after receiving nothing more than a glinting glare from her mother, a scowl from her father, and a neutral look from Harrison—because ostensible peace-keeper that he was, he never took sides—she ran from the table.

The car ride passed by in a blur as Ryley curled into herself, away from the hurt radiating from her mother, and then too soon, they were at the mall. The smell of Abercrombie & Fitch cologne overwhelmed her, fogging her mind, and she took short, shallow breaths to avoid inhaling too much of it. As they began the trek across the gray marble floor, Ryley focused on the plaintive, angsty tones of Lifehouse flowing forth from her headphones. Lifehouse was her favorite, stolen wholesale from her brother Harrison a good seven years ago and not let go of since. Her brother had moved on to Kanye and Coldplay with everyone else, but she considered herself a maverick, a cow in sheep's clothing (she couldn't possibly justify calling herself a wolf). She turned up the volume so her mom could hopefully hear how she was just "Hanging by a Moment;" the song was her current album favorite.

Ryley dragged her feet as they got closer to Claire's. Claire's was the quick stop ear-piercing place everyone went to, located on the first floor of the mall. Her mom overtook her easily, a rather common occurrence in spite of the fact her mother was a generally small woman and Ryley easily towered over her, all gangly arms and legs. But Ryley tended to walk slowly, mulling through things, as she let her feet absentmindedly carry her along. It drove her mother, whose middle name was efficiency, crazy.

Her mom let out a huff now as she turned to Ryley and said, "Do you want me to come in with you or not?"

Ryley shook her head, though she would have liked her mom to insist that yes, she would come. Her mom would have normally insisted and made it her problem, so Ryley could reluctantly and dramatically cave, but now, Ryley's mom just said, "Okay. I'll be at the Banana Republic on the second level."

As Ryley passed her mother, she wanted to skitter closer, touch her hand slightly, and then play it off as accidental, acting annoyed that her mother had invaded her space. They didn't fight, not like this, but it had been a long time coming: a culmination of too many underlying tensions simmering on broil unduly long. Ryley dragged herself through the door and into line, looking down at the floor as she replayed the words she'd said and let herself sink into the guilt.

Eventually, Ryley reached the front of the line and looked up to see a tall blond girl standing before her with low-cut jeans and a casual, white tank; they looked to be about the same age. Her name tag read *Sarah*, the *h* written to end in a playful loop. Sarah looked at her as much as through her and Ryley felt the immaturity of her outfit, of her person.

"Hi!" Ryley said loudly—too loud for the relative quietness of the store.

"Hey." The reply was bored and careless in delivery, a tone removed from the perky, cheerful one she had just used with the girl in line in front of Ryley.

"I'm here to get my ears pierced. I'm pretty old, I know, but I accidentally let the holes close because I just got bored with the earrings I had. But then I realized I should get my ears re-pierced because who doesn't like earrings? So, if you have some availability, I'd love to get them re-pierced. Maybe, also a cartilage piercing? What do you think?" If Ryley hadn't had to stop for air, she would've told the other girl she wanted to get her eyebrow pierced as well.

Sarah stared at her blankly and then after a prolonged pause, said, "Yeah, sure, I can pierce your ears for you, but I have to help these other customers first." She pointed at the line where five or six people were standing behind Ryley. Ryley saw another Claire's employee standing off to the side, texting on her phone. She wanted to ask about her but convinced herself that likely only Sarah was capable of piercing ears.

Ryley meandered around the bright purple store with its racks and racks of earrings, nail polish, and makeup, a supposed dreamland for a teenage girl. A gaggle of girls was huddled around the makeup display, applying eye shadow to each other in turns. Ryley looked down and away, drifting over to the birthday card rack instead and reading the messages inside. She looked back over at Sarah every three cards or so. Over the span of thirty cards, she saw Sarah lead two girls over to a white plastic chair to pierce their ears, even as the other Claire's employee took over at the register. Ryley pictured herself going over, asking what had happened commandingly, but she could just see her voice tremble instead and her hands shake. She was still standing there, trying to muster up the courage to do something, when her mom came in and agitatedly walked over to her.

"What's taking so long?" Her mother's tone was unusually curt, but it was naïve to have hoped her mom would have magically forgiven her after spending twenty minutes in Banana Republic.

"Nothing," Ryley muttered. "I was just about to go over to that employee, Sarah, to see what was going on. I think I was here before two girls who just got their ears pierced, but I'm not sure. Maybe they made appointments beforehand."

Her mom clicked her tongue and irritably said, "Stay here." She shook her head as she walked away. Her mother strode up to Sarah, cutting into her conversation with another girl. Ryley edged closer to them to overhear their conversation so as to appropriately calibrate how embarrassed she should be when she got into the chair.

"My daughter has been sitting over there for twenty minutes. There were two people in line before her when I left her, so I don't quite understand how she still hasn't been seen."

Sarah looked taken aback for a moment, as if not expecting this type of mother with this type of daughter. Ryley's mother was dressed in a manner very typical of a banker's wife, with her silk shirt tucked into form-fitting, dark-wash jeans, her petite stature augmented by heels. She had thick black hair, styled with dark brown highlights, and her caramel-brown skin, unadorned with wrinkles, belied her fifty years of age. Other than their skin color and hair, they looked nothing alike. Her mom had light eyebrows, usually penciled in, small, light brown eyes, and a thin, narrow nose and mouth set in an oval face. Ryley, in contrast, had a round face, thick dark eyebrows set over big dark brown eyes, a wide mouth, and a nose that the rest of her face hadn't yet grown into.

Sarah looked at Ryley once again as if to check that this pair actually went together and for a second, her mom and Sarah seemed to blur together, denizens of a world she could never hope to inhabit. Ryley wondered if it all really came down to presentation. To acting presumptuous, to acting white. Ryley had seen all the moms at her prep school act the same way.

Ryley's mom prompted Sarah impatiently, demanding, "Well? Why hasn't she been seen?"

Sarah fidgeted, played around with her thumb ring, and then eventually said, with an air of forced nonchalance, "Two girls came in with rush appointments. Your daughter didn't seem to be in any hurry and was going on about how she might want her cartilage pierced."

Her mother interrupted Sarah to scoff. "She doesn't want her cartilage pierced."

Sarah looked over at Ryley with a single eyebrow effortlessly raised. Ryley looked down at the floor.

Sarah turned back to her mother. "Okay, anyway, I didn't know how long all that would take, so I just saw people who would be quicker."

"Well, can you fit her in now or can *she* pierce my daughter's ears?" Ryley's mother pointed at the other employee standing off to the side.

"What?" Sarah asked innocently, her head cocked to the side. Her mother's accent tended to get thicker when she was flustered.

"Can the other employee pierce my daughter's ears?" Her mother carefully enunciated the words, her voice frigid.

"Sure," Sarah said shortly.

As Charlie led Ryley over to the white chair, she looked apologetically at Ryley's mom and said, "Honestly, I'm not very good at piercings. Sarah's way better, which is why she normally handles them. I think she's just in an off mood today."

Charlie only looked at Ryley's mom as she spoke, not acknowledging Ryley once. They knew Ryley didn't belong in their world even if her mother seemed to be a question mark for them.

Her mother tightened her jaw and then curtly said, "Never mind. We'll go elsewhere." Turning to Ryley, she said, her voice soft, "Ryley, come on." She lightly rested her hand on Ryley's arm and gave it a quick squeeze before letting her fingers trail down the arm, soothing the nerves she knew would already be aflame. The look in her mom's eyes frustrated her; Ryley didn't want her pity.

Ryley shook her hand off and strode out of the store rapidly, not daring to make eye contact with anyone. Maybe it was worth it to make the effort; to dress like them, to dress like her mom. To at least try to lean into being the same.

CHAPTER 2

SEPTEMBER 2018

———

Ryley walked rapidly, matching her steps to the electronic beat thrumming in her ears; she let herself feel the rhythm, internalize the singer's confidence. Today was her first day of orientation at Harvard Law School, and she felt like her whole life had been building up to this point. She had finally arrived, attending a hallowed institution whose very name caused every one of her parents' friends to say, "You must be so happy." She supposed she was; she didn't know. Regardless, she strutted along now. She would have preferred her heeled boots over the flats she had on; she liked how her boots' startlingly loud staccato strike pattern sounded indoors. Unfortunately, the boots would have looked a bit out of place in late-summer, muggy Cambridge, so she'd gone with her floral designer flats, paired with a dark-blue shirt dress instead. Perhaps it was better that she'd been forced to go with the dress—it did a good job of projecting fun and casual. She repeated aloud that she was the epitome of relatable as she moseyed along in the general direction of campus.

The main building was imposing enough with its white limestone façade but not unduly so. The arches framing the entryway were free of Latin, free of ostentation, and formed three upside-down Us at a reasonable, friendly height. Maybe it wouldn't be so bad. Maybe everyone would be nice and laid-back.

She momentarily paused outside the building, shooting a quick prayer up to the sky, before skipping up the three small steps and sliding through the already-open doors. Her flats slapped gently against the blue and gray tiled floor as she looked around. The corridor was flanked by classrooms to the left and small seating areas to the right. The walls were composed of wooden panels, the light brown shade surprisingly warm although the comfort of the color was offset by the dramatic black and white framed faces of storied professors lining the walls. Clumps of students were scattered along the corridor; she scanned their faces as she walked past, curious to get a sense of her classmates. The make-up aligned with that of past institutions she'd attended: a sea of white with a splash of color here and there. She was unsurprised and slightly appeased by the normalcy of it all.

When she finally reached the reception area, she reluctantly pulled out her headphones, immediately opening herself up to an overwhelming influx of chatter and high-pitched *how are yous*. She was amazed so many people seemed to know each other already. Two seconds later, unwilling to just blankly stare at the check-in people as she waited for the line to move, she pulled out her phone. Fortunately, the screen wasn't blank; she had good luck texts from her mom and a couple of friends from college. She typed slowly, writing out an essay in response to each person, partly because she'd never learned how to be concise and partly to kill time. At least the people directly in front of her were also similarly consumed by their phones.

Three essays later, she glanced up to get her bearings and see if the line had moved at all. Only four more people to go. She began to study the portrait of a professor hanging up on the wall opposite her. He had been captured mid-lecture with his mouth slightly agape. She wondered if the intensity in his eyes was real or staged. She would have liked to ask him how he liked his life and if he'd known what he wanted to do from a young age or if he'd just slotted into it because he was good at it.

Before she got too carried away by her profundity, Ryley found herself compelled to look to her right. A girl was leaning adjacent to one of the frames, staring at her. Ryley calmly waited for the girl to look away, as polite people did. The girl didn't, slouched against the wall with her arms folded in front of her like a shield. She looked to be a mish-mash of different ethnicities. She was pretty, with olive skin, a narrow face, prominent, dark brown eyes, and an aristocratic nose; she was dressed in light-wash high-waisted jeans and a white crop top that spoke of her willingness to make a statement.

As Ryley watched, the girl let her eyes drift down to clearly linger on Ryley's knee. Unwillingly, Ryley looked down and saw that it was ashy and looked dry and ill-moisturized because *of course*, she must have knocked it against a wall when she was doing her power-walk over. She quickly brushed at her knee and then looked back over at the check-in table, hoping the red on the tips of her ears was adequately covered by her hair. She didn't look back over at the girl, except there was Harrison, suddenly walking toward them with his eyes focused on her newly-found arch-nemesis—Ryley was potentially jumping the gun in labeling her so, but having an arch-nemesis was something she thought Law School Ryley should have.

As he neared them, he loudly exclaimed, "Olivia!" He was a second-year at Harvard but had transferred from Cornell, so he was as new to the school as Ryley was. Ryley wasn't surprised he'd somehow already made a friend.

Ryley let them chatter away for a minute or so before poking her body halfway out of line and interjecting with a nonchalant, "Harrison." She impressed herself with the careless way she said his name.

"Rye Bread?" he exclaimed. After pausing to give his shock its requisite due, he asked, "What are the odds I bump into my little sister two feet from my new best friend?"

Ryley shrugged in response, having nothing to say. She glanced over at Olivia, wanting to be formally introduced. She hoped he'd scrap the nickname; Rye Bread was pretty homey and she sounded like a dumpling person. Besides, he no longer had the right to refer to her with such familiarity. They didn't have that relationship anymore; they hadn't had it since she was in high school.

He followed her gaze to Olivia and immediately said, "Olivia, this is my sister, Ryley. She's a One-L here."

Ryley had learned One-L meant first-year from Harrison when he had been going through it. He'd made a show of huffing out irritably the two times Ryley had asked how "first-year" was going during the two times they'd talked in the last year. Ryley had said "first-year" the second time on purpose.

Olivia gave her a smile and a nod of acknowledgment, chirping out "Hi!" as if she hadn't just been eyeing Ryley's scuffed-up knee.

"Hi," Ryley said, stretching her lips just enough to give Olivia a semblance of a smile. Ryley turned back to Harrison. "So how do you two know each other?"

"We're both transfers," Olivia said, responding for Harrison and comfortably setting the dynamic. Turning to Harrison, Olivia asked, "What time did you get back yesterday?"

"Late last night." Harrison had moved in a couple of weeks early and had then embarked upon a two-week road trip with Genie, his girlfriend of two years. Apparently, he'd just gotten back. Ryley had yet to meet Genie. All she knew was that Genie seemed to be an Instagram influencer of some kind.

"Ryley, did your move go okay too?" Harrison queried.

"Yeah," she said shortly. Her mother had come out and helped her. They could have used Harrison's six-one frame and his bodega-store owner vibe when two Bostonians had seen their out-of-state license plate on the rental car and said, "We don't need more outsiders. Get out of here."

Harrison opened his mouth to ask a follow-up, but Olivia interjected once again. "I think you're about to be up. It was nice meeting you." She softened her dismissal with a pleasant enough smile.

In spite of herself, Ryley liked Olivia's confidence and the easy way she took charge; however, determined to have the last word, even though the man in front of her *was* wrapping up, Ryley looked over at Harrison and said, "We should get a coffee soon. Catch up."

He responded, "Yeah, definitely," recognizing her statement for what it was and content to keep any future plans to meet up vague.

Ryley stepped forward to the check-in table. She kept her posture straight and her shoulders back throughout and upon receiving her documents, gave the woman her careful, practiced smile. Ryley wished she could put her headphones back in and get that power walk back as she followed the woman's instructions up the stairs to the temporary breakfast room, but she should play up her approachability.

As soon as she entered the room, she made a beeline for the food, all the better to center herself and get her bearings. An astonishing number of people were packed into what was essentially a glorified conference hall with small high-top tables sprinkled throughout. The crimson carpet and matching curtains might have been a bit overkill, but she supposed the school had a brand to uphold and a favorite color to honor.

Most of the easy-to-eat food was gone—she'd timed her arrival to be on the tail-end of what she imagined would be an uncomfortable meet and greet—and so she made do with snagging the rather pathetic dilapidated bagel sitting there by itself, taken as much out of pity as desire.

She began to slowly and meticulously apply cream cheese to the bagel, but no sooner had she finished with the spread than she was scraping the cream cheese off the bagel and into a napkin. She would not be the putz walking around with cream cheese on her dress. She scoped out the room as she made quick work of the bagel. A couple of tables had huddles that had already progressed from acquaintanceship to best friendship across the span of the morning. Their bodies were turned inward and toward each other; further newcomers were not welcome nor needed. She continued her quick skim of the room and saw a couple more manageable circles to the right, the mélange of bodies replete with welcoming empty spaces. One circle was predominantly white, the other predominantly East Asian and Indian. She walked over to the one predominantly white.

Arriving at the outer bounds of the circle, she slipped in between two boys and plastered a generic, pleasant expression onto her face, asking politely, "Hi! Can I join?"

The two nearest her instantly chorused, "Of course!" Everyone was all smiles on this first day of orientation. Ryley was denied any opportunity to make an introduction though; the blonde across from her didn't stop talking.

"All I'm trying to say is that the Justice's opinion in the immigration ban case, while eloquent in delivery, was not based in context. It was good that the dissent brought up *Korematsu*." The girl was wearing a red sundress straight out of a Kip Moore country song, with her Ray-Bans still perched atop her head and the tan from summer lending a natural bronzing to her skin. Her face was broad and her eyes spaced widely around a dainty, flat nose, before it tapered to end in the form of a neat, small mouth and pointed chin.

In the momentary silence that followed the girl's words, Ryley hurriedly interjected, "Cool, yes. Anyway, hi, I'm Ryley." She punctuated her introduction with an insipid, little hand wave. If she'd had any idea what she was going on, perhaps she could have acknowledged the blond girl's point with some witty rejoinder. She just wanted to get her introduction out of the way.

A doe-eyed brunette quickly glanced at the blonde before introducing herself as Sophie.

The blond girl noticeably flinched at Sophie's squeal of an introduction before saying assertively, "I'm Cassidy, Cass to my friends. Where were you before this?"

Ryley replied, "DC."

"What'd you do there?"

"Drink." The word dropped out almost reflexively.

Sophie and a couple of others chuckled, but she was met with an unimpressed look from Cassidy.

Grimacing slightly, Ryley said, "Just kidding. I worked in consulting. What about you all? Are you from DC as well?"

She directed this last sentence to a boy to the left of her. He looked like a DC-type with his black Warby Parker spectacles and his generally clean-cut look. His blond hair was neatly combed and his button-down shirt carefully pressed. Nerdy, but too confident and self-assured to be labeled as such.

He responded, "Yep, good call! I'm Zeke by the way."

Ryley gave herself a mental pat on the back. From what she'd heard, no one else here would be doing it for her.

Sophie chimed in, "Oh, I love DC; there's always so much to do! I used to love going to Tryst—that cafe in Dupont Circle—on Sundays."

Ryley quickly latched onto the shared point of commonality. "Oh, nice. I used to go there all the time too!"

Zeke scoffed. "Basic."

Ryley ignored him—he was already looking at Cassidy to check her reaction—and continued along with Sophie instead. "Where else did you go in DC?"

As Sophie began listing places, Zeke's too-cool-for-school demeanor proved too hard for him to maintain, and soon he was sharing memories from places much more *basic* than Tryst.

Ryley chimed in with her own stories, naturally embellished to make an eleven p.m. night a two a.m. night, a concert in which she was high off the electronic beat a concert in which she was high off of so much more, and a two-month barely-there relationship a one-year on-and-off affair. She never spoke for long though, providing only enough detail to hint that she was so much more than whatever they, whatever Cassidy, thought the average Indian Harvard Law student consisted of before throwing the conversation back to Sophie and Zeke. Ryley only looked at Sophie and Zeke as she spoke, knowing she was rankling certain members of the group, but she kept her hands from fidgeting nervously by loosely clasping them together in front of her. And even though she never looked at Cassidy, she saw Cassidy re-calibrating out of the corner of her eye, glancing down again at Ryley's floral flats and giving Ryley's watch a second look.

Cassidy eventually interrupted their DC talk, clapping her hands to get their attention. "How about we include everyone? Has anyone checked out the Cambridge restaurant scene yet? During Admitted Students Weekend, my boyfriend and I went to a couple of restaurants in Harvard Square, but none of them were great."

Sophie responded, "Oh, my boyfriend and I checked out Felipe's! We liked it, but we're not exactly high-class."

Zeke responded, "Oh, yeah, not high-class over here either. My girlfriend and I went to Felipe's too."

Ryley would have liked to say her on-and-off boyfriend and she had gone to Felipe's as well, but that really would be taking a two-month affair too far. Regardless, that topic of conversation seemed to die quickly because no one had done anything in Cambridge beyond go to Felipe's with their significant other. Most of them were transplants; from what Ryley could gather, only one of them had gone to Harvard for undergrad. Luckily, even as the last dregs of conversation drained away, a newcomer joined.

Zeke clapped him on the back. "Oh, Cassidy, you worked as a paralegal for Carson & Kline, right? Brad here worked there too."

Cassidy nodded and almost immediately, the newcomer, Brad, asked for a quick primer on what everyone did before getting into Harvard, prompting everyone to stand at attention.

Ryley presented her very standard and unimaginative background as "two years in consulting," delivered with a shrug. Others threw out consultant and paralegal with the same sort of dismissiveness, but all clearly had their ears perked to hear about the expected Rhodes or Marshall Scholar, the McKinsey consultant, or the math PhD. Indeed, when the title of Rhodes Scholar was inevitably dropped, her fellow classmates delivered, in impressive synchronization, hums of admiration, even as they couldn't help but shuffle their feet.

After the last person in the circle had spoken, Sophie said, "I'm so nervous. Everyone here is so smart."

Everyone else, the Rhodes Scholar included, immediately and instinctively nodded. Ryley's nod came two seconds too late. Cassidy, of course, noted that and narrowed her eyes—a shade of brown that would have been friendly on any other person—evaluating Ryley as if to see whether the hesitation had come from arrogance or inattentiveness. Ryley held her gaze calmly.

Fortunately, another girl butted in and interrupted their staring match, wrapping Cassidy in a long hug as she squealed, "Cass! I've been looking everywhere for you."

Cassidy immediately turned to the girl, a move for which Ryley was enormously thankful; her confidence, notwithstanding all her recent posturing otherwise, was about as tenable as scotch tape. As the two started talking loudly, half-in and half-out of the circle, the rest of them awkwardly stood there before Cassidy finally said, "Oh, we're being so rude. Everyone, this is Lily."

People repeated their hellos, but as the conversation continued along, meandering its way once again through people's backstories, Ryley began to grow restless. She wanted to get started and meet the people with whom she would actually be sharing classes—her Section; currently, based on what she could observe from their lanyards, only Cassidy and Sophie would be with her.

Just as Ryley considered taking an unnecessary trip to the bathroom, an usher finally announced breakfast time was over. People immediately clumped together, having already identified friends in their Section, and moved toward the door in tandem. As they exited out into the corridor, Cassidy, who'd looped her arm through Sophie's, slowed her steps to walk alongside Ryley. Ryley gave her a small smile in response before looking ahead down the corridor. She could just make out Olivia and Harrison standing in a loose circle with what looked to be other transfers.

Olivia was looking at them already, her attention inevitably drawn by the sound of stampeding One-Ls. Her brow furrowed as she darted her gaze between Cassidy and Ryley before letting her eyes rest on Ryley. Ryley could feel her judgment and knew instinctively that Olivia had expected something different from Harrison's sister. Ryley didn't care. Harrison had made it clear that she'd never be good enough; she expected nothing different from his friends.

CHAPTER 3

SEPTEMBER 2018

———

After a busy three-day orientation came the first day of classes. Arriving a generous ten minutes before her late afternoon Property class started, Ryley sidled up to a huddle of her classmates already gathered outside the door. They were once again in Wasserstein Hall, the building that had hosted their general orientation. Similar clusters of students were arranged throughout the hallway, all nervously murmuring and occasionally looking down at what appeared to be copious notes covering the assigned readings.

Sophie was speaking. "This professor cold calls like, half the class. Did you know that?" She was visibly preening, armed with the power of insider information, even as she twitched one hand against the other, her enthusiastic happiness the prior week transformed into enthusiastic, wholehearted anxiety.

The circle of students around Ryley let out groans and echoing sighs. Ryley stayed silent as her heartbeat accelerated.

"Yeah, Professor Kilmer is super impressive. You know he wrote the textbook?" Zeke asked, the question not really one, given that he immediately continued, "I heard he decides if you're smart or not by the first week."

"That seems like a rumor meant to scare One-Ls," Ryley piped up. She hadn't quite meant to speak aloud but needed to calm herself, to soothe the nerves that would make her feel completely out of sorts before class even started.

Zeke continued as if Ryley hadn't spoken. "Well, anyway, because he calls on so many of us, I doubt any of the students in the class will remember if you mess up. Especially because we barely know each other's names."

Sophie also ignored Ryley and kept her giant Bambi eyes fixed on Zeke as if he were the authority on all things law school. Others also nodded, soothed now that Zeke had given them permission to be. Ryley clenched her jaw; this wasn't the first time his words had been given an automatic weight hers weren't. She supposed her skinny jeans and floral blouse didn't exactly scream "serious scholar." She should've worn a pantsuit to class; she did look good in a blazer.

Cassidy walked up, her indomitable presence despite her bright blue sundress quickly convincing Ryley that her lack of a pantsuit was not the problem.

"Hey, guys and gals!" Cassidy exclaimed, scooting between Sophie and Zeke and effortlessly forcing Sophie to take a step back. "I have a quick question about the reading—would someone mind confirming that pursuit is not enough and basically, a hunter needs to 'deprive an animal of liberty' and 'subject it to control' so as to own it?'" As she spoke, Cassidy moved her fingers to form air quotes around her thick Property book and the hefty notebook she was carrying in her hands.

Zeke immediately responded, "Yep, that's about right; I think at the end of the day, you should understand that the case is pretty much about showing how no one starts with property rights to anything, and property law revolves around figuring out how to convert anything to individual ownership."

Ryley wondered if everyone else also heard the sweetly patronizing lilt to his tone or if she was just jealous of his knowledge.

Zeke continued, "However, a *Duke Law Journal* article pointed out that in actuality it might have just been a turf war between old agricultural wealth and new commercial wealth."

Cassidy gave him what could only generously be described as a smile of thanks, her narrow lips barely upturning at the corners.

Sophie spoke up in the resultant pause, asking, "Wait, can we go through the major takeaways of the case?" Sophie turned to Cassidy as she said this, her allegiance to Zeke diminished and forgotten in Cassidy's presence.

As they spoke, Ryley became acutely aware she hadn't done nearly as thorough a job as she thought she'd done, scribbling in the margins of the casebook as she had. She looked around at the ring of people and saw them glancing down at outlines laying out the major facts of the cases; some of these outlines were clearly taken from someone else, but others were brand new and freshly made and already spanned at least five pages. Their eyes lit up as they talked and she just felt envy; not of their knowledge but of their passion.

As Ryley kept her silence, she knew she was being mentally lowered in the minds of her peers, even as Zeke boosted himself to the top of "Smart People to Ask to Study With."

Eventually, Cassidy snapped her textbook shut and authoritatively stepped into the classroom without checking to see if anyone would follow. Of course, her entrance catalyzed the rest of them, and the different clusters throughout the hall streamed into the classroom. Cassidy looked pleased if unsurprised by her natural leadership potential.

Ryley merely shook her head, somewhat used to the other girl's sway at this point. At first, Ryley had only hung out with Cassidy tangentially during breaks in orientation, as part of a larger group of students that seemed to inevitably gather around wherever Cassidy was seated; however, after Orientation finished, Sophie had invited her along for drinks on the Saturday before classes started, and Ryley had said yes.

She had found Cassidy, Sophie, and Zeke waiting for her at the restaurant-bar Cambridge Common, a bar right down the street from the law school. The restaurant was homey, with red brick walls made a bit less uniform via interspersed wooden paneling and bright, cheery paintings. Upon entering, she had been greeted by a blast of general warmth and cheeriness, the smell of fried food and beer on tap, and the sound of people jeering at the TV. She hadn't been able to help the smile that had immediately sprung to her face.

When she'd joined them, Sophie and Cassidy were already two drinks in and had been talking about their time as paralegals in New York, name-dropping bars and clubs she imagined she'd have been impressed by if she recognized their repute. She'd listened, nodding along before offering a safe, non-offensive streaking story and another second-class story about riding a moped. Otherwise, Ryley had let them carry the conversation but for prodding for more details or offering the odd snarky remark. She had been content to hoard her words, focused only on how entertaining she found them all. Ryley had liked their confidence and knowledge that they were as important as anyone else in the room. By the end of the night, Cassidy had fully accepted Ryley, Ryley's performance during Orientation and during that dinner convincing her that even though the packaging was different, they were the same. Sophie had been thrilled when Cassidy had hugged

Ryley at the end of the night. Zeke had been oblivious. Indeed, the drunker he got, the more oblivious he was, talking over every girl repeatedly through the course of the night. To his credit, he had shut up when Cassidy began talking over him.

As Ryley passed Zeke now, she gave him a soft, "Good luck," seeing his hands shake slightly in the process of putting his name placard at the front of his desk. Students all around her made beelines for their supposed seats, trying to match the seat map they'd memorized beforehand to the actual seating arrangement of the classroom. The classroom seats were fixed into four rows, each row of seats attached to an unbroken ribbon-like desk. The rows progressively increased in semi-circular length, combining to form a rainbow oriented around the pulpit from which the professor preached.

Ryley found her seat easily enough, located as it was in the back row closest to the door, and just as she was settling in, the professor entered, his six-five stature imposing. The air hummed with nervous energy as each student did their best to appear well-situated and composed for the man. He carried a giant white poster board under one arm with students' pixelated, bug-eyed faces printed out and stuck in squares mimicking the arrangement of seats around the classroom.

After placing the poster board down on the podium and neatly folding his black suit jacket over a chair at the front of the classroom, possibly put there for just that purpose, he launched into lecture. He was of the old-fashioned generation, his antiquated wire-frame spectacles and suspenders on display as he imperiously stalked back and forth in front of them.

He did not bother with a warm-up or an introductory hello and instead called on Zeke not even two minutes into his lecture. "Mr. Smith, please lay out exactly what Pierson and Post were quibbling about."

Zeke responded in a deliberately measured tone. "Well, interestingly, although it may have seemed to be about a fox, it was actually about who would control common resources—landed wealth or commercial wealth."

Professor Kilmer looked at him, unimpressed. "I asked you to lay out the facts of the case as presented on the page, not lay out your hypothesis on what you think is happening."

Zeke's cheeks flushed a vibrant red, but he immediately recovered, delivering the facts quickly and concisely.

Professor Kilmer, appeased, moved onto his next target and Ryley began to breathe normally again, her hands unclenching and her shoulders coming down from where they'd been drawn up to her ears. He didn't linger on anyone longer than a minute.

When he inevitably asked, "Ms. Agarwal, what did Fleta and Bracton think?" Ryley only felt her heartbeat jack-rabbit up at half-speed, staying at fifty miles per hour rather than the hundred it had reached in the past.

Her voice only slightly trembling, she said, "That pursuit alone is not enough to create property rights. That actual possession is necessary."

He gave her a quick, neutral nod and then moved on. She was pleased, thankful she'd gotten that question. One of her greatest strengths was remembering unimportant side details like the one for which he'd just asked. Doing a quick skim around the room, she saw Sophie and Cassidy shoot her a quick smile. Zeke was taking notes.

Basic duty done, Ryley found herself only half-listening as the class continued. She could see she didn't quite get the more theoretical hypotheticals when the answer couldn't simply be found in the pages of the textbook; however, when he asked questions like that, most students' answers only seemed to be in the general realm of right. He always had a clarifying follow-up; she was fine. She was more focused on doing her teenage years right this time; law school was the perfect do-over with its small, high school class size and set-up. She'd be sharing all her classes this semester with the same eighty people in her Section and there were only seven Sections total per class year. She was sure she'd recognize everyone by face, if not name, by the time she graduated.

As she let her mind slightly meander, she was careful to not let her eyes drift too much from the face of the professor. She'd never quite been able to break herself of the deep respect for authority her parents had instilled in her; being too obvious a space cadet would be rude. Finally, inevitably, the professor began wrapping up, and her neighbor couldn't help but breathe out the giant sigh of relief that Ryley felt within. They'd made it through their first class alive, no one's reputation in shreds. Law school was going great!

* * *

Ryley nestled into the crimson leather couch down the hall from her classroom, happy it was Friday. She was tired of being at attention and a section-mate, Ali, had already posted an open invite to her party that weekend in the Section GroupMe, so she wasn't particularly bothered to be sociable in the hectic period right before class started. Instead, she was content flipping through playlists on her phone. She was trying to discover a song that perfectly captured, in retrospect, her feelings about the first day of law school. She liked documenting major events of her life by song and had song choices picked out for things: the first time she had sex ("Boulevard of Broken Dreams" by Green Day); high school graduation ("Send Me on My Way" by Rusted Root); first day of college ("Fall into Place" by Apartment); and twenty-first Birthday ("Die Young" by Kesha).

She didn't bother looking up from her phone when she felt someone plop down next to her, shaking the couch in the process. Her headphones were very visible, effectively functioning as a giant *Do Not Disturb* sign plastered on her forehead. However, a giant hand was unabashedly thrust in front of her phone screen, and she was forced to reluctantly tear herself away from the device. She was pleasantly surprised to be greeted by a warm, relaxed smile from a man she had previously noted was incredibly cute; he was alabaster pale with wide-set blue eyes, large, friendly lips, neatly styled hair, and heavy-set yet carefully groomed eyebrows. They'd said *hi* a couple of times in passing, but he was always off in a rush somewhere.

"Hey, I'm Mark. I like your maroon sweater."

Looking down at his outfit, she saw he too was wearing a maroon V-neck sweater, though tight enough she could just make out the definition of his abs. "Hey. My name's Ryley. I like *yours*."

"Thanks! This is my lucky sweater." He gave her an exaggerated wink.

She smiled, even though she couldn't control her blush and the automatic way she looked down, embarrassingly uncomfortable with any mention of or allusion to sex. After a slight pause, she said, "Anyway, glad you're also wearing a sweater. I wasn't sure if it was too soon to bring one out, but I love fall clothes, so I went for it."

"I say so long as you look good, wear whatever you want." He paused to carefully study her sweater once more and then continued, "That sweater really brings out your skin's undertones. I bet you look dazzling in reds, dark blues, and greens."

She could speak clothes all day. "Literally the colors of my wardrobe. And of course, black."

As she finished speaking, he grabbed the hand she'd been unconsciously gesturing with for emphasis. "Oh, look, you even coordinated your ring to match your outfit."

She actually hadn't meant to, but she pretended intentionality, basking in his attention while gifting him a smug smile and a half-raised shoulder. He intertwined their hands together as he admired her ring, and although she normally didn't like it when people she didn't know touched her, the casual, nonchalant manner in which he did it soothed her.

"Maybe I should send you a picture of my outfit every morning, so you can match to me every day." She flirted safely, knowing without a doubt that he would never be interested in her romantically.

"Please do. Give me your phone and I'll type in my number." After he added himself to her contacts, saving his name with a heart emoji next to it, he said, "I think this is the beginning of a beautiful friendship."

She refrained from rolling her eyes; she had been in need of a cheesy friend.

The rest of the day passed in a blur as she floated in a little bubble of bliss, pleased to have so easily added to her growing collection of friends. Finally arriving home to her quaint one-bedroom apartment, she sprawled onto her black futon couch. The living room was minimally decorated with no paintings or personality to speak of, empty but for a practical wooden coffee table, a desk, the couch, and a black steel-frame bookcase. Feeling unstoppable, she decided to pull up Hinge, her preferred (or alternatively, only) dating app. She never quite enjoyed being on it, but she felt like she was getting left behind whenever she went for too long without using it. Accordingly, she was naturally delighted to see the number of men who'd "liked" her profile once she opened up the app. She'd only changed the city that morning as an afterthought, expecting to get a handful of "likes" that would give her a general sense of the dating scene.

She'd not dated much in the last couple of years, aside from a hook up here and there, and she could rarely stand to see the guy again after they'd been intimate, feeling entirely unconnected. The boys with whom she'd match in DC were also as uninterested in something serious and would leave similarly desultory messages, lacking in any sort of real enthusiasm. Perhaps, though, she could change things here and seriously try to date. It was about time she grew up and played the part of protagonist, the glossy model sitting center cover and not the character set to the side.

After getting through a decent number of profiles, she decided to take a break and give her mother a call. It had been two whole days since they'd last talked and Ryley knew her mother must be missing her. Who wouldn't enjoy talking about Ryley's life and problems *ad nauseum?* She wouldn't deny her mom the joy of hearing about her little cherub now.

"Hi, *beta*. How are you?" Ryley's mom must be at home; she wouldn't have used the Hindi term for darling outside.

"Good, good. Great day today." Ryley bounced her small stuffed turtle between her hands as she talked on speaker phone. Her mom had gotten the turtle for her as a gift, saying it reminded her of Ryley. Ryley wasn't exactly flattered, but she supposed there were worse things to be called.

"You've been having quite a few good days lately." Her mom paused, as if to let Ryley recognize that things were going well for her and she could retire one of the ten angsty playlists she had on shuffle. Her mom continued, almost hesitantly, "Did you end up getting all your readings done, then?"

"No, but that class never cold calls, so it's fine. Besides, Cassidy, Zeke, and Sophie wanted to get drinks yesterday."

"How's that going?"

"Fine. They're cool. Cassidy is cool. She's like Kyle—you remember her? Except I'm actually friends with Cassidy and her crew."

"Oh."

"What?" Ryley asked reluctantly, knowing she'd likely regret prompting her mother for more information.

"Nothing. Just be careful and don't let yourself get so swept up in socializing that you end up sacrificing your studies."

"I'm not letting myself get *swept up* in anything. I'm still doing most of the readings, and if you're worried about Cassidy, I made another new friend. Also, I matched with some cute boys on Hinge today." She pushed the pride into her voice. They'd *just* agreed things were going well for Ryley; her mom couldn't take it back.

Thankfully, her mom retreated. "Okay, okay. If you're happy, that's all that matters."

Ryley tried to read into the tone but couldn't figure it out. She decided to move them along for the sake of both their sanities. "I don't know what that means, but I do know that my college friends are saying I'm killing it."

Her mom stuttered slightly before ultimately saying, "You *are* killing it." And then, because she couldn't seem to help herself, her mom added, "Just take it slow. I don't want to see you get hurt."

CHAPTER 4

SEPTEMBER 2008

———

Ryley hopped out of her brother's black BMW with a little skip in her step, giving her brother a smooth, casual nod of farewell. She was feeling good today. Harrison had let her choose the radio station this morning, and she liked the sense of power it had given her. Usually, she pretended she didn't care what music was playing, but she did. No one could possibly enjoy hearing heavy metal blast in their ears at seven a.m. She knew he did it to mess with her. At night, when she'd press her ear up against his door to better hear the strains of music softly drifting out into the hallway, it was always classical jazz.

As she strolled down the familiar tree-lined concrete path, breezing past the squat high school science building, she was determined to keep her good mood going. She was in her third week of her sophomore year and finally getting into the swing of things, no longer needing an extra ten minutes to get to class. She also no longer darted her eyes away nervously whenever she'd make eye contact with a senior or one of the Legitimate Athletes. She had tried to disguise herself as a Legitimate Athlete last week by carting around her softball bag, but no one cared about softball. Also, she wasn't even very good—she played it foremost to show some level of wholesomeness for college applications and because her parents thought that being part of a sports team was a crucial ingredient in establishing her all-Americanness. But all the Legitimate Athletes could tell she was a Non-Athletic Regular Person (NARP).

The pathway eventually merged into the giant rectangular quad, and she paused for a minute to just stare at the set-up, taking in the boring, beige cafeteria tables and muted dark green umbrellas. The school had done well in cultivating its aura of conformity and professionalism. Given that it was a nice seventy degrees outside, almost all the tables were populated that morning with groups of students lounging and catching up with each other before classes started for the day. The handful of Black students at the school were gathered together on one table, laughing at a joke that would no doubt go over her head; the nerdy Asians, with a couple of mixed in white kids, were gathered on another, also laughing together loudly. Two more tables over, the exclusive crew of attractive rich kids were huddled around a laptop screen.

Ryley would have liked to leave the attractive rich crew with that label and move on for simplicity's sake, but over the last two weeks, she'd unfailingly noticed that even though most of them were white, there was an attractive Indian and an attractive half-Black girl not quite hidden within their midst. Interestingly, these two girls were dressed the same way the white girls were and had the same unblemished skin, curves, and cell phone cover. Also, the same sense of humor if the way they laughed in unison was any indication. They were different but pulled off being the same, and Ryley would've appreciated the chance to observe them more, but sadly, her history class beckoned.

Ryley bounded up the winding staircase that led to the history building, dragging her hand along the tall concrete wall against which the stairs were set sideways to stabilize herself as she climbed. She avoided touching the railing that would most definitely give her the plague, having seen too many a boy pick his nose and then put his hand on it. Ryley knew she had plenty of time, but she always took the stairs quickly to justify the way she'd be gassed at the top; at least sprinting made her distinct lack of physical fitness excusable.

As she pushed open the heavy wooden door of the class-room, she was greeted by a soft hum of conversation. No one in the class was particularly rowdy and an eight a.m. class was too early for most students to put much effort into anything. Ryley plopped herself down next to Josh at her "desk." Instead of individual desks, the teacher, Mr. Weber, had had the mainte-nance staff push long, brown wooden tables together to form a U-shape so the students were looking inward as he paced back and forth in the middle of the room. Ryley looked over at Josh to see if he was in a talking mood. They'd been semi-friends for a while now, sharing classes since they'd both started at Harvard-Westlake in the seventh grade; he was on the baseball team, but he cared a lot about academics and showed it, not infrequently participating in class. Everyone knew he had his heart set on Yale; he wore the sweater almost every other day. His care for academics never pushed him too far out of the baseball team's protective hands though. He was too good at baseball, seen as too much of an overall nice guy, and too attractive to fall out of favor. He had a little pug nose and a wide, generous mouth, complemented by a mess of shaggy brunette hair. The sloppy bangs that covered his pale, slightly acne-prone forehead and fell into his light brown gingerbread eyes gave him a charming, innocent air. Ryley had seen him shamelessly use his puppy dog look one too many times on Ms. Fisher in math when he'd "forgotten" his homework at home.

Josh turned to her now, feeling her eyes on him. "How was your weekend?"

"Good. Didn't get up to much." She refrained from discussing the blow-out pre-mall fight she'd had with her mom on Saturday and the subsequent day-long Summit on Sunday during which they'd analyzed and dissected their feelings.

"The wedding is coming up, yeah?" Josh pulled her back to the present.

"Yep, I'm taking a week and a half off school for it. So not worth it."

"Hm, I can't imagine you in one of those Indian dresses. Maybe you'll come back engaged though, right? Get one of your aunts to set you up with a nice sugar daddy?"

"Ha ha," she said drily. She leaned back into her chair.

"Well, it's been quite the drought for you over here, hasn't it? Have you even kissed someone yet?"

"Yeah, of course, I have," she responded in a tone loud enough to match his, her cheeks flushed. A boy two seats over smirked at them, and she aggressively whispered, "Lower your voice."

He continued unfazed, lowering his voice by maybe one decibel level. "When? You've never dated anyone here and it's not like you're going to any of the parties where shit happens."

"Okay, one, I could have dated someone here without you knowing it—it's not like we're BFFs. Two, it's none of your business, but I have kissed someone. Not at a Harvard-Westlake party but at a party outside." She prayed he wouldn't ask for a name.

"Okay, Ryley, what parties are you going to?" he asked with an exaggerated chuckle. She could have punched him.

"Why are you interrogating me?" she snapped. She didn't know what had gotten into him. They weren't the sort of friends to ask personal questions; sometimes, they compared test answers, and occasionally, they talked about their weekend plans.

"I'm not *interrogating* you. One of the guys on the baseball team was talking about girls the other day, and no one said your name, and I just realized I'd never seen you with someone. I was curious."

Ryley was not shocked that her name wasn't one of the names being tossed around, but it would have been nice. Really nice to get an ego boost instead of feeling like a deflated balloon.

"Well. Curiosity killed the cat." Even she could hear the way her voice slightly went up in pitch as her throat tightened.

"Come on, Ryley. You're going to have to do better than that." He sighed. "Anyway, just put yourself out there more; it's weird that you don't even really try to flirt with guys."

She stared at him for a prolonged moment. Was he trying to tell her something? First the sudden interest in her personal life, now this? He'd look good on paper, make her seem normal. Her parents never much asked her about romantic relationships, but dating in high school seemed pretty high up on the all-American experience they so wanted for her.

Ryley decided to bench any dramatic gestures as the teacher came into the room, but she resolved to focus on Josh going forward and see if he ever looked at her or gave her any special attention. She turned to face Mr. Weber; he was distinguished-looking, with perfect posture, a swimmer's body, and a thick head of silver hair.

Mr. Weber liked her. She'd raised her hand a couple of times during the first week of school—history was her favorite subject, and they were doing the Roman Empire. She liked the story-tale aspect, the intrigue and drama of it all, and had blitzed through the reading, devouring it much like she would any unassigned book she found interesting.

Mr. Weber asked a question now, and when the rest of the class stayed silent, he called on Ryley, offering her a kind smile and repeating the question. "Ryley, what form of government did Augustus establish?"

"A Principate." Unprompted, she said, "Although it superficially had elements of a republic, it was more a monarchy."

His eyes twinkling, he said, "Yes, very good, Ryley—that's what I was going to ask next. What do you think were the advantages of establishing this form of government?"

She opened her mouth to respond but then she saw a boy mocking her out of the corner of her eye, pulling on his ear as she tended to do when nervous. She turned to look at him fully, and he just grinned at her, as if they were in a weird sort of cahoots together. He was a clown, didn't mean any ill will as far as she could gather, but she found herself closing her mouth, nonetheless, shrugging at the teacher instead of saying anything.

Confused, Mr. Weber asked, "No guesses?"

"No."

"Hm, okay. Anyone else?"

Three hands shot up, but Ryley tuned out, not bothering to hear their answers. She wasn't exactly hurt; the boy, Cole, had been too shameless for it to feel like an attack. He poked fun at his friends the same way, shooting them that same goofy, open-mouthed grin after he shouted a *Yo Mama* joke, but she couldn't imagine Cole behaving like that with any of the other girls. Maybe all the boys here really did just see her as one of the guys. Or maybe Cole just thought she in particular a dork and wasn't worried about any blow-back. Although the school had an extensive support system consisting of deans and counselors, she wasn't the type to tattle.

Deciding she would spin in more mental circles later that day when she was bored during softball, she spent the rest of the class tracking Josh out of the corner of her eye. When she saw him glance over at her twice and accidentally "brush" against her when he was throwing his backpack over his shoulder, she regretted being so oblivious.

Fidgeting with her hands and biting her lip—she'd read that the latter action was attractive—she managed to get out, "Hey, want to get lunch together fifth period? You have it free too, right?"

He looked at her in shock before hesitantly saying, "Um. I do have it free, but Ryley, we're like class friends. I'm not trying to be mean, but I don't think you'd get along with my friends. You're a bit... I don't know."

"Oh, yeah, sure," Ryley said, careful to infuse her voice with nonchalance, as she avoided eye contact.

"It's not anything personal. I like you. You just don't get it."

She was a sucker for punishment, so she asked, "Don't get what?"

"Jokes, stupid references," he said semi-sadly, regretting he was the one to have to break the news that she was not with it. Her brand-new skinny jeans couldn't undo a reputation built up over too many years, but at least she was taking steps, finally conceding to the clothing choices offered up by her mom.

"Okay, so what if I don't get the occasional reference?"

"If one of my friends made a joke about going down on someone, would you even know what that meant?" Once again, his attempt at a whisper could do with some work.

"Yes, of course, I would," Ryley snapped, even as she internally cringed, waiting for the inevitable follow-up.

He took a step back at her vehemence, and then in an offensively appeasing tone, said, "Right, of course. So, what does it mean?"

"It's something sexual. I don't feel comfortable saying it." Ryley hoped he would leave her with just a shred of dignity.

"Okay, assuming that wasn't just a cop-out answer, that's my point! You can't even say the words; you've clearly never done it. You wouldn't enjoy yourself around my friends, so why would you even want to come?"

Faced with the undeniable observation that he thought her as out of place as she felt, she finally said, "Whatever. It was just a suggestion. Geez."

"Yeah, okay. Anyway, I'll see you tomorrow. Maybe we can study together or something." He threw the words over his shoulder as he walked out.

"Yeah, sure," Ryley said, unsurprised. Of course he wanted to study with her. He wasn't going to get into Yale on his own. That thought was mean; she mentally took it back.

Unfortunately, their conversation had delayed the hasty exit she planned and it was just her and Mr. Weber in the room as she packed up her bag and he wiped down the chalkboard. In her rush to close the pencil case the first three times, the zip kept getting caught on the fabric, so finally, she paused, took a deep breath, gathered herself, and gently pulled the zip closed. She threw her bag over her shoulder and began walking out of the classroom, careful to avoid eye contact with Mr. Weber.

As she passed near him on her way to the door, he cleared his throat. She couldn't even pretend to act startled and instead just reluctantly lifted her eyes to meet his. They were a pale, faded blue, magnified underneath the wiry glasses he had on.

"What happened today?" As he spoke, he let his hand drop down to rest halfway across the table between them, as if he would have liked to reach out to her.

"Nothing. I feel like I have a reputation I don't particularly like. I decided not answering your question suited me better." They both knew he wouldn't believe her if she said she didn't know the answer.

He took his hand off the table to fold his arms across his chest. His spine seemed to elongate as he took a deep breath in and then actually looked down his nose at her. "Okay. So, you're going to let what other people think affect how you live your life?"

"I don't know. I guess so."

He just looked at her without saying anything more. After a minute of silence passed in this fashion, she walked out.

CHAPTER 5

SEPTEMBER 2018

—

Ryley looked down at the eight different outfits she'd arranged on her sky-blue duvet, each matched to a corresponding pair of shoes lying on the floor next to the bed. Even though she'd drawn her heavy maroon blackout curtains back to see the outfits in the quickly fading natural light, it hadn't helped.

She and Mark were going over to Cassidy's to pregame before Ali's party that evening. It was a simple celebration of getting through the first week of classes. When Cassidy had texted her that morning inviting her over, she'd naturally extended the invite to Mark, eager to bring him into the fold. Eager to be someone *capable* of bringing him into the fold. He'd texted her ten minutes ago saying he was going to be over in twenty. Ryley had originally planned on inviting him up, but she would just have to meet him outside. Ten minutes would not be nearly enough time to finish getting ready, let alone clean up her (light) mess.

Although she wasn't ashamed of the state of her apartment, a neat freak would be, and Mark could very well fall into that category of people. In the living room, the hardwood floors were covered with some stray hairs—she wished she could blame the shedding problem on a dog—and there were some miscellaneous food crumbs on the steel-framed wooden coffee table and the couch standing behind it. Her bedroom was little better with the outfits and shoes out and the makeup scattered along her dresser. She was lucky to have found a one-bedroom apartment cheap enough that she could pay a year's rent with money she'd saved from her business consulting days, but that meant she had no roommate to keep her natural state of slight disarray in check.

Realizing her ten minutes were fast expiring, she forced herself to just pick an outfit, defaulting to simple as her guiding criteria. She threw on a black cotton romper and stacked a couple of bracelets, squeezing her feet into a white pair of Toms to complete the look. Muttering, "I am a hoot and a delight," she hurriedly rubbed the dollop of toner she had squeezed onto her hand all over her face. She then started gliding liquid eyeliner over her eyes, trying to do subtle wings at the corners, only for Mark to buzz into her apartment at that moment, startling her into stabbing one eye with the wand. Of course she'd look like she had pink eye right before the party.

She ran over to the kitchen, took out the six-pack she'd shoved into the fridge earlier that day, and texted him saying she'd be down in a minute. Standing in front of the white-yellow linoleum counter, in a kitchen at most one body-length long—she really didn't use it enough to justify complaining—she took a couple of deep breaths before reaching up and into her liquor cabinet. Her liquor cabinet, so grandly named, consisted quite simply of one handle of gin. She dragged down a shot glass alongside the bottle and quickly poured out a couple of fluid ounces, knocking the shot back in one swift motion. Grimacing still from the aftertaste, from the way her stomach heaved, she did one more and then was running out the door and down the stairs. She felt better already, her energy level high enough that the idea of being packed into a room with eighty loud, drunk people no longer made her want to crawl out of her skin.

As she opened the door to her apartment building, Mark bellowed, "Rye-Rye," his whole face lighting up. He was lounging against the old building's scuffed, red brick wall, with one hand shoved into the pocket of his light-washed cuffed jeans. He belonged more on the cover of a *GQ* magazine than at law school.

She shot him a huge grin and delivered an exuberant, "Hi!" She almost called him *Markie* in turn but that felt too precious and cute. She gave Mark's outstretched hand a quick, obligatory squeeze before turning to begin walking down the street. Ryley went out of her way to purposefully crunch through the red-gold leaves huddled in piles on the sides of the road. She loved fall in Cambridge and the way the humidity sat heavily on her skin, like a constant warm (though admittedly damp) embrace, so different from the dry heat of LA.

As he fell into step beside her, he asked, "Where does Cassidy live?"

"Just a ten-minute walk from here! Cassidy's apartment is right next to Ali's; they live in neighboring buildings. Her apartment is super nice." Ryley was perhaps implying a greater level of familiarity with Cassidy than was warranted; she'd never been over after all, but Cassidy had shown her enough pictures that she'd gotten the gist.

Two minutes of companionable silence later, Mark began to share some of the impressions he had of people in their Section: those who felt comfortable talking at length, those who looked terrified, and so on. Ryley nodded her general agreement, wanting to build their sense of connectedness and not really having strong opinions otherwise. She almost asked him what his opinion of her was but thought it better to not know. Mark seemed to be too willing to be candid and she'd rather keep thinking of herself as a not-yet-recognized star pupil.

All too soon, they arrived at Cassidy's building and were immediately buzzed in. As she traversed the first floor of the modern, newly renovated apartment building, Ryley heard quick, confident steps making their way over what must be hardwood floor before the door at the end of the hallway was yanked open.

"Hey—oh, hi, Mark—you're the first ones here!" Cassidy directed most of the sentence exclusively to Ryley though she flicked her eyes over to Mark in quick acknowledgment.

Ryley just smiled in response even as Mark exclaimed, "Great, we'll get some quality one-on-one Cass time then!" He stepped forward and gave Cassidy a side-hug as he squeezed past her to cross the threshold. Ryley followed, the wattage of her smile increasing, as she saw how much Cassidy's apartment suited her.

They had entered a spacious living room, decorated as if a showroom on a yuppie furniture website. There was a fake, mini palm frond plant in the far right corner of the room and two white frames with the words HOME and LOVE hung on the wall immediately to her right. A regal gray couch, replete with throw pillows saying *the present is female* and *know your worth* lay directly in front of her situated across from what must have been a forty-four-inch plasma screen TV. A sleek glass table set within a silver steel frame, sitting at the center of the room, completed the look.

"So, this is my place! Cara, my roommate, is out. She's in Section Two." Cassidy pointed at the closed door to their left.

She then gestured proudly to another room and said, "My room is through that door to the right." Ryley could see a white wooden bookcase, built in the form of a ladder. The books were stacked such that she could just make out the title of each book serving as a bookend on each of the five shelves. *One L, Just Mercy, Mrs. Dalloway, Pride and Prejudice*, and *The Big Short*. She doubted the book display was unintentional; she did see the opportunity for an easy icebreaker though.

"Oh, *Mrs. Dalloway* is my favorite book," Ryley said.

"It's a good one! Also one of my favorites." Cassidy continued to keep her gaze focused only on Ryley as she spoke.

Mark seemed as unaffected as ever, piping up to say, "I am honored to be in the company of such well-read folk." He threw in a wink at the end, directed at Cassidy, and although Ryley was a bit miffed that Mark had so easily shifted his focus to Cassidy, his body facing hers, his eyes only tracking hers, she supposed it was a good thing. She wanted them to get along.

Cassidy gave him a tight, indulgent smile before turning once more to Ryley. "Ryley, you did management consulting in DC before this, right?" Ryley was not surprised Cassidy remembered; Ryley had seen her observing everyone. She could envision Cassidy coming home every day and typing in information she'd learned about people into an excel spreadsheet.

"Yeah, pretty standard path, I guess. Seems like a lot of us did two or three years at a consulting firm or did the paralegal stint for a bit. Mark, what about you?" Ryley turned her body to bring him in.

"Oh, I worked in investment banking in New York." And then, speaking too deliberately to be believably offhand, he added, "Goldman Sachs. So, law school is quite the shift." He kept his gaze fixed on Cassidy.

Cassidy said nothing in response, but she looked at Mark as much as at Ryley when she suddenly startled, saying, "Oh! Do you two want something to drink?" Ryley wasn't sure if it was the prestige element that had mattered to Cassidy or if she had just wanted Mark to feel like he had to be vetted first, that he had to perform for her.

Mark exclaimed, "Yes, please!"

Ryley nodded too though she was already beginning to feel a touch spacey and unfocused, the shots of gin beginning to hit her system. As Mark moved to help Cassidy with the drinks, Ryley settled into a slightly offset chair in the corner of the kitchen, pulling out her phone by habit. Ryley silently watched as Mark picked out what must have been top-shelf gin, giving Cassidy a beseeching grin. Ryley would never have dared.

Surprisingly, Cassidy only gave a small sigh, and then said, "Fine, but only with you two. Don't let others know I gave you this."

Ryley felt warm, perhaps just because of the gin but also liking the feeling of exclusivity Cassidy's words engendered, especially because she'd seen Cassidy's capacity to be cold. As Cassidy poured their drinks, Mark listed all the men he thought cute in their section, ticking off his fingers as he spoke. Ryley found herself, for the most part, silently nodding along; she could see that Zeke was objectively cute, that David, the only-barely-taller-than-her brunette with the sweet smile, was a looker. Cassidy was much more vocal, unapologetically and adamantly labeling some of the men 100 percent no-gos.

When Ryley got up to get her drink, Ryley realized, for the first time, that Cassidy was a full head shorter. The top of Cassidy's up-do only barely sat at the same level as Ryley's nose. Ryley snorted to herself. Cassidy paused her dissertation on the pros and cons of men in the Section to look at Ryley and, sounding slightly put-upon, asked, "Why are you being so quiet? You must have your eye on someone."

Ryley had the most vivid visual of Cassidy as a chihuahua with a little crown on its blond-wigged head. She pretended the laugh that inescapably bubbled out was a result of her excitement about guys. "Yeah, David is cute! Zeke is all right too." Ryley was feeling light and unstoppable; she'd hit her sweet spot, and if she slowly sipped Cassidy's drink over the hour, hopefully, she could stay at exactly this level. She added, as an afterthought, "Sophie's also pretty."

Cassidy laughed, slightly uncertainly. "Um, okay, yeah, she is." Mark was smirking at her.

Ryley paused, replayed her words, and then rolled her eyes very obviously. "Yes, so I can see when a girl's pretty. Sue me. It's not like I'd ever do anything about it."

"But you want to?" Mark asked, not maliciously—he was gay, for heaven's sake—but with his head slightly cocked to the side, more curious than anything else.

Cassidy just looked uncertain, looking at Ryley closely, perhaps wondering if she'd have to reconstruct the role she'd planned out for Ryley.

"No, I'm twenty-four. If I was going to do something with a girl, I would've done it by now. All I was saying is that objectively, Sophie is gorgeous. I'm sure every guy has a crush on her."

Cassidy laughed, at ease once more knowing she'd read the situation right and they were the same. "Okay, yeah, she's pretty. I don't know if I'd call her gorgeous though." Cassidy then happily changed the topic even as Ryley listened absent-mindedly, focusing on sipping her drink double-time to reclaim the lightness that had been spooked out of her when Cassidy and Mark had looked at her like that—as if they weren't sure she was who they'd slotted her to be.

She was annoyed, especially when she'd never so much as kissed a girl, but the doorbell ringing broke her out of her slight funk, and soon Zeke, Sophie, and some others she recognized from class were entering. She gave Sophie a wave but didn't get up to talk to her. Not that Ryley necessarily would have gone over to her even if the previous conversation hadn't occurred; Sophie was incredibly nice but had been incessantly on-edge since law school started. At least Ryley kept her problems hidden inside, like normal people did.

After everyone had settled into a loose circle in the living room, Sophie clapped her hands loudly. "All right, guys, I just found out some news. David here got into Yale! But he decided to stay with us plebeians." Sophie beamed at David, who blushed, looking down at the floor, no matter that he was the most likely source of such news.

A couple of people gave half-hearted good for yous, but no one prodded David for more information, uninterested in his decision-making process, and fidgeting nervously as they tried to figure out if it was polite to move away from this topic.

Finally, Cassidy said, "I think you made the right choice not going to Yale. I mean, I got into Stanford but realized I'd be miserable and feel claustrophobic, so I came here." Ryley fully expected someone to let out a groan or poke fun at Cassidy for the very obvious plug, but then again, it was Cassidy.

So, instead, another woman piped up, "Oh, yeah, I got a full ride to Columbia—I don't know why, fooled them somehow—but it's hard to turn down a name like this."

Ryley hadn't spoken to the girl yet and couldn't remember her name from class. She was Persian, the only other minority in the room, but hadn't made any effort to come over to Ryley. Not that Ryley had done any better.

A couple more of her classmates threw out the names of the schools they'd gotten into, speaking hesitantly, as if the words were being pulled out of them, as if they had no choice but to prove they belonged at Harvard. Ryley stayed silent; she needed to get a better read of her cohort first and see if this peacocking was just first-week nerves or the norm before she said anything.

"Well, regardless, we're heap-toppers now!" Sophie chimed in.

"What's a heap-topper?" Mark asked.

The others looked at him horrified; even Ryley raised her eyebrows.

Sophie asked, aghast, "Did you not watch the pre-orientation video?"

"No." Mark kept his head high. He was well-positioned so that his sharp jaw was highlighted by the soft glow of Cassidy's lamp. Lowering his head in shame would have ruined the effect.

After a slight pause long enough to make anyone other than Mark uncomfortable, Sophie replied, "One of the professors referred to us as that in the video. We're at the top. We've made it." Sophie earnestly delivered the last line, as if a messiah showing Mark that Harvard was indeed the promised land by the power of willing it alone.

Eventually, they moved on to a new topic, and the tension hanging taut over the room finally abated; people relievedly broke into smiles. Ryley settled back into her chair, using her phone as the effective shield it was as she tapped out a text to a college friend that could easily be sent tomorrow. No sooner had she sent off the text consisting of nothing other than a generic recap of her week than Cassidy came over, asking, "Everything good?"

"Yeah, just catching up with a friend." Ryley looked up at Cassidy, waiting to see what she wanted, curious to know why she'd come over to Ryley when she had her full crew on hand.

"You know, I was super nervous to come here and have people not take me seriously. Having not gone to a feeder school or anything."

Ryley considered asking which school, realized it would show she was as pedigree obsessed as anyone else, and instead murmured, "Oh. Well, you definitely seem on top of it to me."

Cassidy stayed near her, as if hoping for something more, possibly wanting Ryley to absolve her, but Ryley would be of no help. She really was just taking her cue from others.

CHAPTER 6

SEPTEMBER 2018

———

Zeke pushed Ali's apartment door open without even trying to knock, falling into the door more than anything else. There was no way a knock would be heard over the noise spilling onto the stained, water-marked hallway. A whoop of welcome sounded out as they filed in; Ryley had had no deeper exchange than a hello with most of the people at the party, but she appreciated the sense of celebrity she experienced. She was also at peak drunkenness; they'd stayed at Cassidy's later than expected, and the drink Cassidy had made for her was hitting her in all the right places.

Carrying her six-pack very obviously—she was not a free-rider, she was an upstanding member of society—she made a beeline for the drinks table. The urgency with which she made her way across the room was slightly ridiculous, especially because all she did when she reached the table was to place the Stellas on it and proceed to stand there, mulling over whether she even wanted another drink. Ryley looked back at the rest of her group and saw most of them still stuck in the hallway near the door. The apartment was rather bland like her own. There was no art decoration anywhere and the living room and kitchen—the two rooms in which they were all gathered—only had the most essential pieces of furniture. She appreciated the apartment owner's taste. If she ever exchanged more than a hello with Ali, she'd tell her.

Ryley focused once again on the drinks table, picked up a Stella, and proceeded to peel the paper from the top of the bottle with undue care, revving herself up to talk to the nearest semi-stranger. David, *Yale David*, walked up before she had to leave the safety of the table. He offered her a brief, absentminded smile before turning to reach for a beer from one of the other assorted six packs. David hadn't made an effort to get to know her at Cassidy's earlier that night, but then again, she had just been clumped to Cassidy and Mark.

"Hey, I'm Ryley. We didn't get a chance to speak at Cassidy's." Ryley broke the temporary silence that blanketed them now.

David was just about the same height as her five-nine—her height was a consistently alternating source of pride and anguish—his eyes a beautiful hazel green set underneath thick black eyebrows and a shock of black hair that contrasted nicely against his tan skin. His full mouth settled permanently in a half-smile, and his nose, on the larger side, lent him a friendly, more approachable vibe. David's generally easygoing air and subtle attractiveness made him a good, natural draft pick for Cassidy's crew.

"Hi, I'm David." He gave her another slight smile even as his eyes flicked over to Sophie. Sophie and David probably already had a thing going on; half the single people had brought someone home the first weekend after Orientation. She waited to see if he would step away, and although he shifted his weight, he paused, ultimately deciding to give her a chance.

"Yeah, I think we were in the same breakout group a couple of times during Orientation?" Ryley asked, tapping her fingers against the bottle and keeping her tone light-hearted and unaffected, even as he continued to look between her and Sophie. One more look at Sophie and she'd run back to Cassidy and Mark. Quickly skimming for the two, she located them still standing by the front door.

"Oh, yeah, yes, you're right. We were in the same breakout group," he replied. He was truly doing the least. That being said, Mark was grinning at her from behind his shoulder. She'd press on for now.

"Right. So, good first week?"

"Yeah, you know, it *was* good. I mean law school is obviously hard, and I don't think I've ever done this much reading in my life, but I like it. It feels right." He took a swig of beer after he finished speaking. He was holding the bottle precariously between his thumb and index finger, and she had half a mind to tell him to hold it properly before he dropped it and splattered her.

Fortunately, the half of her mind that wasn't an uptight grandmother prevailed and she forged ahead. "That's great! You know, I can tell that you like it. You never look stressed when I see you."

He leaned in slightly now, canting his body toward hers. "Yeah, I really like all our classes even if the sheer amount of work blows. I think it's just about getting that balance right—making sure to do the things that need to get done while carving out time for myself to do things like this." He finished with an offhanded shrug. He took another swig of the precariously held beer. She thought about inching her feet slightly away, but the mindfulness podcast her dad had forced on her a month ago, which was making all the waves in the corporate circles, had emphasized the importance of staying present; she needed to focus on the cute, smart boy in front of her and enjoy the conversation for what it was.

"You know, I agree. Even if it's challenging, law school feels right. I feel like I'm always behind though. How do you keep up?"

"Oh, it definitely takes diligence to strike the balance. I have to work out in the mornings at eight on the dot; otherwise, it just doesn't happen. And I go straight to the library after classes and study for at least five hours before letting myself go home to do something else."

"Got you. Sticking to a schedule makes sense." She rocked back onto her heels, thinking they'd forged a decent enough connection for the day.

"Yeah, it's been a relatively easy transition for me because of what I did before." He left the hook dangling there and she was too stupid a fish not to bite.

"What did you do before law school?"

"Boring stuff, not worth talking about." She couldn't pull out now; he was resting a hand on her arm, invested.

"Hm, okay, try me," she said.

He explained his job in finance and she nodded along enthusiastically. David wasn't insufferable, just driven, she decided, and he would pause intermittently, to see if she was still engaged. Ryley invariably was.

Sometimes, David turned the conversation back to her, asking her about her life before law school, and she'd recite the same lines she'd said to others during Orientation, making sure her intonation was upbeat and spontaneous. Then she'd toss the metaphorical talking stick back to him, and he'd take it gladly.

As she got more comfortable, she started poking fun at him, softly, testing him out; she brought up facts she'd learned five minutes ago and took possession of them with a familiarity reserved for exchanges between two longtime friends. David laughed loudly; out of the corner of her eye, she saw others look over at them. She kept her eyes focused on David's face, even as she gestured with her arms more than necessary, animating their conversation.

She wondered if others thought they were hitting it off, if he thought they were hitting it off, if *she* thought they were hitting it off. Eventually, their conversation tapered to a natural stopping point, and she let the pause linger this time, waiting to see what he'd do. He looked over her shoulder, and she opened her mouth to beat him into being the first person to say she needed another drink. Or that she needed to use the bathroom seeing as they were standing near the drinks table already.

Before she could say anything, he called out, "Olivia! Come over here." He stayed standing near Ryley.

Ryley half-turned her body to face Olivia. She remembered her. Olivia was Harrison's friend. This time Olivia was wearing a tube crop top over flowy lounge pants, her dark brown hair twisted tightly into a bun. Ryley didn't know why Olivia was making such an effort to stand out. She was at law school, not Coachella. Ryley was well within her rights to make jabs like that; she'd been to Coachella. She made a mental note to mention that more.

"Olivia, what are you doing here? I didn't know you were friends with Ali?" he asked, while giving her a side-hug.

"We had a couple of classes together in undergrad," Olivia responded before looking over at Ryley.

David jumped to introduce them. "Olivia, this is Ryley—she's in my Section. Ryley, Olivia—we both went to Harvard for undergrad."

"Hi," Ryley said neutrally, curious to see if Olivia would acknowledge they'd met before.

"Hey, you," Olivia responded with an air of familiarity Ryley wouldn't have expected. "How did your first week go?" Her lips were stretched into a wide smile, her obsidian eyes trained on Ryley with an intensity that surprised her. She'd have thought she was too conventional for a girl like Olivia and David wasn't exactly winning awards for being counter-culture.

"Good! Not as bad as I was expecting and I'm slowly getting to know people in my Section." She gestured at David as she said this, pausing to see if he wanted to chime in. He didn't, looking down at something on his phone, so Ryley continued, "What about you?"

"About the same as you. Harrison's been a doll." Olivia said his name slightly possessively, in a way that made Ryley want to assert her sibling trump. She refrained. Olivia could have him.

Before either girl could decide if they wanted to push the conversation forward, David spoke up. "I have to get going. I want to get up early tomorrow to do the readings." He hesitated and then turned to Ryley and asked, "Can I have your number?"

He was cute; Mark had listed him on his Eligible Bachelors list. She responded with an earnest, "Yes!"

He gave her his phone, and after she handed it back to him, he commented, "Oh, cool spelling of Ryley. Is it Indian?"

Ryley saw Olivia grimace, but Ryley ignored her—she didn't understand why Olivia was still standing there in the first place—and gave him a smile. "No. I think my parents just wanted me to have a unique name without giving me something Americans would have a hard time with."

"Got it. I don't know many Indians. You're my first!" He gave her a huge smile as he said this.

She didn't quite know what to do with her face in response. Seeing her expression, he hastened to say, "No, like I've met Indians before, of course I have. But I've never been friends with one. Not that I have anything against Indians. I just feel like sometimes there's a cultural divide or something, and I don't know how to relate. You're different, you know? You're not like Indian-Indian. It's cool. You're cool."

Ryley saw that the tips of his ears had turned bright red and hurried to interrupt him before he could continue. "Oh, yeah, totally get what you mean, no worries." He hadn't meant any harm; she was flattered if anything. She noted his use of "friend" though and decided she'd have to dissect that later in the night.

David, still slightly flushed, gave her a flustered smile, a wave, and then walked away, barely nodding a goodbye to Olivia. The dichotomy between this David and the David of five minutes before was startling.

Olivia stayed near her after David had walked away, evaluating her silently. Ryley would have liked to know what she was thinking, like if she thought Ryley and David would make a cute couple. She wanted to ask, to get an objective perspective from a girl like Olivia who oozed confidence and who had boys eying her even now. Instead, feeling awkward, Ryley said, "I'm going to get a drink." To make it seem like less of a brush-off and because they were already right next to the drinks table, she asked, "Do you want anything?"

Olivia responded, "No, I don't drink." Ryley nodded and said nothing further, turning her body half away to get another beer. She opened her mouth to ask what Olivia did to decompress then, but Olivia was already walking away. Before she got too far though, Olivia turned back to Ryley, said, "I think you could do better," and then slipped away into a crowd of people huddled by the kitchen.

PART II

NOVEMBER

———

CHAPTER 7

NOVEMBER 2008

———

Ryley was running late, but she desperately ran her hands along the carpet, trying to find her lucky necklace. It was a simple silver chain with an elephant pendant, and because the chain was so long, she could usually keep it tucked away and hidden underneath whatever shirt she was wearing that day. She especially needed it today, but she had yanked it off when she had woken up in the middle of the night only to feel it choking her. Of all the ways she'd imagined herself dying, asphyxiation by elephant necklace was not one of them (she had a sad preoccupation with death and the idea of being taken from the world too early for people to appreciate the talents of one Ryley Agarwal).

As she raced around her room, she heard echoes of conversation drift in through the open door; two seniors named Callie and Carly were sitting downstairs, talking with her mom. Both were broad-boned brunettes with pleasant, potentially bland features. They were the captains of the softball team and had barged into her room ten minutes ago, rudely waking her from a dream in which she could talk to dolphins and was saving them from extinction. They were at her house at eight a.m. on a slightly foggy Saturday morning in order to "kidnap her"—i.e., take her to IHOP in her pajamas for a team bonding brunch. At least she'd had her grown-up pajamas on: a cotton gray tank top over plain navy bottoms. She was thankful her mom had forced her to change out of her normal, ratty sleepwear last night and was thankful she had been too tired to lecture her mom about overstepping.

She wished her mom had also done her the courtesy of stuffing away all the childhood Beanie Babies perched on the window sill and of tucking away all the photos displaying her with braces and a bowl cut. Luckily, her room was otherwise devoid of personality: she didn't have posters of anything, the walls were a neutral beige, and her black, nondescript metal bookcase was filled with schoolbooks and very standard assorted fiction and nonfiction. Even as Ryley changed up her haircut, updated her wardrobe, etc., her mom still encouraged Ryley to express herself fully and without filter within the four walls of her room, but Ryley didn't know what she should fill her walls up with. She didn't know who Inside Ryley was and didn't want to make the discrepancy between Outside Ryley and Inside Ryley worse than it had to be when she was whole-heartedly committed to developing an Outside Ryley that fit.

After five more minutes of fruitless searching, she finally gave up on finding her necklace and went downstairs. Her mom had Callie and Carly chuckling merrily away, and Ryley found herself momentarily unsure as she stood there hovering in the doorway, not wanting to intrude. These girls intimidated her with the casual, offhanded way they talked about alcohol, boys, and drugs.

Upon seeing Ryley hovering there uncertainly, her mom quickly and assuredly beckoned her in. "Girls, looks like Sleeping Beauty is ready to go. Now I can finally go get my iced coffee." Her mom shot her a fond smile as she said this, even as the two seniors laughed. Her mom was as talented as ever at playing a part; she knew her mom would just make herself a cup of *chai*.

"Well, girls, you should get going. You don't want to be late." Her mom, seeing Ryley still frozen by the door, decided to get up and physically nudge Ryley along.

Callie and Carly thanked her mom profusely as the four strode across the formal black and white marble tile that made up the rather imposing foyer to the house.

As they exited, Ryley's mom said, "You two will keep an eye on my girl, right?"

Carly nodded and said, "Of course, we'll look out for Rye-Rye," before heading over to the car.

Ryley's mom grabbed her arm before she could exit, gave her a quick side hug, and said, "Ryley, relax, and have fun. Give them a chance."

Ryley responded with a small, tight smile and followed the two girls out the door.

* * *

Ryley entered IHOP slightly grumpy but determined to keep an open mind. She loved her sleep, and so far, the morning hadn't been worth cutting into her required eight-hour minimum. Ryley had chimed in with the odd comment here and there but stayed mostly quiet on the car ride over as the two seniors had bickered over radio stations in a light-hearted, familiar way. They'd picked up one other girl, Kyle, who Ryley still didn't know very well and who hadn't made any particular effort to speak to Ryley, closing her eyes immediately. Kind of a buzzkill.

As they walked deeper into the restaurant, Ryley looked around; she'd never been to this IHOP before. The tables were the same beige brown as the walls, and this IHOP looked identical to others she'd visited in that they'd chosen to do nothing in the way of actual ambiance. The smell of maple syrup and melted butter did warm her soul though. She followed the other girls into a semi-private dining area set off from the rest of the restaurant with a wall that only went up to her hip. All the other girls on the team were already seated, gathered four to a table.

Everyone in the room shouted, "Finally!" upon seeing the captains, and Carly and Callie made good-natured heckles back while pointing Ryley and Kyle to the two open seats remaining near the other sophomores. As the two quickly and quietly took their place, the captains immediately started speaking, pontificating on the importance of teamwork and what the softball team meant to them. Ryley was charmed by the wholesomeness of it all. She liked how the captains made eye contact with each of the sophomores in turn and how Carly held Ryley's gaze when she said, "Welcome to your second family." When their speech came to an end, they waved over two other seniors who carried a large, brown box up with them.

After pausing for dramatic effect, Callie said, "Now for the fun part! We're going to call each of you forward and give you a cardboard plate with a word on it that we thought fit you. You will also get to wear one of these fun purple boas!"

Carly followed up, saying, "First, Ryley."

Ryley pulled a face but stood up to the sound of what was at least enthusiastic clapping. The one benefit of going first was that no one was tired yet.

She walked briskly over to Carly and Callie, keeping her gaze fixed on the box to calm her nerves. She wished her heart wouldn't thump so fast; she felt light-headed.

"Ryley!" Callie exclaimed as she came closer. "We decided to give you *safe* because you're a good, wholesome kid. We look forward to corrupting you!"

Ryley gave them a hesitant grin in return. She disliked how they'd infantilized her, but then again, she did have a collection of Beanie Babies on her window sill and she'd not had the chance to make any substantive progress in rebranding herself. At least they'd implied she was one of them now.

Carly, seeing Ryley's slightly pained smile, said, in an undertone, "Don't be embarrassed. *Safe* is good! And besides, we're going to cure you of that real quick. We always have a legendary pregame for Homecoming!"

Given that Ryley only tentatively nodded in response, Carly lightly grabbed on to Ryley's sleeve before she could walk away and added, "You're family now and you'll have more fun if you relax—channel your mom!"

Carly's efforts to comfort her appealed to her more than her words did, but nevertheless, she shot Carly as genuine a smile as she could muster and wrapped the unappealing boa around her neck. She felt only *slightly* resentful of Callie and Carly as she heard the words some of the other sophomores got. Kyle, who Ryley had yet to see show any emotion other than general standoffishness, had gotten *party girl*—which was two words, not one. Uptight, perfectionist Maddie, who had yelled at Ryley for messing up a play, had gotten *spirited*. Ryley stopped paying attention after that.

The rest of the breakfast continued without incident until Anu, the one other Indian on the team, intercepted Ryley as she was going up to the buffet table for a second serving. Anu had a sweet, round face, big brown eyes, and thick black hair she usually wore in the form of a tight braid. She was short, clocking in at a more normal Indian height, and stocky.

"Hey, your mom called mine to see if I could bring you over to our house directly, so she wouldn't have to drive all the way here just to go back to the Westside. Are you good to leave in ten?" Anu's parents regularly invited hers over to one of their Indian-centric gatherings that took place once a month, but those always felt like a secret, done as a sort of escape into an alternative world for their parents.

"Oh, yeah, that would be great. Thanks for the ride." Ryley was curious how the drive with Anu would go; they'd never hung out one-on-one. Anu was a junior and kept mostly to herself at the practices they were just beginning to have, given that softball season didn't start until the spring. Furthermore, only a couple of Indians chose to hang out with each other inside the school bounds; most stayed separate. Perhaps they too feared being labeled a FOB (Fresh Off the Boat) or feared they would come off as making no effort if they didn't at least hang out with the East Asians. Importantly, the East Asians had critical mass, with enough people they didn't seem to care what the rest of the school thought of them. In contrast, there were only five or six Indians per grade, hardly enough to form some sort of wolfpack.

After around twenty minutes elapsed—the aforementioned ten minutes in Indian Standard Time—the two said their goodbyes to the rest of the team. There was little fanfare apart from Carly giving Ryley an over-the-top hug, having decided it was her solemn duty to take Ryley under her wing.

Anu immediately turned on the radio station and popped the top upon entering her convertible. With the wind and the music, it would be almost impossible to carry a conversation, not that Ryley minded. She was content to sit in relative silence as she let herself relax, already dropping shields she no longer consciously registered putting up. They didn't have anything in common, but Anu was as, if not more, out of place. She'd seen Anu's childhood bedroom that had all the expected posters of Justin Timberlake and Edward Cullen from *Twilight*. But Anu also had a lightsaber propped against her closet door and had numerous Bollywood movies and dance sequences saved on her computer.

Anu's parents frequently made Anu perform *Bharatanatyam* (a type of Indian classical dance) at their gatherings, and although Anu would moan and drag her feet, she was so good at dancing that Ryley was invariably awed. That being said, the two times they'd both been invited to the same Sweet Sixteen Blowout party, Anu had not danced at all to the Britney Spears classics blasting. Instead, she'd stayed in the corner, awkwardly bopping up and down on her feet. Ryley had done the same awkward bopping up and down, but at least she'd been in a circle of friends.

Indeed, though one would be justified in thinking otherwise, Ryley had more than enough "friends." She just had no Starsky to her Hutch, no Timon to her Pumbaa. She used to be close to a couple of girls, Jane and Lisa, who alongside her had been part of a larger established fifteen-person friend group. They'd go to the movies, have the occasional sleepover, talk about things like The Red Hot Chili Peppers and *The Fresh Prince of Bel-Air*, and life was good. However, everything had changed once they'd begun tenth grade, leaving the middle school campus and arriving at the upper school one. Jane had gotten into her studies and liked playing up that she was a nerd, and Lisa had gotten into boys and singing, and began to hang out with the cool, artsy kids. Ryley disliked talking about material outside the confines of class and so lacked the outward academic intensity necessary to hang with the former but also lacked the nonchalant ennui necessary to hang with the latter.

Without the protection of Jane and Lisa, she soon realized she was unfortunately not all that close to the broader friend group. The epiphany had come when she overheard two of them talking about a Secret Santa/Friendsgiving Extravaganza and realized they'd planned it without her, Jane, and Lisa—quite aggressively in October. So, although she still sat with them at lunch and still went with them to the movies, she was sourcing her options. She couldn't forgive a Friendsgiving slight, and maybe she could hang out with high schoolers who lived the lives they showed in the movies.

All too soon, they arrived at Anu's house and Ryley walked up the familiar cobblestone pathway, ducking under a loquat tree peppered with small white flowers. Ryley, Anu, Harrison, and a couple of the other Indian kids had spent an afternoon in the spring plucking the small golden orbs and eating so many they'd all passed out, queasy, in the soft, freshly mowed grass with their sacks of loquats dumped beside them. It was one of her favorite memories of this house—the easy, wholesome fun, the way Anu's mother had come out and brought them freshly-squeezed lemonade, while Anu's father had run to get them a ladder to get the hard-to-reach loquats. Even before Anu pushed open the white wooden door, Ryley could hear tinkling laughter and shouts of Hindi as someone told the punchline to a joke. As the two girls entered the kitchen, the women, gathered at the table, immediately turned to them; the men were most certainly gathered outside.

Ryley's mom was in the middle of recounting stories from the fourth day of her cousin's seven-day wedding, but immediately stopped mid-story to ask Ryley, "How did the event go?"

Ryley gave her mother and the rest of the women a generic summary of the event, leaving out reference to the word assignments. That detail would be shared with her mother privately. Blessedly, Anu lost interest and left the kitchen as soon as Ryley began talking, so there was no one to fact check her generally upbeat, positive review. Her mother eyed Ryley suspiciously, undoubtedly knowing she was giving her audience a heavily redacted version of the event when the normally loquacious Ryley finished her overview in two minutes.

Regardless, her mother didn't push and began talking about the wedding again. Ryley tuned her out. She had felt incredibly ill-at-ease during that wedding and had no desire to relive the experience during story-time. Over the week-long objectively joyous affair, her extended family had flipped between English and Hindi easily, getting impatient with Ryley as she'd stumbled through wedding traditions core to their culture. They were almost overwhelmingly warm and loving, pushing helping after helping of food at her, but she could sense their surprise and dismay at how foreign she was. Although Ryley's mother had not said anything, she'd seen the way they had looked at her mom disappointedly. As Ryley had predicted, the earrings had done minimal damage control.

Feeling claustrophobic, Ryley yanked the screen door open, causing an unfortunate screech that sounded like a dying hyena to resonate through the house before settling down near her dad. She liked the cadence of his measured, confident voice as he talked about the economy. She began to nod along, happy to be sitting with the men, and happy to show support for whatever her dad was saying.

Unfortunately, her enthusiastic nodding caused him to turn to her and ask, "Oh, Ryley, what do you think?"

Flinching inside, she offered her half-baked opinion, formed on the basis of three articles she'd read.

Her dad didn't say anything for a couple of moments, but then he exclaimed, "Isn't the American education system wonderful?" and she felt like a star once again. Unfortunately, too soon, the men inevitably fell back into speaking in Hindi, forgetting where they were momentarily as they riffed off each other, transported back to home and jokes she didn't understand.

Every time this group of Indian transplants gathered, Ryley would see them shed their American shell and emerge whole, and she would've liked to join them and pull out a fully developed Indian self from inside; however, her Indian self was a larva at best and even less developed than her American one. That had been made transparently clear at the wedding. So, instead, she tried to respect the order of things in this safe space of theirs, and when the women inevitably came to serve the men snacks, Ryley reluctantly and sadly hopped up to join them in bringing out everything for the men. She would've liked to ask why this was the done way, why this dynamic existed, but she stayed silent. She wouldn't have minded so much if she had the easy possessiveness, the fond nostalgia for a home no one could doubt she belonged to, instead of looking through the window at them.

CHAPTER 8

NOVEMBER 2018

———

Ryley skidded into Property, barely getting settled into her seat before Professor Kilmer started talking. They'd lost about a fifth of the class at this point; these students had realized attendance wasn't actually mandatory and didn't count toward the grade, so they'd just started skipping, deciding they might as well learn from supplements and materials online than risk being humiliated through a cold call. Ryley had yet to miss a single class; she couldn't fathom the idea of not showing up at all. A lifetime of being a participator could do that to a girl.

She swiveled her head around now to see if David was there. He also had yet to miss a single class, and there he was, shooting her a grin from the front row. He was quite serious and regularly spoke in class, but he would only ever raise his hand to give a measured, unique opinion. Nothing that could be read off textbook pages. Certainly, he had never played coy about his ambitions: he wanted to be a judge, someone of influence, and had made clear that academics would take precedence over everything else for him. But he showered her with compliments and emphasized her social fluency and level-headedness. They'd spent the last couple of months feeling each other out, and he'd finally asked her out last week; they were planning to get dinner together that night. She was thrilled she was doing the grad school experience right. She didn't let herself think about it much beyond that.

As Professor Kilmer glanced over at her now, she realized she hadn't finished setting up and belatedly pulled out her name placard though she would've liked to keep it in her bag to see if he remembered her name. She forced herself to start writing as the professor began his lecture in earnest, finding it helped her to pay attention and prevented her from completely drifting off. It was only when Mark raised his hand to ask a question and launched the class into a discussion about ethics, outside the scope of the homework assignment, that she gave herself permission to start drawing little stick figures with small, pointed swords engaged in a furious war with each other. She drew upside-down Vs on all their heads, gave them all slight chests and hips, and felt good about it. She was unfortunately limited by her artistic capabilities, so she couldn't come up with too ornate backstories for any of her characters, but she'd replaced her daydreaming with doodling out of necessity. She was trying to focus, and she only allowed herself to doodle when it was an absolute necessity for her brain to take a mental vacation during class; during those not infrequent occurrences when Mark asked a question unrelated to the subject matter.

She was still generally confident she would pull through, that everything would be okay when she buckled down and started studying for finals, but her recent memo performance had startled her. In their Legal Research and Writing class, a hallmark class of One-L, they'd been tasked with writing a memo summarizing the rule of law on a given issue. The "grade" didn't count for anything and instead was just meant to serve as a temperature check of sorts, in case certain students such as Ryley were deluded enough to think they were doing fine when in reality they weren't. But Ryley refused to let herself worry about it. She knew it was just a fluke. She hadn't given the work her all yet.

Ryley looked back up at Professor Kilmer as she scribbled her initials in a loopy, lazy signature at the bottom corner of her doodle only to suddenly find him looking back at her. She froze, frightened, feeling out of sorts entirely. She'd thought he would be engaged with Mark, who'd recently started participating much more, possibly to help compensate for the fact that Zeke had started participating much less after the first month. Zeke was still only ever diligently and furiously taking notes, but his opinions on the casebook readings were no longer an intrinsic part of the curriculum.

As she heard the passion rising in Mark's voice as he spoke again, she forced herself to look away from Professor Kilmer and at Mark, even as her hands began to slightly tremble. She knew what was coming, but she could barely get Mark's words to filter into her brain, and all she could think about was how sad it was that Pluto had been demoted from planethood. She didn't even like astrology.

As she'd predicted, as soon as Mark finished speaking, Professor Kilmer called on her. "Ms. Agarwal, do you have any thoughts?"

Ryley hemmed and said, "I'm not sure," her voice audibly shaking and embarrassing her further. She had no idea what was going on; she'd zoned out for at least the last ten minutes. Unwilling to let her off the hook, he asked Mark to repeat himself. Mark said something about a lawyer's role morally to always do the right thing for their client.

Ryley hesitated and then finally said, "I think it's important to always try to do the right thing, but if a partner were to ask me, a first-year associate, to do something I considered morally gray, but it wasn't against the law, I think it would depend on the situation and what's at stake. I wouldn't presume to know better."

Professor Kilmer said nothing and instead nodded at Mark, who had immediately raised his hand again.

"We need to look outside ourselves and push ourselves to make a difference. There are too many people who think nothing needs to be done if they have the safe harbor of the law. But the world is the way it is because of people like Ryley, because people stick with being *safe*. Because people just go along with the existing way of doing things. We need to recognize that we have more power than we think we have." Mark's voice was wavering too, in a way that was especially noticeable because he was normally so calm and composed.

Ryley shrunk into herself, keeping her gaze firmly locked on her notebook, feeling the flush spread throughout her neck as she looked down. She'd been called *safe* before, but not in this context. Then, the word had been used to signal she was too naïve, too immature. She'd grown up and had learned how to behave, but now the word was once again being used as a weapon against her, this time to signal she'd done too good a job at learning the rules. Mark had only ever been nice to her, had seemed to genuinely like and respect her, but she should have known something was going to give. The water had been too calm.

She listened with only half an ear from then on as others raised their hand and continued to validate Mark's point. Cassidy spoke in an emotional, ringing tone. Even Sophie, rarely a participant, raised her hand, confirming that although it took strength to push the envelope forward, it was a moral necessity.

As the class finally ended and Ryley avoided making eye contact with anyone, feeling incredibly exposed, Professor Kilmer called out, "Ms. Agarwal, could I speak with you for a moment?"

Ryley felt the choking tightening of humiliation in her throat and a concomitant pressure behind her eyes, but she kept her head high and simply nodded as others made a show of turning their heads to gawk at her. A couple of students hesitantly approached the lectern, used to staying after class to discuss the finer minutiae of the cases with the professor. He cut them off with a "Not today," and the two shot Ryley half-pitying, half-baleful looks as they exited. After the last of her Section-mates had left the classroom, Ryley forced herself to leave the safety of her seat and approached Professor Kilmer, situated commandingly in the center of the room.

He heaved a sigh as he looked at her standing in front of him, uncertain and contrite. She'd never been asked to stay back by a professor in her life—at least in regard to doing something bad.

"Ryley. When I've called on you, you've always delivered good answers, and you have potential, reciting some of the finer nuances of the fact patterns; however, you lose focus frequently. You need to build up your stamina and you need to learn how to think about the law." He paused to check in with her, to see if she had anything to say for herself. She didn't.

She forced herself to maintain eye contact, even as she clenched and unclenched the fist she had jammed into one of her pockets.

He continued, "I bet you did well before just based on your knowledge of facts and details and knowing more material than the next guy. Here, though, you need to become smart in learning how to interpret and apply the law. By refusing to meaningfully engage in class discussion that will push your understanding of the material and allow you to learn the law beyond the facts on the page, you are crippling yourself right out the gate. Learn from your fellow students; learn how they present their opinions in a convincing way."

Seeing she was rather frozen and unsure of how to appropriately respond to his unsolicited advice, he gave her a fatherly pat on the arm before adding, "You don't have to want to ace this class or spend every waking moment studying the law, but you owe it to yourself to develop the skills to interpret cases and to learn to argue generally so that when you find the area of law you love, you can hit the ground running."

Ryley finally responded, "Yes, got it. Thanks for the advice. Makes sense." She took a step backward, hoping she could be excused.

"How did you do on your closed memo?" He was not quite done.

"Fine." She didn't want him to think he was right about her, that he had her pegged. Given his long look, she was sure he didn't believe her anyway. She wouldn't have believed herself.

Thankfully, he didn't seem to have anything more to say, so Ryley repeated her thanks, said, "I'll try harder," and walked quickly away at his nod. Ryley jammed her headphones in as she walked toward the door, hoping to disguise, or at least blend, the ringing in her ears with music. In the past, the more things went off the rails, and the more anxious she got, the worse the ear ringing was; headaches usually followed. She drew in a breath through her nose and expelled it through her mouth in a measured count. The professor's talk after the graded memo was a bit too much of a one-two punch, and she pulled out her phone to text David asking for a raincheck. However, upon exiting the classroom, she saw Sophie and Cassidy there waiting for her.

After making inadvertent eye contact with the two for a split second, Ryley immediately veered to the right. If called out about it later, she would say she'd been in a rush. Naturally, Cassidy was not to be so easily dissuaded and reached out to tug on Ryley's coat sleeve, grounding her to a stop.

"Hey, hold up for a second. What happened in there?" Cassidy asked, her voice coated in a velvet layer of care and sincerity, her brown eyes soft like melted caramel.

"Nothing. He just noticed I've been drifting off in the last two classes or so and wanted to check in on me," Ryley answered, smoothing out the story and packaging it incredibly neatly on the fly. She doubted her composure would last long, however, and thought it prudent to cut the conversation short. "Well, I have to get going." After being met with blank expressions, Ryley said, "In a rush and all."

"Yes, yes, of course. But you don't even have two minutes?" Cassidy asked, managing to make the request more of a command than a question.

Ryley stuttered when put so overtly on the spot and finally said, "Sure, I have one minute."

Sophie took the lead this time. "We wanted to make sure you were okay. You looked pretty upset earlier today. You know Mark means well, and we hope you didn't take our agreement with him personally; I think we all just want to try to make the world better, to not just accept the status quo."

"Yes, sure. Okay." Ryley didn't think petulantly saying she wanted to make the world a better place too would win her any points.

"That's not much of a response." The reprobation was clear in Cassidy's tone.

"I'm not quite sure what you want me to say," Ryley said, flinching when she heard how heavy and resentful her words sounded. "Sorry. I mean, I get it. I'm not mad at him. Or you both. But I do have to go. Excuse me."

"Glad we're all in agreement and there are no hard feelings." Cassidy waited until Ryley nodded before switching her tone to be light and airy once more. "Have fun on your date with David tonight. Let me know how it goes."

Ryley gave them both quick grimace-smiles—those were her specialty—and strode rapidly away. Mark must have told Cassidy of her date. She decided she should go after all; even if the day hadn't been a good one thus far, she could possibly recover with a win in the romantic sphere. She'd rush over to the gym to get a quick workout in to decompress though. Short-circuit her mind.

The concept of alone time, which had once been so crucial to her, was non-existent, and she began to wonder if she'd made up the fact she liked being alone. David had begun to rub off on her and she found herself liking how having a jam-packed schedule made her feel. She'd fallen into a rhythm of sorts—classes in the morning and afternoon followed immediately by a workout and a couple of hours of studying in the evening. She'd also joined a law journal and signed up for a couple of Saturdays' worth of work, so she felt she was really leaning into the whole law school thing.

There was never a time she was not doing something and on weekend nights, she was usually just getting more drunk than necessary with Mark, Cassidy, David, and whoever else was free in that group. She hadn't expected there to be as much drinking as there was in law school, but she'd been fast disabused of the notion. There was a student body-organized drinking event every Thursday and beyond that, there were happy hours, casual hangs, and house parties; as a drunk third year had told her when he pulled her gleefully aside, lawyers had the highest rate of alcoholism.

It was good to be busy or to be drunk. It was good to have no time to think.

CHAPTER 9

NOVEMBER 2018

Ryley broke into a light trot as she exited Wasserstein Hall and made her way across the speckled gravel toward the gym. She was cutting it close timing-wise, but she was sure David would prefer a slightly late, endorphin-buzzed, first-date Ryley to a distracted, slightly depressed one. Mark hadn't even stayed back to talk to her, booking it out of there instead. She'd wait for him to reach out to her.

It was just beginning to get noticeably cold in Cambridge and she deeply regretted wearing the California cold-weather coat that was slimming but entirely useless. As yet another gust of wind managed to sneak its way under her turtleneck, she was quite sure her body had entered into some state of shock. Desperate to get indoors, she road-runnered her way past the library, only briefly skimming the Latin scrawled across the front. She didn't understand any of it, but then again, she'd always been of a more practical bent. Practical notwithstanding the fact she had no real life skills and had chosen to take French, a language spoken by, at most, one percent of Americans. Harrison used to joke that she'd be the first person to die if a group of them were stranded on a deserted island (Harrison and Ryley had been huge *Lost* fans back in the day).

She rounded the corner of the library, narrowly avoided hitting a tourist with his camera out, and gratefully took the last few steps to get into the blessed warmth. She looked back to see what he was capturing as she pulled open the door to the gym. Perhaps he had found an angle of the law school she'd want to replicate later for her Instagram. It was a simple shot of the library, with the lawn before it, made significant only because of the lighting. Because the sun was beginning to set at the offensive time of 4:30 p.m. Ryley needed to get out, go someplace where everyone didn't suffer from severe sun deprivation. Maybe she and David could go on a couples vacation to a nice beach house. She'd never done that with a boyfriend and would love to check it off the bucket list.

Striding into the rather ordinary red-brick gym (the law school had clearly designed buildings in line with how they thought students should organize their priorities), she was startled to find it surprisingly packed. She let herself heave a small, pathetic sigh and made her rapid way up to the locker room; hopefully she could snag the one open treadmill. After a quick deck change, she put on a *Mood Pop* playlist and then, feeling it, embarked upon a dramatic, fast walk out the locker room. Unfortunately, her walk was cut prematurely short when she immediately collided with another girl upon exiting the room.

"Oh, sorry," she said or perhaps shouted. She had zero volume control when her headphones were in. Taking a step back to check for casualties, she realized the girl clutching at her elbow was Olivia. She apologized again, though the way she was semi-laughing the second time around probably took away from the perceived genuineness of it. She hadn't bumped

Olivia all that hard, and Olivia was just standing there in an over-the-top lime green sports bra with an over-the-top eyebrows-scrunched, eyes-squinted-in-pain look on her face.

Ryley gave another muted laugh-snort before she finally gathered herself and asked, "Are you okay?"

"Yes. Though I don't see what's so funny. You could've knocked me backward down the stairs and then I'd have been dead." Olivia leaned back against the wall as she spoke, unnecessarily flexing her abs. It was barely a two-pack—more of a zero-pack.

"Okay. But you're not dead, so this is all a moot point." Ryley considered walking away, but Olivia was still lounging against the wall, so she continued, "Anyway, what's up? How's life?"

Olivia gave a generic, "Good," but didn't rush off, simply letting the word hang there in the space between them. They weren't the talking type of friends though they did happen to see each other almost every day, if only ever in passing. They both usually just gave each other brief smiles whenever they made eye contact, though sometimes, Olivia seemed to forget how to smile, and Ryley would have to hold a prolonged smile to show her how it was done. So, sometimes, Ryley pretended not to see her.

As the silence dragged, Ryley took a step back and lifted her headphones to shove them back into her ears, prompting Olivia to noisily exhale through her thin, patrician nose and ask, "Everything good? Killing One-L? Harrison always talks about how smart you are."

"Yeah, it's going great! Super great. The people are nice, the classes are going well." Ryley wasn't lying. She would pull through; she knew she would. Professor Kilmer and Professor Suh—her Legal Research & Writing professor, who had given her the lowest possible grade on her memo—just hadn't seen her brilliance yet. Ryley was surprised Harrison was talking about her, though. She barely mentioned him to her friends.

As if cued by her thoughts, Harrison appeared at the bottom of the gray concrete stairwell. He shouted, "Olivia, I didn't know you were friends with Rye Bread!"

"Oh, yeah, she's a doll," Olivia said, keeping her gaze trained on Harrison. Harrison shot Ryley a bemused look.

Ryley shrugged though she considered telling Olivia that she couldn't pull off saying "doll." That was the second time she had used the word. Instead, Ryley said, "Hey Harrison. It's been a while." Harrison had shorn his hair. He looked surprisingly good in a buzz-cut, his strong, prominent forehead and jaw contrasting nicely against his short hair, though his nose did stick out a bit. She'd like to say that she at least had grown into her nose.

"Yeah, it has! These past few months have flown by. You look like you're living it up."

His enthusiasm made her feel slightly foolish. She dialed up her engagement level. "Just trying to make the most of things!"

"Do you spend any time studying?" He followed up with what she supposed could be a joking tone. Maybe she needed to scale back on her social media posting.

"Yes, *of course,* I do," she said, frowning down at him. She could do without a lecture now. Seeing how easily he fell into the role of big brother, she realized he must have missed being condescending to someone. "Anyway, how're you doing? Happy to be a Two-L?"

"I'm fine. It's all right." Ryley couldn't blame him for his concision. It was hard to catch up on two months of life in a gym stairwell with Olivia carefully evaluating them, ping-ponging her eyes between the two of them. Ryley looked at Olivia to see if she'd add anything to Harrison's words.

Surprisingly, Olivia did choose to chime in, saying, "I think I miss all the friends I made my first year. Some of the people here are particular. And kind of judgey. I still don't feel like I belong."

"I can see that," Ryley said, hoping the soft tenor of her voice was conveying the right amount of sympathy without dipping into pity. Because she was a good person, she chose not to draw attention to how Olivia seemed to make an effort to stick out with her dress sense and general don't-mess-with-me attitude.

Despite Ryley's angelic intentions, Olivia looked at her with her thin lips pressed together as she grumbled, "And how exactly can you see that?"

Harrison, who had moved up to be near them so he was no longer shouting, jumped in before Ryley had to respond, saying, "Oh, I've talked about this with Ryley some, so she gets where we're coming from." Ryley didn't want his protection, and she opened her mouth to say something to that effect, but he loudly continued, "Anyway, Olivia, as you know, I totally agree. It's like everyone's already formed all their cliques and stuff. I feel like some of them think they're smarter just because they got in from the beginning."

He paused to take a breath before pushing on in a more mellow tone. "It's definitely an adjustment, I don't know. I mean, I get that it's worth it to come here for the name, but I miss my friends at Cornell. And of course, it sucks that I'm even farther from Genie. Hopefully it'll end up being worth it."

Genie, Harrison's picture-perfect girlfriend, had stayed in New York. Although their conversation in September had been too short for Harrison to adequately extoll her virtues,

Ryley had heard him go on about Genie forever at the dinner table last Christmas. Ryley wondered if she could get away without asking about her.

Fortunately, she remembered she was in a rush and so opened her mouth to excuse herself, but Olivia jumped in before Ryley could say anything. "All things considered, we're doing a pretty good job of it, Hari." There was a distinct possessiveness and familiarity with which Olivia said the nickname.

"How's Genie?" The words tumbled out of Ryley's mouth, quite against her will.

Olivia made a point of snorting loudly, staring at Ryley with a mix of amusement and irritation. Ryley blushed and looked away from her quickly. Harrison just looked between the two of them, confused.

"She's good. The long-distance is obviously hard, but she's coming for the Harvard-Yale game, so hopefully you both can meet her then."

Olivia said, "You know how excited I am to meet your girlfriend, right, Harrison?"

"Yeah, of course. I feel like I'm going to become the third wheel." Ryley could feel Olivia's eyes drilling a hole into the side of her face; she kept her gaze on Harrison.

Turning to exclusively face Ryley, Harrison asked, "How did you do on your closed memo? I heard you all got it back."

"Fine," Ryley said shortly. She hoped their mom hadn't told him about her grade. She'd kill her if she had.

"Okay, well, let me know if you need any help." He paused after he said this.

Ryley responded with a rather ungracious, "Sure. Thanks, will do." They both knew she wouldn't be coming over to him for help anytime soon.

Likely hit by the same unfortunate memories, he rather abruptly said, "I'll let you go. I know you One-Ls are busy. We should definitely meet up soon though." He was making a farce of their relationship, saying such generic things.

"Yeah. Anyway, I should go. I'm running late for a date already." She felt no shame in skating over his dismissal of her not moments before. She would be the one to formally end the conversation.

She waved bye to him and nodded to Olivia before squeezing past them to get to the door leading to the gym floor. As she opened it, Olivia called out, "With David?"

Ryley just gave her a half-smile in response and continued on her way out, blasting *Mood Pop* on high.

* * *

Ryley beat David to Alden & Harlow; he had texted her while she was at the gym saying he needed thirty more minutes to complete the readings, which had suited her just fine, especially because the stairwell conversation had delayed her. She wanted time without David to settle into the ambiance of the restaurant. Alden & Harlow was of the sort that refused to seat anyone until everyone had arrived, so she stood by the hostess, observing. It was casual in a purposefully intentional way that demanded guests recognize its charm. The tastefully tatted, stylish waiters smoothly scurrying around further added to a brand that screamed unassuming in a deliberate, expensive way. Mark, who kept track of every new hip restaurant and bar, had recommended the place. All the people in the restaurant were classically upscale Cambridge— nice sweaters or button-down shirts the norm, the occasional dress an anomaly.

Ryley was wearing a tight, navy blue mock neck which she'd tucked into ripped jeans. Although she usually skewed more conservative in her clothing, sometimes she couldn't resist purchasing a piece or two to mix things up. The clothing was cut well enough that she felt at ease, though she'd have matched better to Olivia than to David, who was stepping up now in a plain, black button-down shirt. He leaned in automatically for a hug and she let it happen.

"Have you checked in yet?" he asked, keeping a hand on her arm.

"Yep. I'll go and let them know you're here as well." She refrained from tucking her arm behind her back. She'd gotten comfortable enough with Mark and Cassidy that she didn't mind when they touched her now, but David touched her so frequently that sometimes she wanted to take a step back, feeling like they were moving too fast—notwithstanding the last two months they'd spent getting to know each other.

"I don't mind checking in for us," he replied.

She hesitated, waffled some more, and then ended up saying, "I've got it."

He responded with a raised eyebrow and an uncertain, "Um, okay."

When he offered to order for the two of them, she let him. After he'd placed the order, he said, "Interesting class today. Mark was really fired up."

"Yeah." She fiddled with her beer bottle as she thought about how to quickly move on.

"I liked what you said. I think you were being realistic! People get caught up in their own righteousness."

She decided she wouldn't mind staying on the topic a bit longer after all and expanded willingly. "I mean, I obviously see his point. I was just saying that in the real world, it's not as black and white. And it's not fair that everyone chimed in and supported him. It's easy to be a maverick when people automatically give you the benefit of the doubt and you have nothing to lose. It's harder when you have to prove you belong in the first place."

"Yeah, Ryley, of course. But it's not like you're exactly on the outside here either, right? You're an inside-the-lines person if I've seen one. Come on, people accept you." He punctuated his statement with a chuckle.

"They accept me *because* I am inside the lines. Now I'm being called out for that, for playing it *safe*. There's no winning."

"Ryley, not to be mean, but you're playing the world's smallest violin," he said, half-chuckling again. "Don't let Mark's one comment get to you. I like how normal you are. You make people feel comfortable. You make *me* feel comfortable. You're not one of those annoying people who gets offended about every little thing so people always have to be watching their words around you." He leaned forward across the table to rest his hand on hers.

"Yeah," Ryley said quietly. She shouldn't let Mark get to her. She would continue ignoring Mark until he apologized though.

David continued, "I think we all have to perform somewhat to fit in. I don't think it's such a bad burden to bear. It's what makes you successful." There was a soft, barely-there edge to his words as he gently chided her for trying to disown exactly what her key value-add was. He was right.

"Yeah, you're right. I just got stuck in my head," she conceded, though she slid her hand out from underneath his. "Anyway, I didn't get a chance to ask you about your weekend earlier. What'd you get up to?"

They ended up talking about nothing and everything for the rest of the evening and skipped from light topic to light topic, laughing eagerly whenever the opportunity arose. Both wanted the first date to be a success, so with the aid of numerous drinks, the two happily stayed until closing time. They dawdled outside the restaurant for just a bit longer after that, not quite ready to call the evening to a close. Eventually, though, after two disjointed strings of conversation too many, they parted ways. He gave her a warm hug and a gentle kiss on the cheek, drawing out the embrace; she liked it, felt he'd earned it, that they'd both done good work that night. Polite as ever, he offered to walk her home, but she declined. He lived right near the restaurant and she wanted to use the walk to sober up and reflect on the date.

As she made her way up the cobblestone path, she couldn't help the smile that came naturally to her face. Despite the small disagreement in the beginning, he seemed to have her best interests at heart. She had a good feeling about the relationship; it felt like it had actual staying power this time. He was undoubtedly going places given his drive, his scholarly mind, and his calm demeanor. He'd also paid for the meal even after she'd made a couple of good-faith protests. He wanted to treat her like a lady.

She put her headphones on, wanting to boost her mood further and memorialize the moment with a song. What if she'd found her life partner through a swoop of good luck after striking out for so long? She loved, more than anything else, the absurd normalcy of meeting her potential husband in graduate school.

Her mom called as she was scrolling through her playlists and she eagerly took the chance to recap every aspect of the date in excruciating detail. She decided to leave the class incident and the talk with Professor Kilmer for another time. She'd already shared her closed memo grade and her mom had brushed it off like she had, saying it was a fluke. There was no need to cause unnecessary panic.

As she finally entered her apartment and ended the call with her mom, her phone lit up. Fully expecting to see David's name attached to a text thanking her for a wonderful night, she was startled to see that it was Harrison saying, *Hope your date went well. It was good seeing you.* She'd ignore the message for now but respond in a day or two. It was potentially time to bury the hatchet and move on.

CHAPTER 10

NOVEMBER 2008

———

Ryley kept her headphones jammed firmly in her ears. She was listening to The Pussycat Dolls' "When I Grow Up" to try to get in the mood. She heard her mom speaking, pretended she couldn't, felt her mom's glare, and then pulled out her headphones.

"What?" Ryley asked, her tone slightly petulant.

"How're you feeling?"

"All right." Ryley sighed. "I don't know if this is quite my scene." Ryley's mom was dropping her off at Carly's house. The night of Carly's "legendary" Homecoming pregame had finally arrived.

Her mom responded, "Just take a breath, and be your nice, normal self. If someone gives you a cup, sip at it so you don't stand out, but don't have more than one or two sips."

"Okay," Ryley mumbled, fidgeting with her phone. People weren't as moronic as her mom seemed to think. Her *Miss Congeniality* makeover had yet to convince everyone she was cool.

"Ryley, you're the one who wanted to come to this. Do you want me to turn around?" Her mom's hands were clenched tightly around the steering wheel, and Ryley could hear the tiredness in her tone. Although her mom had quit her strategy consulting job to raise them, she regularly helped her dad clinch deals, and Ryley's mom and dad had spent the whole day figuring out how to close a prospective client.

"No, I'm good," Ryley said, making sure to draw the *O* sound out. She'd recently stumbled upon a whole collection of whale songs when she was looking for new forms of white noise to drown out Harrison's trumpet playing, and she liked how the whales wailed their *O*s.

"Okay, great. I know you'll be fine. And if you get uncomfortable, call me, okay? I'll come in a heartbeat. Or Harrison can take you home. He's going to be at Homecoming too."

"It's fine. There's no way I'm going to make him leave early. He'll think I'm so lame."

"Ryley, he acts tough and all, but you know he would never judge you. He loves you." Ryley would 100 percent disagree on the judgment bit, but he was probably a better choice for a getaway driver than her mom; he'd be quick and smooth leaving. And he'd already be at the scene of the crime, so Ryley said nothing and just pulled on the red shirt with the *Go Wolverines!* plastered across the front, ridding it of imaginary wrinkles. As they pulled up to the curb in front of Carly's house, Ryley began revving herself up. Going straight to Homecoming from a pregame with the softball girls would be good for her. It would definitely help refurbish her image.

As Ryley sat there, giving herself a pep talk, her mom softly chuckled before reaching over the console to yank her into a hug, pressing a kiss into her hair. "Go now."

Ryley let out a long-suffering sigh but finally pushed the car door open, waving bye to her mom, even as her mother's car stayed stationary. She wouldn't leave until Ryley had entered Carly's house. Ryley stepped gingerly onto the grass, pulling at her shirt once again and running her fingers lightly against one of her eyebrows. She'd only recently begun getting her eyebrows threaded as part of the whole makeover routine, and she hated every second of it. The Indian cosmetologist who saw her would always tell her that her "eyebrows looked like a man's" without fail and yank out the hair mercilessly. Ryley knocked on Carly's door and then ran a couple of fingers against her traumatized right eyebrow again as she waited for Carly to open the door.

A second louder knock and phone call later, Carly threw open the door, giving Ryley a bear hug and a giant smile though her glazed eyes seemed to look slightly through Ryley and beyond. Ryley offered Carly a shy smile and a small flap of her hand.

Carly exclaimed, "Rye-Rye! Come in, come in. All the girls are already here. I've invited the baseball guys over too, so they'll be here in about thirty and then we can all leave together to go to the game." Ryley gave what she hoped was an enthusiastic nod and stepped gingerly across the threshold.

All the girls were lounging on bright, patterned cushions thrown haphazardly on the carpeted living room floor, the couches pushed to the side. Two of the seniors sat huddled on one of the couches, whispering to one another. As Ryley watched, one threw her head back, almost knocking down one of the paintings hung up on the white crepe wall. The painting looked expensive, but Carly didn't bat an eye as she pounced on the two girls, half-sitting on one with carefree disregard. Ryley turned her feet toward the girls sitting on the floor. A couple of them gave her small waves; most, however, kept their eyes focused on Kyle. Kyle was in fine form, holding court.

"At this point, I've called him a friend a billion times, and I've blown him off to go on a 'date' that's just me hanging out with my dad, but he really doesn't want to get it."

"Oh, no!" a couple of the girls interrupted to half-laugh, half-moan.

"Right? So eventually, I have to just be straight with him, and I say, 'I think you're really sweet, but I promise I'm not going to change my mind, so please move on to someone else. Besides, date me for a month, and you'll be begging to go back to being friends.'" The other girls laughed, charmed by Kyle's perfect blend of self-deprecation and entertainment value.

Ryley was curious to know which boy Kyle was talking about and pondered what it must be like to inspire that sort of devotion in someone else. Kyle was definitely beautiful in a sort of classical way, but she'd always thought boys preferred less muscular girls, and Kyle was built. That being said, she was bleach-blond and funny, and in theater and Improv. A real renaissance woman.

Ryley settled down on one of the open seat cushions toward the periphery of the group as Kyle matched wits with another girl there. Ryley listened to them casually discuss boys, last week's party, and Mr. Newton's impossible exam. With nothing to contribute, she stayed silent, focused on taking it all in and listening to the careless, self-assured way they talked. As Kyle circled back to discuss "the boy"—though Kyle must have shared his name at some point given the way three-quarters of the girls smirked when she said that—Ryley focused on the bouquet of scents around her. She loved the grown-up smell of perfume; she picked up vanilla on one girl, citrus notes on another, and sandalwood on a third.

Eventually, at some point in Kyle's repeated story, Carly walked past Ryley and leaned slightly down to say, "Oh

Rye-Rye, take whatever you want from the table. My brother bought a bunch of stuff for us."

Ryley hesitated and then said, "I'm good for now." She hoped Carly wouldn't make a big deal of it.

Carly responded, "Okay, but we're playing *Never Have I Ever*, so you'll need something." She then turned to the larger group of girls and repeated herself, causing all the girls to get up and scurry over to the drinks table.

Ryley hoisted herself up, got a head rush because she'd gotten up too fast, stumbled, gracefully, of course, and trudged her way over to the table. She found herself next to Carly at the back of the group as they waited for girls to pick out drinks.

Ryley racked her brains for something to say and finally just landed on, "Who was the boy Kyle was talking about?"

"Just some guy named Josh. He's on the baseball team and thinks he's way cooler than he is, but he means well."

Ryley considered poking fun at Josh, bringing up to Carly that he'd had the nerve to lecture her about having no game, but she decided the poor boy had been punished enough. She simply said, "Oh, I know him."

"Yeah, he's a good kid. He just needs to grow up." Ryley could get behind that sentiment. As Carly got pulled into another conversation, Ryley let her gaze drift to the far side of the room where Anu was sitting. Ryley had yet to go over and say hi, but Anu had not been making any effort to socialize, texting on her phone all evening. A couple of the girls half-heartedly called out to Anu, urging her to try something, but Anu was steadfast in refusing. Ryley knew where Anu was coming from; Anu's parents were the type to stay up until Anu came home and would freak if they smelled alcohol on her. Ryley was thankful she didn't have to deal with that.

Pulling up to the drinks table, she dithered, saw Carly grab a Bud Light, and then grabbed one too—she liked the Clydesdale horses from the commercials. The metal can was also an added bonus, obscuring the volume of beer inside; she'd easily be able to take the beer to the bathroom and dump most of it. Movies showing drunk people unwittingly speaking their unfiltered truths and making fools of themselves were the only form of anti-drinking propaganda Ryley needed to see.

When Ryley turned from the table, she saw there was only one open cushion left, located next to Anu. Ryley went over to Anu slightly hesitantly, leery of others thinking she was not making an effort to blend in by going to sit next to the one other Indian. Ryley made a show of taking a swig of beer as she sat down. She was trying.

"Hey Anu," Ryley said, confident and level. The slight hesitance marking her tone during the entire evening was notably absent with Anu.

"Hi." Anu's response wasn't very encouraging.

"What's up? I don't see you hanging much with the team," Ryley said, letting the words trail away, allowing the unsaid question to linger.

"Yeah, they're not my vibe." Anu fidgeted with a cushion.

"Got it, got it," Ryley said for lack of anything better. She couldn't agree. She wanted the team to become "her vibe." After a few more seconds of silence, Ryley asked, "So who do you hang out with?"

"No one you would know. None of them are Indian. They're all juniors involved in artsy stuff."

Ryley dropped the names of two juniors in her honors calculus class to show she did know juniors who weren't Indian. Anu stayed silent, texting someone on her phone. As Anu smiled at the response, Ryley tried to surreptitiously peek and see if the name was masculine or feminine. Maybe Anu was too good for the softball team because she had a boyfriend on the sly. Anu turned her phone over. Ryley couldn't even bring herself to be embarrassed; it wasn't like she had anything better to do. Finally, the game started.

"Okay, never have I ever done coke."

"Never have I ever done oral."

"Never have I ever done a keg stand."

Ryley hadn't done anything, clearly. She didn't even bother faking a half-lift, like she was considering drinking, like she'd done something that came anywhere close.

"Ryley, your turn."

Saying she'd never kissed a boy would be horrific; she tried to think of something more hardcore.

"Never have I ever had sex." About half the girls drank. Not bad.

Kyle shouted out, "Ryley, play your cards right tonight, and we can change things."

Ryley forced herself to make a chuckle-like noise, even as she considered what it would be like to just get it over with early. The game continued for some rounds more and Ryley sipped her drink cautiously. She didn't like the light buzz that began to run through her, making her feel entirely out of sorts. She felt like she was slightly floating and could see herself letting her guard down and spilling all the feelings out. She stopped sipping.

She surreptitiously glanced around, but no one was watching her. They were all too fascinated watching Kyle and Carly consume their drinks with alarming rapidity. As Kyle nonchalantly talked about all the things she had done, Ryley felt a surge of surprising resentment run through her. Ryley wished she knew where Kyle got the courage from.

Soon, the baseball boys were ringing the doorbell, and because everyone was running late, they almost immediately left for the football game. Before leaving Carly's house, Ryley made a quick run to the bathroom, and with a huge sigh of relief, dumped her beer down the drain.

* * *

Ryley was seated next to Kyle and Josh in the eighth row of the bleachers. Josh had cajoled Kyle into being in his car and Ryley had asked to be in it—he was the only baseball player she knew. But Josh had taken a wrong turn, so by the time they'd arrived, everyone else was already settled into the bleachers and they'd been relegated to the outskirts of their softball-baseball group. Although it wasn't too cold a night, they were comfortably into sweater weather, and Ryley wished they could have sat in the center of the grouping and been afforded the protection of body heat. Ryley's sweater was slightly on the thinner side and pulling the sleeves over her hands and tucking her hands between her crossed legs was doing nothing in the way of generating even an iota of extra warmth. Beside her, Kyle and Josh seemed relatively unaffected by the wind chill, but they had drunk significantly more than she had; she'd heard that alcohol made people less sensitive to the cold.

As others jeered at the football players, Ryley looked around her, taking in the general merriment and the carnival air. The large, fluorescent outdoor stadium lights shone a spotlight on the field and on the parking lot to the right, where dozens of food stands were set up. The stands were staffed with parents handing out cotton candy, samosas, boba tea, burritos, falafel, and so much more. Josh and Kyle, citing hunger pains, had demanded they go over to the food stands immediately upon getting there, blitzing past the drumline and the milieu of people wandering along on the dark red track that formed a natural perimeter to the football field. Ryley had followed them even though she'd eaten beforehand, wanting to keep her hands clean and not risk spilling.

When Ryley, Josh, and Kyle had swung by the Indian food stand so Kyle could get a samosa, Ryley had been surprised to see the line spilling out twenty people deep. As she had breathed in the smell of fried onion and garlic wafting outside the confines of the tent and into the open air, Josh had nudged her, asking her if she was happy to see the stand's popularity. She'd nodded. The Indian food was inescapably a representation of her in a way that no food would ever be for him.

Josh nudged her again now. "So, how'd you like your first softball party?"

"It was good, I had fun." It wasn't like she could say anything else; they were surrounded, but she could appreciate his politeness. And she *had* liked the thrill of living up to the high school movie experience instead of just watching it.

"Yeah, good group of girls," he said fondly, a tad too presumptuously. Kyle looked at him and shook her head but said nothing.

Ryley, not wanting the conversation to so quickly sputter, asked, "How about you? What did you do beforehand?"

He puffed out his chest slightly. "I actually hosted our pregame. My parents were away, so I offered up my home. Don't worry though, I didn't drink much. I took the wrong turn because I'm a moron, not because I was buzzed."

Ryley was gratified he'd thought to assure her, that he'd predicted the thoughts going through her mind. Before she could say anything, Kyle butted in.

"What the hell, Josh! You should have had all of us over. We wouldn't have needed to go to Carly's to pregame then." *So much for sisterhood.* Ryley's thoughts must have shown on her face because Kyle followed up by saying, "Whatever. We had fun. You all missed out coming as late as you did."

As she finished speaking, Kyle pulled out a flask and pushed it at Ryley. Ryley passed it over to Josh.

Kyle groaned. "Ryley, don't be such a buzzkill. You barely drank at the pregame. Come on. Loosen up. Show Josh what he missed out on by not inviting us."

"I am loose. I just don't want that right now."

"What, like you'll want it in five minutes?" Kyle loudly scoffed.

"Yes, if I have to keep putting up with you," Ryley muttered.

Kyle didn't ask her to speak up and instead said, "Come on, live a little. Break a couple of rules. Lose the stick-in-the-mud image." Kyle always had a loud speaking voice, and it seemed alcohol only exacerbated her volume. Some of their neighbors were turning to look at them. Ryley clenched her fists and prepared to "accidentally" knock the flask down as she grabbed for it.

Before she could take a course of action that she would have very obviously regretted, Josh piped up. "Kyle, come on. Leave it."

Kyle turned to look at Josh, her voice still unnaturally loud and her eyes slightly unfocused. "Oh, playing knight in shining armor for Ryley here? Found your newest girl to woo?"

Josh exclaimed, "No! No, definitely not."

Ryley tried to calm herself even as she felt her head beginning to pound. She would rather not have been so clearly shown how offensive he found the idea of being into her. He was nice to everyone and unthreatening, even if he tried to play at being a Jock™. She wanted to leave. Kyle in a rather rapid, startling about-face, then parried with, "What are you trying to say? Ryley's not good enough for you?" Kyle started to lightly sway from side to side as she spoke, seeming unable to find her grounding.

Josh sputtered, "What? Of course she's good enough for me, but I don't think about her like that."

Ryley looked down upon hearing the casual finality in his tone. She'd never been attracted to him beyond thinking he was good on paper, but being good on paper counted for a whole lot at this moment in time, so she found herself hurt now. Especially given that he'd thrown himself at Kyle god knows how many times. Kyle had, perhaps, wanted to put them into stark relief on purpose. Indeed, she'd calmed down now that her point was made, no longer swaying, her eyes focused, as Ryley watched her type out a surprisingly coherent message to her dad.

Josh shot Ryley a semi-apologetic look in the face of her continuing silence, which she did not like. *Really* did not like. She craned her head to see who else was in the bleachers and saw her de facto friend group two bleacher stands over. Her fade-out was supposed to be gradual and/or non-existent depending on how things went with the softball girls, and one of her old friends had just invited her to see *Twilight*. She jumped up out of her seat without another word and walked over to the hot dog stand, a stand close to her friends but with a line lengthy enough that it would buy her some time to calm down before she talked to them. She would take them up on their *Twilight* offer.

As she stood there, she realized it was truly moronic to have joined this particular line. The smell roiled her stomach; she was vegetarian. She could've thought this out better. But she couldn't very well step out of the line in case Kyle and Josh were looking at her—though they probably weren't.

Before she could take any definitive action, Harrison walked up to her. "Ryley, hey. How's it going? Mom said you were nervous about tonight."

"It's going great." Her words did not sound convincing. She didn't want to talk to him and looked down at her phone.

"What happened?" he asked in a tone that demanded honesty.

"Nothing. It was dumb. Just two people making a scene. A guy said he was not into me very loudly because a girl was goading him."

"Oh. Don't sweat it, Ryley. You're just looking at the wrong people. They don't understand you." He pulled her out of line, knowing she couldn't possibly want a hot dog, and dragged her along until they stood outside the Indian tent. He must have led her here because he automatically felt safer as well. "Maybe hang out with people who are more your speed? Who are happy talking about school, video games, and things like that? That's what I did."

"How is that my speed? I don't play any video games and I hate talking about school outside class." She knew she was being purposefully obtuse, but she would rather be alone than play into the Indian tech geek stereotype. Besides, she was already redoing her brand. She was just slow on the uptake, finding it hard to live one life on the outside when she was still trying to figure out who she was on the inside. Perhaps, that was why Harrison had allowed himself to be siloed to Indian tech geek—refusing to wear the shirts their mom bought for him—deciding he'd spread his wings later when so many people didn't already have a set preconception of him.

Harrison paused, looking down at the floor as he gathered his thoughts. Eventually, he said, "Okay, those people might not be your scene, but is the softball-baseball crew really who you want to be hanging out with? Every person is white, except for you, Anu, and George."

"So?" Ryley snapped.

"So, that could be why they're not interested. Right now, you're a second-class version of a white person. They're obviously much better at being white than you are. You won't have to be the odd one out if you just hang with the Asian group." His voice was offensively bland and matter-of-fact even as he insulted her.

"I'm not a second-class version of anything." She didn't bother to respond to anything else he said; her right eyelid was spasming. Although she'd initially begun rebranding herself to prevent interactions like the one at Claire's from ever happening again, her goal had transformed in the process of buying new clothes and starting to hang out with the softball girls. White people were the ones with power, the ones who invariably seemed to make the rules, and the ones who were undeniably the protagonists of the Great American Life in the Twenty-First Century; their faces were all over every TV show, every movie, every newsroom. She wanted to show she belonged with them.

As the silence settled around them and Ryley stared sullenly over Harrison's shoulder, he held up his hands in a placating gesture. "Okay, never mind. Forget I said anything, but please don't forget, you're wonderful the way you are." If he didn't sound so earnest, she would've thought he was mocking her by responding to her with such a canned phrase.

"AKA, if I continue down my current path, you think it's a recipe for disaster?" she asked.

"I'm not going to make any predictions. All I'm saying is that you're wonderful the way you are and people will come to see that when they're ready for you," he said, his big brown eyes solemn and sad. Pity most definitely got too much airtime at the expense of empathy.

She bit out, "I mean, it sounds like you're giving me euphemisms instead of just saying you think I'm a weirdo. And that I'm going for normal people who are out of my league."

"No, nothing about leagues, no comparative aspect. I'm just reminding you that the Ryley I see in front of me is a good egg. Mom wants us to feel like we fit in, yeah, but she doesn't want us to lose ourselves in the process," he said earnestly, leaning down toward her. At six feet, he was a half-head taller than she, his black caterpillar eyebrows and thick black hair unrulier than her own. He had no pushy cosmetologist crossing all bounds of propriety with him.

"Okay. I'm going to go." Even though her parting line was delivered flatly, she felt a (small) wave of fondness for Harrison wash over her. Every time he'd said she was wonderful, a little part of her had grown stronger. She wouldn't tell him that though.

CHAPTER 11

NOVEMBER 2018

———

The day of the Harvard-Yale game had finally arrived. The overcast sky and an ever-present chill in the air warned of the cold freeze that would inevitably overwhelm Boston. Ryley was fully prepared to let off steam in one last hurrah before clamping down to study for finals. They'd all gathered at a bar dedicated to pre-game activities though none of them were actually going to the game.

As they stood at the bar, waiting for their drinks, Cassidy gave her a warm squeeze and smile, affectionately twirling her hand through Ryley's naturally wavy, unnaturally high-lighted hair. Cassidy commented, "Oh, you look so pretty. Today is going to be a good day."

They were both already three drinks in, having pre-gamed at Mark's beforehand. Ryley gave Cassidy a warm smile back, noting just how much she liked complimentary, slightly drunk Cassidy, who'd managed to gather a crew of fifteen or so people for the game. Even when Cassidy was temperamental and snappy, it always seemed excusable, and when she was feeling generous toward someone, the intensity with which Ryley had seen Cassidy focus on the other person was admirable. Ryley was nervous to see what Cassidy was like during a study group though. Cassidy had been consistently leading a study group two days a week over the last couple of weeks, and although usually a solo studier, Ryley had finally mustered up the energy to ask to join. She was going to her first study session after the game.

Finally, the bartender served the two girls their drinks and Cassidy and Ryley began the laborious shuffle back to their table, squeezing through bodies, packed like sardines, in the classic Boston bar. The walls were painted bright red with random pictures of American flags sprinkled throughout and the hardwood floors were expectedly grimy from too much spilled beer. Indeed, Ryley's hands were drenched. She'd been double-fisting with two glasses of Sam Adams and had already sloshed a decent bit of the beer over her hands and onto Cassidy. Cassidy hadn't seemed to notice though, so Ryley kept her mouth shut.

Mark was standing off to the side of their table, speaking with David. Ryley and Mark still hadn't talked out the events of three weeks ago in which he'd called her out for being *safe*. In the days immediately after that class, she'd just ignored him, only ever skimming her eyes past his when they were in group settings. Last weekend though, even if not exactly apologetic, he had bought her free drinks a couple of times, never saying anything but forcing the drinks into her hands. Given that Ryley wasn't one for direct confrontation, she'd taken the peace offering for what it was and had decided to move on. That being said, they'd still managed to avoid spending any one-on-one time together.

As Ryley and Cassidy drew near now, Mark shot Ryley a huge smile and obnoxiously proclaimed, "Well, well, well. I can't believe I get the honor of having our Section's newest, hottest couple keeping me company." Ryley and David had decided to go exclusive yesterday. It felt like a natural progression after four easy, carefree dates and it wasn't like either was interested in pursuing anyone else.

David gave Mark a shy, pleased smile in response, but Ryley just rolled her eyes and said, "Shut up." Her words carried more of a bite than she would've preferred. She was potentially not the best at letting things go.

Cassidy piped up, "One of my friends in a different Section was talking about the two of you. Honestly, this place operates like a high school. I'm sure everyone will know Ryley is off the market by the end of the day."

Ryley said drily, "I'm not sure how many people were shopping at that market."

Mark retorted, "Ryley, Ryley. Let's not go fishing now. Some of us are still single and would love to have even one person at our hot dog stand."

Ryley snorted. "Sure, Mark, because you don't have guys throwing themselves at you."

Mark shrugged sheepishly, although he couldn't quite hide his mouth twitching up at the corners. Turning to Ryley, he said, "But let's celebrate! You are now the seventh person to pair off with another law student even though we swore to each other we wouldn't date in the One-L pool." Mark shook his head exaggeratedly in disappointment as he finished speaking.

Cassidy clapped her hands. "Yes, let's celebrate! Oh, you guys, I'm so excited. You'll finally get to meet my boyfriend. He should be here in about twenty minutes!" She paused to squeal for joy and then asked, "David, do you have friends from undergrad scattered here already?"

"Yeah. A bunch of them are over there. I'll wave them over."

After he walked away, Mark said, "He's cute." Cassidy earnestly nodded.

Ryley looked at them with a cocked eyebrow. "Okay?" They'd hung out altogether plenty of times before this; it was hardly the first time they were meeting David. Though he did look particularly good that day with his black hair neatly styled and his hazel eyes reflecting a beautiful shade of gold.

"It's just that there's this whole hesitant vibe about you. Like you're waiting for the other shoe to drop. Be happy, Ryley!" Mark exclaimed.

Ryley should be happy: she was at Harvard Law, she had a boyfriend, and she had a good crew of friends. However, the set-up felt unfortunately, innately temporary, as if something was on the cusp of giving, and the whole edifice would come crashing down. She could see herself becoming Ryley of high school, Ryley on the outside, once again. Mark calling her *safe*, her closed memo grade, Professor Kilmer's talk—those had been the warning wobbles. She knew she'd be fine; academics had always been her saving grace when everything else went belly-up, but she couldn't shake her premonition of looming disaster.

Finally, Ryley responded to Mark, deciding carefree Ryley was who everyone would much prefer to be around. "Yeah, my set-up is pretty good right now. I'm happy."

Cassidy gave Ryley's arm a quick squeeze of acknowledgment before changing the topic to be about herself, undoubtedly more interesting subject matter. "This will be my boyfriend's first time visiting. I'm so excited. He's been on rotations at New York-Presbyterian—number one in New York—so he hasn't had a chance to breathe. I'm so glad he's finally going to make it out to meet everyone."

"We know," Ryley and Mark said in tandem, having heard about Cassidy's boyfriend in increasing detail for the last month. Ryley half-smiled to show she meant no harm.

"Yes, whatever. Anyway, I think you both will really like him. All my friends like him."

Ryley and Mark nodded in response, their marching orders received. Then Sophie and Zeke were shouting for Cassidy to meet a friend of theirs, Cassidy was flitting away to join them, and it was just Ryley and Mark. Ryley considered scooting away.

As if to preempt her, Mark started speaking immediately, his voice loud. He was easily five drinks in. "It's been a minute since it's just been you and me."

"Yeah." Ryley didn't elaborate, uncertain of where he wanted to take the conversation and uncertain if she wanted to follow.

"Look. I didn't mean to hurt your feelings, but I obviously did. Cassidy came by my apartment last week to catch up one-on-one and told me off for calling you out like that."

"Oh, that was nice of her," Ryley interjected. Every time Ryley tried to typecast Cassidy in some sort of way, Cassidy would show another side of herself.

Mark nodded before continuing in a rush, as if desperate to get it all out. "But sometimes, I feel so suffocated, and I'm so tired of people just going along with the establishment and not pushing themselves to do more. I'm sorry if it came off like I was attacking you—I'm just so frustrated. I'm tired of trusting people in power; I'm tired of keeping my head down, and I had to get that out. You were just a casualty in it all." His lower lip was slightly jutting out, the corners of his mouth downturned.

Ryley leaned against the side of the booth, the weight of the conversation bringing her down, but she was glad drinking had allowed Mark to open up. Conversely, Ryley'd only grown to like drinking when she figured out that a drunk Ryley, although sloppy and stumbly, wasn't one to bare her soul. Drunk Ryley only let out third-rate secrets and instead became obsessed with taking pictures to show sober Ryley everything she'd missed.

Ryley heaved a deep sigh before saying, "Honestly, I saw your point. Even then. I just felt hurt that our friendship meant so little that you didn't care if you hurt me just to get your point across."

Mark looked flummoxed and grabbed ahold of her hands, his baby blue eyes wide and contrite. "No, Ryley. I value you, of course, I do. I feel like I can be myself around you. Though I wish you'd trust me more and actually open up to me. I feel like I don't know anything real about you. You *hide* yourself."

Ryley fortunately avoided having to say anything in response because David was suddenly upon them, flanked by people. One of said people was Olivia, who hadn't looked over at Ryley and Mark yet, caught up in conversation with another girl. This time, Olivia was dressed in a surprisingly understated fashion. Ryley had the same oversized Harvard sweater on.

David sidled in to be between Ryley and Mark, standing close enough that their arms brushed. As he leaned in to give her a quick peck, Ryley turned her head so that his kiss landed on her cheek; she was not a fan of PDA. Olivia looked over at Ryley at that moment—because why not?—and made no effort to hide the way her lips curled up into a smirk. Relationships took time. Olivia didn't get it and was too quick to judge. Ryley would learn to love him even if the emotional connection she was hoping for was taking longer to develop than she would've thought.

After some of David's friends briefly introduced themselves, Mark took center stage and easily began to dominate the conversation, telling a story from his college years. Ryley was used to it, as was David, and both were more than happy to stand in silence, except for the occasional chuckle or emphatic "Oh, my god!" Eventually, Ryley started to lose interest in Mark's story, having heard it before, and looked over at Olivia again to see that Olivia was already staring at her.

Olivia shot her a quick smile and then confidently made her way over to Ryley; she said nothing other than a semi-quiet, "Hi," not wanting to interrupt Mark in his flow.

Ryley turned her body to face Olivia, slightly stepping out of the conversation circle to do so. "Hi, how's it hanging?" No one said that anymore. Ryley could have kicked herself.

"Good. Nice seeing all my undergrad friends. Nice seeing you. I don't think I know how to function anymore without seeing at least one Agarwal a day." Olivia and Ryley had continued to see each other in passing nearly every day and Olivia still regularly hung out with Harrison from what Ryley could gather from Harrison's Instagram Stories—Ryley refused to follow Olivia on Instagram first.

Ryley smiled. "Glad I can be of service. At least Harrison looks like he's living it up in New York." Harrison had ended up driving down to New York on Friday, having to accompany Genie to a work party she "absolutely could not miss." Harrison had texted Ryley about the schedule change a week ago, worried Ryley was making plans around meeting Genie. And although Ryley had told David, Cassidy, and Mark that she might have to ditch them for a couple of hours or so to meet Harrison's girlfriend, she'd responded to Harrison in an unnecessarily flippant fashion, saying she'd forgotten Genie was even coming up for the Harvard-Yale Game.

Harrison had not responded to that text, though last night, he had posted a beautiful picture of him and Genie all dressed up on Instagram. Genie was a short white girl with faded blue eyes and platinum-blond hair that was most certainly a dye job. The photo had effectively showcased her nose piercing, stacked bracelets, and a couple of tattoos in Hindi easily visible on arms that said she was a regular at Pilates. Her pale, petite frame had contrasted nicely against Harrison's larger build, his mocha brown skin, and thick mop of hair.

Ryley gave voice to her thoughts, saying, "They both looked gorgeous in that photo."

"Yeah, they did. We're going to have a blast getting wined and dined this summer." Harrison was going to a Big Law firm in New York although she hadn't known that the same was true for Olivia.

"You're working Big Law in New York?" Ryley kept her tone neutral though she pictured Olivia as more of a public interest person or as counsel for a random startup. Anything but a serious corporate New York lawyer.

"I mean, I'll probably apply to do a clerkship, but yeah, I'm going to spend the summer at a law firm in New York and I'll likely rejoin for at least a bit after the clerkship," Olivia responded nonchalantly. It seemed Olivia was doing as traditional a path out of law school as possible. Ryley knew it was unfair to feel let down, but she'd thought the other girl would say something crazy that would show her just how many avenues were open to her after graduation.

"Got it, cool. I'm also thinking New York." Ryley had no strong leanings amongst the few places urban enough to be the only real options available to her, but she was thinking

New York by sheer process of elimination. "I don't know what I want to do though," Ryley offered, unprompted, making herself seem more mysterious than she was.

"One hundred dollars say you end up in Big Law," Olivia retorted matter-of-factly.

"We'll see." Ryley normally would have conceded the point, but she liked keeping Olivia on her toes, especially because Olivia seemed to enjoy poking at Ryley in turn, occasionally smirking at her like she knew something Ryley didn't.

"Okay, so what do you think you'll do if not Big Law?" Olivia pushed.

"I don't know, Olivia," Ryley responded with a slightly curt edge to her tone, suddenly feeling foolish. The past six years of her life had been focused on collecting gold stars, on getting to a place where she felt good enough, and she'd always known the future would probably be more of the same, so she didn't know why she was trying to be cute now. Olivia was right. Ryley would probably just join some law firm and rise up the ranks. She needed to take a step back though, feeling overwhelmingly claustrophobic. David's arm was pressing too much into her and one of his friends talking about clerkship applications in too high-pitched a voice was getting to her. She needed breathing room. She put the remaining Sam Adams in her hand down and began to step away.

"Hey, wait, hold up a sec. You good?" Olivia lightly tugged on Ryley's sweater sleeve, grounding her to a halt. They'd completely stepped out of the friend circle now.

"Yeah. I am. I was just getting overheated."

Olivia looked at her disbelievingly, biting her lip slightly. "Okay. You know, everyone's figuring things out day by day. You could stay in Big Law, go in-house, or do something completely outside the law. So many lawyers become writers or work in finance. We have *so* many options." Ryley gave Olivia a soft smile. Even if Ryley had always secretly liked Olivia's bravado, she found she liked an Olivia who explicitly showed she cared even more. However, David butted in before she could say anything in response.

"I didn't know you two were friends! You've been talking just the two of you for way too long. I want in!" David didn't seem annoyed that Ryley'd effectively turned her back to him, but he moved his arm to be resting against hers again. "You know Olivia is super impressive, right, Ryley?"

Olivia groaned even as Ryley said, "No, I didn't. But I feel like you want to enlighten me?"

David continued, "Well, Olivia graduated Summa from Harvard four years ago and then went on to start her own non-profit."

Ryley would have liked to know more about Olivia's backstory, but Olivia said, "Okay, David, thanks. Let's cut that off here. Anyways, I was not expecting to see John make the trek out from California for this. That's some commitment."

Ryley inevitably tuned them out as they started talking about people from college, though they both did make an effort to consistently give her relevant backstories. Ryley made up for the way her eyes very obviously drifted during that conversation by staying with David, even as Olivia and Mark left to catch up with other friends. She subsequently tagged along with David and his friends to another Boston bar, popular with Harvard undergrads, though she would have liked to stay behind with Mark and Cassidy or get to know Olivia better.

However, when she'd swung by to check in with her Section friend group, most had shooed her away, emphasizing she take the day to get to know David's friends better rather than stick with them. The one exception had been Cassidy, who'd wanted Ryley and David to hold off leaving so they could meet her still-soon-to-arrive boyfriend. Mark had overruled Cassidy by clamping his hand over Cassidy's mouth; seeing Cassidy's face flush red even as her cheeks puffed out, Ryley had skedaddled rather than bear witness to the aftermath.

Ryley made it her mission to make David feel special that day. She liked being part of a unit and the idea of having someone when Mark inevitably partnered up and Cassidy moved in with her boyfriend. So, trying to be the best girl-friend she could be, she recited a tasteful line here and there from the many stories David had regaled her with over the past couple of months, making his friends believe they were closer and more intimate than they were.

Indeed, in response to her efforts, David's face lit up and his wide lips stretched into a smile. "Isn't she the best?"

Ryley found it interesting that they seemed to get along as well as they did—Ryley's intimacy hang-ups aside—given that he continued to say things suggesting he had only hung out with white people before meeting her. On their last date, before he asked her to go exclusive, he'd told her he never pictured himself with an Indian, immediately insisting he meant "no offense," as she was contemplating whether to get offended or not. From a quick Facebook stalk later that night, she'd decided that given the way his life had been lived thus far, it was unsurprising he felt this way. He'd come from a small town in North Carolina, which seemed to only have white folk, and he'd appeared to have almost exclusively white friends in college. Ryley had given herself a high-five when she'd realized she'd broken David out of his mold, or alternatively, behaved so effectively white that he felt right at home.

After David finished telling the story of their first date, of course, leaving out any mention of the small disagreement they'd had in the beginning, his best friend said, "Man, you seem really happy."

If possible, David's smile stretched further as he responded, "Well, we're very new, but I have high hopes." David tacked on, almost as an afterthought, "I knew I was interested in her after we met at one of the first Section parties of the year. A friend told me she didn't think Ryley would be interested, so I was slow in asking her out."

Ryley frowned and asked, "Which friend?"

David froze, clearly realizing his happy, drunken glow had caused him to lower barriers he'd normally have firmly intact and stuttered, "Oh, nobody you know. Just a guy. You don't know him."

He'd said *she* a moment ago, so Ryley simply said, "Olivia?" and the manner in which David's eyes darted away was tell enough. She decided not to dwell on it and risk ruining the generally happy mood around her but stored the knowledge very firmly in her Grudges compartment. She switched the conversation back to being about David's friend and felt David's visible exhalation of relief, even as he pulled her slightly closer.

When she finally reached home for the night and plopped into bed—Ryley still hadn't slept over at David's and wasn't sure how much longer she could put it off—she found she was somehow not surprised to receive a message saying, *hey. Harrison gave me your number. good seeing u today. see u around.* Ryley would throw a like onto Olivia's message tomorrow.

CHAPTER 12

NOVEMBER 2018

———

Ryley's phone screen lit up with a text from Cassidy, letting her know which study room they were in, as Ryley made a beeline for the cafeteria even though she was already running late. All the treadmills had been taken once again so she had had to dither around on a mat. By the time a treadmill finally freed up, she was running so late that the stress of keeping Cassidy waiting effectively canceled out any endorphins she could have hoped to gain.

Ryley made it to the cafeteria in record time, making a game of weaving through the bodies without cutting pace. She gave muttered, canned *excuse mes* and *sorrys* even as she continued squeezing between people and cutting around them. She wasn't shaving more than a couple of seconds off her tardiness, but at least she was moving faster than everyone else. Going straight to the Grab-N-Go section, she grabbed a power bar and a Gatorade, a too-frequent meal choice of hers. She strode over to Jenny to check out. She liked Jenny even though she had taken to offering Ryley her advice each day because Ryley came to the cafeteria every day. Her mom had made sure she knew how to make some basic

Indian dishes—*gobi aloo, bhindi and tofu matar*—before she left for college, but Ryley had a pathological aversion to cooking, so here she was for the umpteenth time.

Jenny rang up the four white people before her without comment, but of course, gave her a "Honey, you've got to put some more meat on those bones," and then Ryley was through the crowd. She liked how all the cafeteria workers had adopted her, giving her free food when she realized too late that she'd left her credit card at home one day, or giving her a "you look so pretty!" on the days she had taken special care with her presentation, throwing on a wool dress with tights because she'd needed to break up the monotony of skinny jeans, sweater, and thick overcoat.

Just last week, Leo had said, "It's so good to see you here, working hard. We need more of us here." He wasn't Indian, just someone else who was non-white. She'd given him an instinctive nod of thanks and a smile as he had handed her a helping of pasta, even as Cassidy, standing next to her, had shot her a confused look, silently urging her to correct him. Ryley had not explained the incident later, even as Cassidy had let the silence rest between them on their walk back to the classroom. Ryley hadn't even known where to begin, instead talking about a story from her prep school days. Cassidy had immediately relaxed and hooked an arm through hers.

Ryley looked down at her phone now to see another text from Cassidy. *I've relocated to room 1057 if you ever arrive.*

As she rounded the corner and skipped down her preferred choice of side stairwell, she ran abruptly into Mark at the bottom. Taking a few steps back to properly look at him, she said, "Oh, I just texted you—why'd you skip class?"

He shrugged in response. "I wanted to work out. But wait, what's going on with you?"

"Nothing, why?" she asked, giving her outfit a once-over. She had thought she looked cute today.

"You look kinda ill?" Mark shot her a hesitant half-grin and reached out to grab her hand loosely.

"Excuse me?" Ryley scooted to be closer to the large window framing the side of the stairwell, breaking his grip in the process. She leaned against the glass pane, soaking in all the warmth she could. She was leaving for Los Angeles tomorrow and Thanksgiving couldn't come soon enough.

"It's fine, you just need to hydrate more and make sure you log those hours of sleep and your skin will be back to its usual Milky Way glow." He moved with her to lean against the glass pane as well.

"Great. Thanks, Mark," she responded in a flat tone. The four nights following the Harvard-Yale game had been rough ones and the dark patches under her eyes must be unflattering. Usually a strict devotee of eight hours a night, she had only been getting five hours of sleep as she had tried to churn out a legal memo due the day after Thanksgiving break and had begun the transition into Finals Ryley. That Ryley pored over every single detail of the textbook while factoring in time for her brain to shut down, even as her fingers typed out mindlessly regurgitated synopses of the cases. She could not fathom how certain students (i.e. Zeke) had kept this pace all year, consistently staying in the library until two in the morning, but she'd always been more of a sprinter than a marathon runner. That being said, she was not going to cop to the fact that she was increasingly getting as stressed as everyone around her, especially when Mark seemed just dandy.

Faced with her continuing silence, he said, "You know I'm just being real with you. That's why you keep me around."

Ignoring her wrinkled eyebrows, he continued, unfazed. "Anyway, you won't believe what happened to me this morning. I ran into HB on the way to the cafeteria, and although he's way too crazy for me, he could not take his eyes off me!"

HB stood for Hot Brian. Ryley had gotten used to Mark's code-names within two weeks of knowing him. She, however, could not find it within herself to fake excitement and felt that she had been given too short a shrift to be annoyed. Wanting to soak in her sulk a bit more, she said, "Well, your skin has its usual pasty glow, so I can see why he was staring."

Mark laughed in response. "Got it out of your system?"

Ryley gave him a sheepish shrug and smile and then said, "I'm going to the study session with Cassidy, Sophie, Zeke, and David. You didn't respond in the group chat. Are you coming?"

Mark paused, mulling it over. "I wasn't planning on it, but why not? I want to see how you handle Study Group Cassidy. She went after Zeke last week when he started speaking to her in his professor voice."

Ryley cringed preemptively. "Well, hopefully, this will be good for me. I want to do law school right." Left to her own devices, she would never have joined, but Professor Kilmer's words had continued to circle around her brain at night and she wanted to make sure she wasn't too far behind. Her mother had also brought up *Legally Blonde* the other day and Ryley wanted to at least do the whole study group thing once.

Mark reached for her hand again. "I think study groups are definitely worth it. Though people, as in Cassidy, can get pretty argumentative, so be prepared for that. Are you heading there right now?"

She let him keep ahold of her this time. "Yep. Do you have your stuff with you?"

He nodded in agreement and they began to make their way over to the study room, arms lightly brushing. She'd begun to look forward to his touch, given how non-presumptuous and affectionate it was. He also never acted annoyed when she'd shake his hand off, and she shook him off less and less as they began to spend more time together in the aftermath of their talk at the Harvard-Yale game. She hoped she would reach that point with David soon.

As they walked over, he asked, "Did Cassidy tell you she and her boyfriend are taking a break?"

"No!" She was unsurprised that Cassidy had shared the information with Mark and not with her, especially because she and David had left before meeting Cassidy's boyfriend. Ryley would have to do a bit of penance and validate Cassidy's role in her life, especially if she had a boyfriend now and Cassidy didn't. "How was his personality? I wish I'd gotten a chance to meet him."

"You didn't miss out on much. He seemed like he looked."

Ryley responded with a light laugh. Although she'd not seen him in person, she'd left little heart emojis in a comment on a picture Cassidy had put up on the Sunday following the game. Cassidy's boyfriend had been only slightly taller than Cassidy, with mousy brown hair, vintage, round wire spectacles, and a shy, tentative smile. They must have broken up almost immediately after Cassidy had taken the photo.

Ryley finally responded, "I'll see if she voluntarily brings it up; otherwise, I'll let it lie."

Their conversation tapered off as they finally reached the study room in which Cassidy sat ensconced with her back to the door. Ryley thought better of making the girl get up to let them in and instead shuffled around in her bag. She fished out her ID and pressed it against the card reader to gain access to the study room. She supposed the school only wanted to allow veritable scholars of law access to the facilities though she found it hard to imagine anyone trying to infiltrate the rather barren law school study rooms. Perhaps it was to preserve the veneer of prestige? Remind students the Harvard name unlocked doors that otherwise stayed closed. As they swung open the door, Cassidy kept her gaze on her textbook, though her fingers twitched distractedly as her body betrayed her desire to acknowledge that another being had entered the room.

Ryley cleared her throat. "Sorry I'm late. I picked up a stray on the way."

Cassidy looked up then. "Oh, hey Mark. Well, Sophie just stepped out to go to the bathroom and Zeke and David still aren't here. They went to get coffee from Hi-Rise and the line is supposedly a disaster."

Ryley checked her phone to see if David had texted if he was going to be late or had offered to get her a coffee. He hadn't. She didn't let herself get irritated. It was Cassidy's study group and she was the one they needed to report to. Ryley wasn't irritated.

As Mark and Ryley got settled, Cassidy asked, "Want to look at the contracts assignment? I doubt the professor is going to read the mock answer, so it would probably be helpful to do it together."

They nodded and Ryley hauled the heavy textbook up out of her bag to start going through the material.

Cassidy looked at her aghast. "What are you doing?"

"Flipping to the relevant readings?"

"You should download the *Libya* outline from Too Dope instead. It got a DS last year," Cassidy said. Too Dope was an outline bank every student knew about: students from past years uploaded outlines laying out and explaining subject material and indicated the grade they'd gotten in the class so students would know they could be trusted. A DS, or dean's scholar, was the highest grade a student could get.

"I would rather create my own outline," Ryley answered. That was a bit extra. She hadn't needed to share that.

"If you would rather create your own, then you can do it on your own time, Ryley," Cassidy said, a tad exasperated. "I, for one, have been supplementing the *Libya* outline all year with my own notes, so it's basically my own. But for someone who hasn't started on an outline, i.e., you, *Libya* is a good starting point."

Ryley muttered, "Okay," and navigated to the database and downloaded the document. Ryley decided not to mention that she had in fact started on her own outline, if only a quarter of the way done, and pushed down the part of her that wanted to force Cassidy out of the protagonist role. Ryley could play as good an Elle Woods as Cassidy. She'd never seen an Indian successfully pull off blond hair though.

As they started going through the question and discussing the fact pattern of the case they'd been provided, Ryley found every answer she gave was rebutted by Mark and Cassidy.

"I think there's a question of whether there is even sufficient consideration to make this a legitimate contract," Ryley said.

"Hmm, no. I don't think that consideration is really at issue," Mark replied, almost immediately.

Ryley insisted, "But the buyer is not obligated to do anything or give up anything. It just says, 'whatever amount they choose to order.'"

"Ryley, that's a side issue you shouldn't waste time on in the exam; it's clearly an enforceable contract. There is good faith built up between the two parties. It's understood that the buyer was going to buy something," Cassidy said. "Let's move on to the economic duress bit."

In the study room setting, Cassidy and Mark spoke even more confidently than they normally did, playing up the formality of their speech, throwing around words like "dispositive" easily. As they continued, Ryley found herself contributing less and less, especially because they seemed ready to disagree with everything she said. Unfortunately, Ryley hated arguing, and especially arguing with friends; this was summarily disadvantageous to anyone training to be a "zealous advocate"—which was, according to Harvard, their *raison d'être*.

When David, Sophie, and Zeke eventually trickled in, she found herself growing even more tentative. She tried to reflect on the fact that she loved that David, Mark, and Cassidy had such strong personalities, inevitably competitive but transparent about their drive. And all three had shown they cared about her; Ryley unapologetically excluded Sophie and Zeke from her reflections. They'd never broken past being Group Friends and never spent any time one-on-one. Ryley decided, as she sat there quietly, half-absorbing what they were saying but mostly evaluating the relationships, that David, Mark, and Cassidy were the people with whom she felt closest at law school. Picking a fight wasn't worth losing their companionship. So, instead, she became gradually more sullen and closed off even as Cassidy became more dictatorial and David continued to look to Cassidy over Ryley.

Finally, a mere forty minutes after they'd started, Ryley said, "Hey, I think I should get going. I forgot I had scheduled a call." She would have to trust herself and her intellect to deliver her to the top. She'd always learned best by solo studying after all.

Cassidy sighed. "You know what, Ryley, that's not believable at all. We can see through you when you huff off and pretend you're fine."

Ryley had quite shockingly never been directly called out on her propensity for sulking by anyone outside her family, so she sat there for a bit, stymied. Finally, she said, "I honestly am tired and I feel like you all have strong opinions." She began to gather her books to give her hands something to do and her eyes somewhere to look.

Cassidy wrinkled her little button nose. "Yes, we do have strong opinions. We're lawyers. It's our job to know how to argue."

David chimed in before the two could continue their back and forth. "Okay, Cassidy, that's enough. Ryley, I'll text you tonight. Maybe we can get dinner?"

Ryley nodded at him, grateful for his intervention though she could have used his support about thirty minutes ago. He had been too busy staring at Cassidy and focusing on bantering about the material. Gathering her books, she said, "Okay, well, I have to get going, but I'll see you all in class tomorrow."

Mark gave her a sympathetic smile and waved her off, ever the perfect diplomat.

As Ryley turned to go, Cassidy added as a seemingly off-hand afterthought, which meant it was anything but, "I've seen you hanging out with Rohan. He would fit in well with the study group dynamic. He always brings in that policy perspective no one else is thinking about."

Ryley responded to Cassidy's not-quite question with a non-committal nod. Ryley was not going to ask Rohan to join on Cassidy's behalf when she felt like she might have just been kicked out—or kicked herself out—of the study group. Besides, "hanging out" was a strong term for the one ten-minute talk they'd had in the semester. He'd wished her a *Happy Diwali* to celebrate the Indian new year earlier in the month. They'd talked about what their parents used to do in celebration—all the candles they'd light, the Bollywood dance performances they'd make their kids learn, the sudden upswell of Hindi around a house in which it was otherwise notably absent—and had then parted ways. Ryley had not made any effort to talk with him since.

Things would have been different if they'd connected as Americans first, using her learned definition of American, which was necessarily constrained to sharing a similar love of Chipotle, Beyoncé (or Rihanna, she wasn't picky), brunch, drinking, and Obama, but Ryley hadn't wanted a friendship primarily based on shared Indian heritage. She didn't need to connect through her Indianness when she knew she belonged in America.

As Ryley pulled open the door, Cassidy commanded, "Wait," and, deciding to be more direct, said, "Can you ask Rohan to join?"

"I think you'd have as good a shot. I've talked with him *once* in the last month." Ryley turned once again to exit out of the room, but Cassidy's irritated clucking sound stopped her.

"Still, you know him better than I do, so I think it's worth it. He's never made any effort to come over to me." Cassidy seemed to think over her own statement for a second or two and then added, "It must be because I'm too white. Your whiteness is at least on the inside. Come on, I bet he'd open right up to you."

David was half-nodding along, almost questioningly. Mark opened his mouth and then closed it, looking to Ryley for direction. Ryley gave a short, barking laugh of disbelief. Even as Cassidy had validated her for essentially being white, for being just like them, she still looked to Ryley's brown skin and thought it a prop that automatically connected Ryley with all other Indians. That all Indians, if they wanted, were one and the same. Ryley bit out, "Oh, yes, I forgot. The fact we're both brown is an instant guarantee of friendship."

Cassidy didn't stutter or apologize as Ryley had expected. Instead, Cassidy rolled her eyes and returned her gaze to her laptop, letting a nice, neat tension settle in the room. During the pregame to the Harvard-Yale game, Cassidy had warned Ryley she'd turn into a bit of a lunatic as finals approached, saying the statement with a what-can-you-do shrug. Even Mark had tried to prepare her, but Ryley found herself incredibly disappointed nonetheless. Ryley left the room without another word.

PART III

FEBRUARY

—

CHAPTER 13

FEBRUARY 2009

—

100 percent. Ryley loved getting tests back. She kept her face neutral; the exaggerated Joker grin she wanted to let crawl across her face would be obnoxious. She let the small seed of contentment sit like a warm coal at the bottom of her stomach.

"Class, overall good job at doing a phenomenally mediocre job. Some of you could have used the help of a curve, but I curve it off the highest score. And in this case, the highest score was a hundred." Mr. Weber let his eyes rest on hers, as he said "a hundred" and Ryley gave a slight, barely noticeable nod in acknowledgment. She dropped her eyes to her desk shortly thereafter; she didn't want his sustained gaze to give her away. The competition was intense, and as sophomores, they knew their grades this year and the next would be crucial for college applications. She'd rather not have a target painted on her back, though she knew her classmates already had a sense of her. Students were constantly sniffing each other out.

As if to prove her point, Josh decided to stretch his body, managing to twist his head in the process so he directly faced her. She casually flipped the first page of her exam so the score was obscured just as he casually dropped his eyes down.

Raising his voice to be heard over the rain beginning to pound at the window, Mr. Weber continued, "History is a hard subject. I get it, but I do not reward laziness. I gave a seventy percent to those who said World War One began because of the assassination of Franz Ferdinand and then went into depth about meaningless details. Please do not word-vomit and expect me to be impressed. See me if you have questions, but let's turn to the assigned reading."

Ryley took notes mindlessly, automatically transcribing the words Mr. Weber said without digesting them. Instead, she focused on the small seed of happiness within and nurtured it, wanting it to grow and fill her so she could backlog the feeling of contentment and pull it out on a sad day. She was usually swift to squish out feelings of self-satisfaction and smugness, reminding herself of things that could have been done better, or areas in which she was lacking, but she let herself enjoy the success for now. Mr. Weber had looked at her with such approval that she had felt genuinely special, like it was undoubtedly good she was the way she was, that nothing needed to be changed about her.

As the clock hit 8:45, Mr. Weber immediately cut himself off and said, "Until next time then." He was punctilious and never started late or stopped late and had never gotten the names of Asian students confused nor those of the Black or Hispanic students. She liked him. Probably also in large part because he liked her.

As she started to pack, she pondered what to do with the free Friday evening she had awaiting her. Usually, she had softball practice, followed by practicing the piano for a couple of hours, followed by homework. Her parents had asked her to stack up on extracurriculars for her own good and Ryley hadn't minded, knowing she had to be exceptionally well-rounded if she was to get people to give her a chance. The latest statistic being thrown around was fifteen percent. Elite colleges, the ones that would open the doors to bigger and better things, only allowed Asians to fill up fifteen percent of their incoming class and a basic level of academic excellence was taken for granted. She needed to be good enough to outcompete the other Asians vying for those same spots with extracurriculars, showing she was more than her GPA. Or, as her college advisor put it, more than another "grade-obsessed Asian."

But tonight, softball had been canceled because of the thunderstorm taking LA by surprise. Naturally, that had become the only thing anyone could talk about, and she'd had at least ten conversations about the shocking weather; not that she had anything better to talk about.

She saw Josh waiting for her out of the corner of her eye. As she finished packing up, he explicitly asked, "How'd you do on the test?"

"Fine, fine," she said, keeping it generic as much to irritate him as to preserve her academic anonymity. He'd not done enough subterfuge to justify asking her directly. He should have tried to peek at her exam at least two more times.

"How did you do?" she finally asked after he said nothing more and just stood there, fidgeting with his backpack strap as he waited for her to finish packing up. She stopped pretending she was looking around for a pencil she knew she'd already put away and swung her backpack over one shoulder. Her painful attempt at a power play had lasted long enough and was, quite frankly, unnecessary. She had quickly moved on from the debacle that was Homecoming, deciding it wasn't even worth it to nurse a grudge. Leaving a quarter of the way into the game had made enough of a statement, and it wasn't like she could demand an apology from him for speaking his truth.

"Okay. Definitely not top of class like you." He left the words there as a hook. She stayed silent.

As they were exiting the classroom, Mr. Weber called out, "Ryley, fantastic job."

Ryley turned to him with a pained, grimace of a smile, said, "Thanks," and turned to face straight again.

"So, you got the hundred," Josh said loudly. Too many people were hovering around outside the classroom and more than a couple of heads swiveled to look at her. Ryley's ears burned, but at least the brown of her skin would camouflage the red flush she could feel painting her cheeks.

"I never said that."

"Mr. Weber essentially said it for you."

She would have liked to tell him to shut up, but she was sure Josh thought he was bragging for her in that deluded brain of his. He didn't know of her single-minded campaign oriented around fitting in such that a simple portrait of Indian academic excellence paired with her "stick in the mud" image, as Kyle had called it, was doing her no favors; even colleges didn't want that.

Harrison came up before she could formulate a rebuttal that would concisely and accurately encapsulate all her thoughts. "Oh, yeah, she's a little brainiac. You should see the amount she reads."

Ryley was startled to see Harrison ground to a halt next to her. They rarely interacted at school. Ryley would prefer that he stick to that pattern.

"Okay, Harrison, don't you have band practice to get to?" Harrison was as loaded up on extracurriculars as she was, though he was a senior.

"No, I'm skipping class. It's not required. Also, I know I said I'd give you a ride home tonight, but I want to go to the mall and watch a movie with some friends. Can you get a ride from Mom?"

Harrison was off to Princeton and although he'd been an incredibly serious student through most of high school, once he'd gotten early admission, he'd decided to become a social butterfly. People had accepted him with open arms. As she'd noted at Homecoming, he'd leaned into being a tech geek, dressing carelessly on purpose and comfortably playing up his nerdiness. He hadn't bothered to show that he was on the same playing field as the jocks or the clique of rich, white kids and had never challenged the existing social structure with its preset stereotypes. Instead, he'd just been infallibly helpful and kind even when people were rude to him.

The black BMW he drove her to school in every morning was the only nod he ever made to their family's wealth. But even the BMW didn't stand out amongst the Audis, Mercedes, and Lexuses that packed the school's parking lot, so people were comfortable treating him like they'd treat an adorable puppy. Ryley disliked it, but she supposed he was happy, so she kept it to herself. After all, his method seemed to be working for him.

"Ryley?" Harrison prodded her. Josh stared at the two of them. Ryley wished Josh would buzz off.

"Yeah, I'll call Mom and ask her," Ryley said shortly. She had just gotten her driver's license, but they still carpooled together and Harrison unfortunately got priority over the car. He was only two years older.

"Wait, didn't you say you lived close?" Josh asked, absent-mindedly running a hand through his shaggy mop of hair.

"Yeah, like a fifteen-minute drive." Ryley was confused why he cared.

"I'm not doing anything. I can drop you off after school."

"Hm, okay." She realized her surprise made her sound decidedly ungrateful, so she added, "Thanks. I appreciate it."

"Solid, man. Thank you," Harrison echoed. Then he was bouncing away like an overgrown rabbit. He called out over his shoulder, "Congrats, Einstein."

Most of the students from their history class were still gathered in the small patio that doubled as a general locker area outside the classroom. A couple of them shot her long looks. Harrison was not the type to actively sabotage or embarrass; he was too good for that. That being said, he was the type to let himself get in the way. Because *he* would have liked everyone to know he got the top score, that meant *she* wanted everyone to know she got the top score. Never mind that she was intensely private about her grades and she'd never share anything meaningful about herself if she could help it.

Ryley and Josh agreed to meet by the parking lot after school and parted ways for the day. Neither mentioned the possibility of getting lunch together.

* * *

Ryley and Josh made their way to his car in relative quiet. Ryley was still slightly surprised by the offer but she decided not to look a gift cow in the mouth—that's what her mom always said, simultaneously poking fun at the Indian obsession with cows and her penchant for getting idioms mixed up.

When they stopped outside a red Mustang parked only two cars down from the empty spot where Harrison's car was usually parked, Ryley was surprised. She'd had no idea their parking spots were so close together. It wasn't like they were really friends, though; hence, she was still slightly confused about the current state of affairs. As they got settled into the car, Josh proudly began droning on about the horsepower of a Mustang. Ryley tuned him out, compiling a list of potential reasons for why he was suddenly being so nice to her in her head.

Eventually, as they were peeling out of the parking lot, he asked, "Where do you live?"

Ryley tried not to make how tightly she was holding onto the car's handlebar too obvious as she chirped, "Just off Mulholland. I'll direct you when we get to my cross street."

He scoffed. "You'll direct me? Ryley, sometimes you talk like a robot."

"And sometimes you talk like a moron." Ryley had not meant to say that aloud, preferring to keep her more pointed retorts to herself to write down and laugh at later, but the never-ending number of things to tweak and fix was getting to her. She wanted access to the script everyone else seemed to be reading off that fed them the right slang and dialogue lines.

Josh stared at her in shock for a couple of seconds before he suddenly started to laugh. "Nice one, Ryley."

They passed the rest of the short drive in relative silence, letting The All-American Rejects' "Gives You Hell" transition to Britney Spears' "Womanizer" without comment. Ryley would have liked to slip in some subtle nod to how musically cultured she was, but she couldn't figure out how to do it after she'd sung along to Britney Spears' hook chorus. It had been unintentional, a result of being too focused on pretending she was texting a friend when she had just been typing random letters into her Google Search.

Eventually, Ryley decided to ask, "So what are you doing this weekend?"

"Just baseball practice. And then I'm probably going to go over to Taylor's. He's having a party for the baseball team. I thought he invited the softball team."

"Yeah, he did. I blanked," she said quickly. Too quickly. She was in the middle of rereading *Mrs. Dalloway* for the third time anyway, and she could hit up some of the friends in her extended friend group if she truly wanted to socialize; she'd continued treading periphery friend land quite successfully. As they got off Mulholland and started getting close to her house, she began to guide him through the side streets.

As Josh made the final turn onto her block, he said, "It looks like you live pretty close to Taylor. If you want, I can pick you up on my way over."

Ryley fiddled with the seatbelt as she weighed what to say. Although Josh was usually nice enough, he never put himself out like this and something felt off now. Ryley couldn't quite bring herself to ask him directly.

Instead, she said, "Oh, yeah, sure. That would be great. It'll save me from having to get a ride from one of the girls."

"Okay, cool." He didn't exactly sound enthused. She would have liked to snap that she didn't need his pity if that's what he was inviting her out of, but she also really didn't want him to take back the invitation. So she said nothing, even as he drove up to her front gate.

"Whoa, nice house," he said, slightly taken aback. "I did not expect you to live somewhere like this." The house looked a bit like a mini castle with its regal cobblestone exterior, stained glass windows, and a pointed little tower spire situated front and center with ivy hanging off the trellis upfront.

Feeling skittish and uncomfortable, she didn't acknowledge his words and rather abruptly hopped out of the car with her backpack in hand, leaning slightly against the car to say through the open window, "Thanks for dropping me off and for offering to take me to the party tomorrow. I seem to be racking up favors with you." She punctuated her last statement with a light-hearted laugh. He smiled back at her but didn't argue with her words, just giving her a small wave before driving off. She looked forward to spending the rest of the night alternating between replaying that interaction in her mind and stressing about attending a party to which she had not quite been invited.

CHAPTER 14

FEBRUARY 2019

———

Pass. Pass. Pass. Pass. Pass.

Harvard graded on a curve as follows: fail, low pass, pass, honors, and dean's scholar. Only a very unlucky few, if any, got fails. The majority of students, around seventy percent, received some type of pass with the rest getting some type of honors. In the pass bucket, most got regular passes, though a handful of students got low passes should the professor choose to give them out.

In the honors bucket, most got regular honors, though a handful of students got awarded dean's scholar.

Ryley had prepared herself, almost lazily, for one or two honors—in shorthand, Hs—as a worst-case scenario. She was used to others knowing much more than she did through the course of the term and then suddenly, having everything come together at the end, as she pulled late night after late night. Awakened out of her hibernation earlier than usual by Professor Kilmer's call-out, a large part of her had almost thought she might get a dean's scholar or two.

She had made plans to get lunch with David today, but she canceled, claiming illness. He would probably guess she'd not done as well as she'd hoped but there was nothing to be done for it. At least, to belie suspicion, she did look physically ill. She'd been unable to sleep; whenever she closed her eyes, all she could see were the passes (Ps) circling around her in a ring. She thought she'd read it wrong the first two times. The dean of Career Services had said one H was average and most students could eke out one by skillfully prioritizing a class or two. She'd been arrogant, delusional, and somehow dropped into being below average.

She was finally broken from her on-again, off-again stupor by the sound of her alarm going off. She had known to give herself a ten-minute alarm or she'd never rally for class.

She threw on a thick jacket that made her look like the Michelin tire mascot (except her marshmallow padding was black) and yanked on long calf-length snow boots, aggressively shoving her feet in to get through the narrow ankle bit of the shoe on the first try. All she did was get her feet stuck and give herself hefty bruises. Eventually, five calming breaths later, she figured it out.

When she exited her building and stepped into the courtyard, she couldn't control the preemptive shiver that went down her spine. People had been posting Instagram Stories all morning about the "winter wonderland" that was Boston, but she knew it was all a façade—a mass societal delusion to make the cold more bearable.

She plodded her way to campus, clomping along like a horse. They had a new set of five classes for the spring semester, but at least only the professors were new and she was with her Section, the same set of students from the first semester, for the majority of them. She'd stupidly been in the student lounge last night when the grades announcement came out and had witnessed enough jagged crying spells—timed, with an alarm, to last no longer than ten minutes because even emotional breakdowns were scheduled in law school—that she knew many were nursing the same sort of disappointment. She would rather not trade sorrow. She'd carry on alone.

As she swung open the door to the main law school building, she felt a body fall into step alongside her own and half-turned her head to see Cassidy. They were on undeniably and unfortunately good terms and Ryley was forced to take her headphones out. After Cassidy had so clearly highlighted the fact that she thought all Indians were fundamentally and undeniably connected by color of skin alone, no matter how different their personalities, the two hadn't much talked; however, during Thanksgiving break, Cassidy had ended up texting Ryley a couple of links to music videos she thought Ryley would like. Since Cassidy had never watched a music video in her life, Ryley had taken the olive branch for what it was.

Ryley finished shoving her headphones into her pocket and looked over at Cassidy again to see her sporting a beaming smile. It was the sort of beaming smile Cassidy undeniably practiced in front of the mirror for the inevitable time she was proclaimed Justice of the Supreme Court. Ryley offered a sure smile back as Cassidy carefully evaluated her expression.

Finally, Cassidy asked, "And how are we today? You look a bit under the weather." When Cassidy was truly feeling herself, she'd sometimes adopt the lofty tone of an eighty-year-old debutante.

"I'm good, but yeah, I think a little sick," Ryley said. Good to plant the seeds now.

"Got it. Let me know if I can get you anything! I'm feeling so good! You know, just super happy today."

Ryley wondered if Cassidy would be like this all morning, making clear to the entire class just how good of a mood she was in. Ryley stayed silent.

Cassidy continued speaking, unbothered. "Excited for this semester? Heard we got a full bench of hard-asses."

Ryley forced herself to respond with a similarly light and breezy tone. "Ha, yes. It'll be interesting. At least we're no longer sparkling new." She pointed to a random student walking ahead with a rather long face, his backpack bulging with what were likely brand-new casebooks. "I'm sure he came in bright-eyed and bushy-tailed, and look at him now: broken down by the world and One-L."

Cassidy laughed loudly, too jovially for the rather average quality of Ryley's "joke," and said, "What doesn't kill you makes you stronger."

They entered the classroom as Cassidy spoke and Ryley turned to her and said something nonsensical in response. She wanted a distraction, wary of the way in which she felt numerous pairs of eyes rest on and evaluate her. She kept a small, even smile on her face and after not paying attention to whatever response Cassidy gave to her nonsense, made a bee-line for her seat. Only after falling into her assigned seat did she quickly look up to scan the classroom. It was mostly full. She had cut it extremely close on purpose; students usually liked sliding in at the two- to three-minute mark, providing themselves with just enough time to get settled and engage in superficial small talk without providing too much time to make apparent their small talk only spanned the same four topics. Ryley only had enough in her to last up to the minute mark so she had planned accordingly.

Next to her, she heard Sophie and David three seats down switch from weather ("Oh, it's so dreary out, isn't it? I should invest in a vitamin D lamp") to workload ("These readings took forever. I just ended up going online to read an outline") to law school scandal ("Did you hear that Section Three had to bring in a mediator?") and finish up with general tiredness, stress, and anxiety ("Another day here. How do you think I'm doing?").

David was unusually relaxed and laidback. Normally, he was rereading his notes right before class, but now, he paid Sophie an impressive amount of attention as she vented her need for a break. He'd most certainly done well. Ryley would pretend she was in a rush to get to her next class and hold off speaking to David until tomorrow; she'd rather not go through with him what she just went through with Cassidy.

One of their new professors for the semester called the class to order, his low rolling baritone effortlessly carrying over the noise. "All right, class, I know some of you are feeling thrilled right now, and others are feeling not so great. But everyone can't get honors, and for some people, it just takes longer to get things right, so don't give up. I got all passes first semester and then I built myself up. Your life is not over. You will live another day."

Cassidy and a couple of others smiled in response to his pep talk. Many kept their faces blank.

As he began lecturing, Ryley forced herself to pay attention, taking diligent notes throughout although a large part of her wanted to stick it to them and give up trying entirely. Academics had been her cornerstone. Academic excellence was the one area she'd thought she could take her sense of belonging for granted, where she didn't have to bend to the way others did things. Ryley kept her pencil steady, reminding herself that everyone was observing each other, looking to see who was beaten down, and who was staring morosely down at their paper instead of paying attention.

At one point in the class, she felt the professor's eyes rest on hers briefly and her heart rate picked up by habit, but he almost seemed to look through her as he skipped on to the next student. She recognized and felt in every fiber of her body the complete non-importance she would have in this man's life. He would continue to train his focus on his publications and his eloquent theories of legal history and perhaps the random bright student in which he found a mind rivaling his own. She was just a cog in the wheel of students passing in and out of his classroom. Here was someone who had no expectations of her and it was almost freeing that she wouldn't be able to let him down. If she wasn't on the path to making something of herself to begin with, then she hadn't fallen off that path with an academic performance that had summarily knocked her out of the running for being any sort of legal savant.

As soon as class wrapped up, Ryley was out of her seat and heading toward the door, prepared to say she had to run home before her next class if anyone stopped her. No one did. David half held up his hand, but Ryley just pointed at her watch, and although Mark gave her a smile, he didn't make any effort to step away from his conversation with Cassidy, who continued speaking without pause. Ryley was relieved.

Unfortunately, she still had an awkward fifteen minutes before her elective class started and it was taking place in a room located only one floor up, so she decided to make a quick run to the cafeteria for lack of anything better to do. Walking briskly through the corridor, she managed to narrowly avoid running into Professor Kilmer, who had just walked through the doors of the building. He had his standard giant whiteboard full of cutouts of students' faces clasped firmly under one arm.

"Ryley! How are you?" He stopped walking to face her.

"Good, good." Then after looking over her shoulder to make sure no one she knew was nearby, she asked, "Um, can I come see you about my exam?"

"Yes, of course. Why don't you come to my office tomorrow morning at nine?"

"Okay, yes, sure. Thank you." Eager to finish the conversation, she took a step back, saying, "I'll see you then." After turning around and taking a few more steps, she suddenly realized how rude she'd been and horrified, she said, "Wow, I was rude. How are you? Is your semester off to a good start? Are you enjoying the first snowfall? Or maybe you're used to the snow and can see that it just sucks." She felt unhinged.

He gave her a slight smile. "I'm good. I'll see you tomorrow." And then, to save her from herself, he began walking confidently (and rapidly) away.

Ryley let out a huff and decided to skip the cafeteria and head up to the second floor for her next class. She could hear her classmates' voices and knew she'd be caught in a giant pack of them if she stayed anywhere on the ground floor. Taking the stairs rapidly, she decided to kill some time in the bathroom, guaranteed a solitude she wouldn't likely get in the cafeteria.

After five minutes of sitting on the toilet seat cover and clicking through a couple more Instagram Stories containing artsy pictures of snow, Ryley lugged herself over to the conference hall hosting the Negotiation Workshop, her elective class. It was a large class. Around 120 people had signed up, so it made sense that their first introduction to the course took place in a giant conference room. They'd rolled in plain brown tables with eight black metal chairs arranged neatly around each one. The room had crimson carpeting, crimson drapes, and wood-paneled walls. It was a mirror image and across the hall from the room that had held their orientation.

Going from table to table, she finally found her name tag slightly off to the side and settled into her chair gratefully, heaving a sigh. She was still one of the first ones there, so she pulled out her phone again. She clicked through a couple of spam emails before getting bored and deciding to leave her inbox count at 1,520. It was a lost cause.

"Well, look who it is." Ryley jerked her head up to see Olivia standing across from her.

Ryley let out a snort of amusement, unable to help herself. Naturally, for the one class in which there was the potential for overlap with other class years, she would overlap with Olivia. And naturally, Olivia would be assigned to her table.

"What's up?" Ryley asked.

"Nothing much. I'm still feeling things out and trying to decide which classes I should stay in for the semester."

Olivia settled back into her chair, propping her feet up on the seat in between them. Olivia wasn't wearing snow boots, just plain black booties that paired well with her dual-colored turtleneck sweater. Although Olivia must've had a time getting to school in those shoes, Ryley was easily jealous of her entire outfit. Quite frankly, Ryley could see she'd been envious of Olivia's dress sense all along, which broadcast how much Olivia didn't care what other people thought. Ryley could use a bit of that mentality right now.

Ryley considered urging Olivia to stay in the class in case this was one of the ones about to get the axe but then decided they didn't have that sort of relationship, so she stayed quiet and nodded instead. Olivia stayed quiet too, so Ryley turned back to her phone, feeling still more tense and wanting something to break a silence that felt more loaded than it should have.

When Harrison showed up out of the blue and plopped down at the table with them, Ryley only barely managed to keep her face and tone neutral. "Harrison?" If Ryley hadn't seen Olivia walking by herself enough times in passing, she would have thought they never spent any time apart.

"Hey, Rye Bread. Mom didn't tell me you were taking this class." He shot Olivia a casual smile of hello as he spoke.

"Well, it's not like she has my schedule memorized. I don't tell her everything."

He loudly scoffed, but Ryley continued, undeterred. "Harrison, I raved about this course nonstop after I visited for Admitted Students Weekend. Obviously I was going to take it. Why are you taking it?"

"Olivia was talking about it and saying how excited she was, so I decided to try it."

"Of course." Her words only came out slightly snarky. Olivia just smiled in response.

"Anyway, I'm going to go back to my table. But before I leave, Ryley, I'm having a pregame for Winter Formal if you want to come. You can bring a couple of friends...and your boyfriend." Harrison paused hesitantly on the word *boyfriend*, as if he wasn't sure if he should make Ryley aware of how much their mom talked about one to the other.

Ryley started nodding instinctively. She'd already decided it was high time to at least superficially move on from the grudge she'd been nursing for almost ten years at this point, and right now, she wanted to be around family. She wanted the grounding his presence would provide her.

Seeing her immediately nod, Harrison continued in a more confident, enthusiastic tone. "Awesome! Genie's coming to town! And for real this time, so she'll be there."

"Oh, it'll be great to finally meet her." Ryley was curious to see if Genie was as perfect as Harrison made her out to be. Her mom would be thrilled that someone in the family was finally meeting Genie. In fact, she would be thrilled Ryley and Harrison were even hanging out in the first place. She'd long ago given up on forcing them together after she'd gotten their individual sincere assurances that even though "the like was gone, the love was still there" (Ryley had coined that phrase). Indeed, Ryley should call her mom right after class. They hadn't talked for three whole days; she was probably worried that her daughter's rather rare lack of communication was a result of Ryley being run over by a car.

Olivia chimed in, "Fantastic. I can't wait to meet the girl who has my friend consistently pining and moony-eyed for her." It was time to move on from pondering Olivia and Harrison's potential romantic entanglement. Ryley snorted even as a sheepish grin snuck across Harrison's face.

"Okay! I'm excited. I'll see you both later." With that farewell, Harrison walked away.

Their table began to fill up with other students, and shortly thereafter, the negotiation professors began their introduction to the course, explaining the rules for the first exercise. Once the professors had finished speaking, people immediately began proposing possible courses of action.

Ryley, however, was taking a bit longer than the others to understand the introductions and stayed quiet. She couldn't think clearly, feeling pressured to perform and prove herself academically in a way she hadn't before.

Olivia naturally took a leadership role, unapologetic in organizing a plan of action for the eight of them, but she was nice and patient with Ryley. She showed the side of herself that had come out at the Harvard-Yale Game, singling Ryley out and asking her what she thought even though a majority of the table had already spoken. Ryley could see why Harrison liked her as much as he did.

As the exercise progressed, Ryley let herself focus on Olivia and the way she ignored other students' groans as she asked Ryley for her opinion on something that had already been decided. And for a moment, Ryley stopped worrying about how everyone would react if they found out she was a failure after she'd tried so hard to do nothing but be a success in other people's eyes.

CHAPTER 15

FEBRUARY 2019

——

"Hi, Professor. Thanks for meeting with me," Ryley said, distinctly feeling her sense of inferiority vis-à-vis him, made explicit by the contrast between his intimidating, plush office chair and her simple, hardbacked metal one.

"Yes, happy to do so." As he leaned back into his chair, wisps of white hair waved hello to her before settling gently down onto his crown once more. His fingers were steepled and his shoulders relaxed. Of course he was at ease—his intelligence was not on the line here. She looked beyond him to gather her thoughts. His office was bare but for a bookcase bursting with thick legal tomes, a couple of Hallmark-perfect family pictures laid out on his desk, and a potted plant in the corner.

"Um, so I went through the exam and went through some sample answers I saw online, and I was a bit confused because I thought my answer said the same thing as ones you liked. Not that I'm doubting the fairness of your grading or anything. I'm just confused." She clasped her hands together to prevent any further gesturing on her part.

"Well, I have a hardcopy right here, so I can pull it up for you if you would like?" he offered, surprisingly gently.

"Sure, okay," she said, and then for the first time since walking into his office, she leaned back into the chair, her spine no longer ramrod straight.

He was silent for a couple of moments as he looked through her exam. Finally, he said, "You spotted most of the issues, and you were right on the cusp, but you didn't show the level of knowledge necessary. The students I gave honors to played at the edges." He paused, as if to check if she was listening, and she immediately started bobbing her head rapidly (though given that she had no idea what he meant, she may as well have been off in one of her daydreams).

"You spent so much more time detailing the rules of the cases rather than applying the rules of the cases to the issue at hand and tracing through each issue carefully, showing you'd given deliberate thought to how each side could argue. In your policy answer, you just throw a lot of material on the page."

He paused dramatically and she could see that here was the punchline. "Look, your exam showed me you did all the readings, but I don't see a strong, cogent answer here that shows me how you, Ryley, think. Yes, I get that you play it *safe* and don't necessarily want to share your own opinion, but that's what we're encouraging you to do here. To argue something, to demonstrate a sophisticated understanding of the subject matter, and not just parrot back material to us."

She tried to digest his words. They made sense in theory, but she was too busy feeling personally attacked. There had been no need for him to unduly emphasize *safe* the way he had. Also, in truth, a not insignificant part of her had come in for an "It's okay, you tried," or an "I can see you're brilliant, but I was tired when I graded your exam."

He finally chose to break the ensuing silence, asking, "How did you do in your other classes?"

She paused, considered fibbing, but then said, "About the same." She couldn't help but break eye contact as she said this, ashamed and angry that she couldn't tell him this performance had just been an aberration and she was smart. When she looked back up at him, he was nodding, unsurprised.

And then her mouth was moving of its own accord. "But I'm smart. I am. I've been the top of my class at incredibly competitive institutions." She'd never been classified a word-vomiter or a parrot!

He sighed. "Ryley, you may have been at the top of the class at other institutions, but you're in the Olympics now. Being top of your class before means nothing. This is a whole different league."

Again she was rendered silent. This time she was too busy trying to process her self-image shattering even as wave after wave of dizziness made her lightheaded. She'd had anxiety attacks before, previously in social situations when she was made aware that something was fundamentally off with her, but never in an academic one. She would have liked to tuck her head down and sit in a corner, but she didn't exactly have that option. Maybe Professor Kilmer wouldn't mind if she shoved his lone bamboo plant aside and claimed the spot as her own.

He seemed to recognize something was going on in her head or had just pegged her as something of a space cadet because he continued to happily carry the conversation for the rest of the meeting. Of his own accord, he went through some of her answers in more depth, pointing out the core issues he thought she'd missed. She wrote everything he said down, her pen scribbling across the page. If he'd asked her to repeat a single thing back to him in the moment, she would've been incapable of doing so.

She left his office rather robotically and immediately went home, thankful the class this morning was one she could skip. She'd never skipped a whole class before, but she'd also never been called a parrot. All that was echoing through her head was that she was not smart when it came down to it. That at the end of the day, she didn't have a single original thought in her head. She found herself devastated as a part of her identity was forcibly removed and taken from her without any say on her part, and she gave herself the necessary time to blankly stare at her bedroom ceiling.

Five minutes into her stupor, she saw her phone light up out of the corner of her eye. It was her mom calling.

She considered not answering, but she wasn't a martyr and the idea of some cheerleading appealed to her.

"Hi." She kept her pose, lying spread-eagled on the sky-blue duvet irritating her with its cheerfulness. At least the rest of her room was suitably gloomy with her walls and ceiling a dark green unadorned but for cracks in the plaster.

"Hi. How did the talk with your professor go?"

"Fine." She waited for her mom to prod her, so when she delivered the subsequent in-depth play-by-play, she could tell herself she hadn't wanted to share in that amount of detail and it had been her mom's doing. Ten minutes later, Ryley finally wrapped up.

"That wasn't that bad! Look at how invested he was in you and in helping you. I doubt he would have been like that if he thought you were dumb and without hope." Her mom's perky tone made her dig her fingers into the duvet.

"I never said I was dumb and without hope," Ryley said flatly.

"I was summarizing general themes." Her mom slightly laughed as she said this and Ryley couldn't help but smile in reaction though she found none of this the slightest bit amusing.

"You're paraphrasing when my very essence is on the line?"

"Are you sure you don't want to go into acting? Now that you're proving mediocre in law, it could be time for a career change."

"Mom." Ryley tried to sound upset, but she couldn't contain the laugh that bubbled around the word and soon they were both laughing, which Ryley supposed had been the whole point.

"Ryley, you know I will never think you're anything less than brilliant, and I know he said the bit about the Olympics, but I don't think he was saying you lack talent." Her mom's cheerleading felt flat.

"I think he *was* saying that, and regardless, I'm done for. Law firms will see my Ps and think I just squeaked into Harvard and don't deserve to be here. Career Services said I had to get at least one H to be competitive. If I don't go to a certain tier firm, everyone here will know I didn't do well."

Although her mom tried chiming in, Ryley was in full flow and continued talking over her unapologetically. "My life is over; the mirage is ruined. David texted me saying both he and Cassidy were asked to be research assistants for one of our professors. Obviously they did well. Once people find out I got all Ps, they'll think I don't belong. You know how grade-obsessed everyone is here. I'm back to being on the outside."

"Ryley, you're jumping all over. You need to calm down. Breathe with me." Her mom had shifted to her dictator tone, used whenever Ryley was getting too overwhelmed and spiraling. Knowing she had no choice, Ryley mimicked her mom's breathing, although she had a few choice words she would've liked to say instead.

Once her mom was assured Ryley was occupied taking deep breaths in and out, she said, "Okay. Your life is not over. Yes, you stumbled, but you've stumbled before, and every time you've brushed yourself off and gotten back up. I know it hurts, but you have second semester and all those networking events. And you've gotten good at living two lives—you don't need to tell anyone your grades. You know what to say and what to do. You know how to tell people what they want to hear."

Ryley couldn't argue with that and supposed her mom had done all the problem-solving Ryley would have otherwise kept herself distracted with. "I'm so tired of pretending." The whisper fell unintentionally from her lips, the stress of the day getting to her. Not wanting to hear what her mom had to say in response, she quickly said, "I didn't mean that. I haven't forgotten how hard I fought to get here. I have to go. I have to hang up."

"Ryley, you don't have to—"

Ryley interrupted, insistent. "I have to go. I need to do the readings. We'll talk later, okay?"

"Okay. I love you no matter what. You know that."

Ryley did know that, but she was scared. The wobbles she felt before were nothing; the whole edifice was in danger of collapsing and she'd spent too long developing the construct and living within it to turn back now. She hung up with a quick "you too" and disconnected.

* * *

Ryley decided to meet David for a coffee before her 3:15 class. She'd blown him off for the last week in the aftermath of grades coming out and didn't particularly want to cross over from being "under the weather" to just being a bad girlfriend.

She walked the path she'd walked hundreds of times already, cutting through Wasserstein Hall to get out of the cold and striding past the classrooms and through the student lounge to get to the tucked-away alcove. The cozy fireside nook with the small café stand was her favorite place to do the readings. The chairs were upholstered with vibrant, patterned fabric that brightened the otherwise nondescript brown wall paneling and brown hardwood floor.

Ryley wouldn't have minded if everything was brown and black (like her), but she supposed others wanted some color and happiness to break up the monotony. She considered the café to be a second living space given that she spent all her time studying there. Although the café was packed enough during the day, she was usually the only one there after the barista service stopped. David would always retire to the library for more "serious" work, liking the hardcore scholar sort of vibe. Ryley found the library too intense, given the glares other students sent her when she inevitably knocked her water bottle over.

Ryley stepped up to the counter now, happy to see no line and happy to see her favorite barista. She always gave Ryley a small glass of hot water free of charge in which she could soak her teabag. The two would usually talk on and off at closing, and the barista had developed a soft spot for her after seeing her holed up in the café too many times toward the end of last semester.

Ryley gave the barista a large smile of thanks and a wave and walked over to the offset nook, seeing David with Cassidy and Mark all clustered next to the fireplace. She hadn't realized it was a group outing.

"Hey, guys!" She let the surprise in her voice ring out.

"Hey, Ryley. Cassidy and Mark were sitting nearby, so I invited them over. Didn't think you'd mind," David responded.

"Oh, yeah, totally fine." Although a girl sitting in a chair right next to Cassidy began packing up her bag, Ryley turned away from them to drag over a chair from a couple of yards away. Hopefully they'd see the way they were putting her out. She'd thought David had wanted to check on her and connect one-on-one, but it had been ten days since grades came out and he'd asked to get lunch. She knew she'd hurt him. She knew she wasn't pulling her weight and had been pulling away from all her friends in order to avoid any talk of grades. Both Mark and Cassidy had texted her a couple of times in the last few days, and she'd blown them off too with flimsy excuses.

As Ryley got settled, they continued talking about a reading for the elective class they were all in (with the exception of Ryley). She stayed silent, waiting for anyone to change the topic. No one did, so she decided to bring up Harrison's pregame, using it as a peace offering.

"Oh, before I forget, are you all planning on going to Winter Formal? Harrison is having a pregame for it."

"That'll be fun! It'll be nice to meet some new people," Mark said instantly. David nodded in agreement, his wide lips stretching into a smile. Ryley relaxed some; since she'd arrived, that had been the first time he'd smiled at her.

Cassidy hemmed and then said, "I think I should be able to make it, but I know Soph and a couple of other girls had talked about going dress shopping before."

Ryley quickly responded, "Oh, I'm sure Harrison would be fine if a couple more people came. I can post in our group text."

"I can do it. If it's from me, they'll see it's all in the same plan and not like they have to choose." It went unsaid that they would all choose Cassidy over Ryley. Cassidy didn't really look at Ryley as she spoke, clearly still a bit miffed. Ryley would send her a link to a cat video later today; Cassidy was into those.

For now, Ryley just said, "Okay great, thanks." Changing the topic, she asked, "Are you all going to the recruiting event tonight? I'm thinking of going."

"Well, if you have at least two or three Hs from first semester, you're good to go. No need to go to those," David said off-handedly. The self-assuredness she'd seen when he was talking to Sophie in class was on display once again. "You can totally figure out who got all Ps though. Did you see Garrett last week? Or Lyla? They looked devastated and they both acted like they were so smart first semester. Even Zeke looked a bit down but probably only because he got three Hs instead of four."

Ryley knew he was only speaking this way because he couldn't fathom that any of them, his crew, had gotten all Ps. She kept her face neutral, nodding along.

Cassidy jumped in. "Whatever, I'm going to go. I want the free drinks. Ryley, you want to meet up ten minutes before to walk over?"

Ryley immediately nodded, mentally taking back any mean thing she'd ever thought about Cassidy. As a matter of fact, for all her showmanship, Cassidy had not brought up her research assistant position once, downplaying any talk of grades after that first smug day.

Mark added, "I'll come!" He was quick to say, "Nothing better to do." He spoke so confidently that possibly he did have nothing better to do, but she wondered if he too had stumbled. Plans made, Ryley relaxed as the four continued speaking, jumping from topic to topic for the next thirty minutes with relative ease.

As they chatted, Ryley tracked David, trying to figure out if something was going on. Although he looked at her a normal amount, she felt as if they were, in fact, just four friends hanging out. He didn't look to her nearly as much as he used to nor try to scoot his foot against hers or brush his fingers against hers under the table. She could feel her relationship with David losing its newness and excitement. She'd continued to push off sex and her behavior this past week wasn't exactly winning her any points. Maybe it wouldn't be her grades that ended them after all.

CHAPTER 16

FEBRUARY 2009

Ryley hopped into Josh's car. "Gives You Hell" was on again. Josh was crooning along, belting out the chorus line with gusto; he was likely thinking of Kyle. Eventually, thankfully, the song came to a close, but other than a simple "hi" when she came in, Josh had yet to say anything. Ryley racked her brain for an icebreaker; he was the one doing her a favor after all.

"So, you excited?" Good. Not a dumb question at all.

"Yeah. I like Taylor and he always throws the best parties. Because his parents know he's having them, they always leave top-shelf stuff around."

"Got it, cool." Taylor was the captain of the baseball team and not even that good-looking, but his general air of well-being and success more than made up for any deficit. Ryley had yet to see him single in the six months she'd been on campus. He seemed to have a Rolodex of girls on hand, kissing a new one in the quad every week. That was likely a stretch. Every two weeks.

"Are you excited? This is like your first party-party, right?"

"Yeah, I've never been to one of these before. Glad I finally get to see what all the hype is about." She pushed her hands under her thighs in an attempt to stop fiddling with the seatbelt. Ryley's nerves were getting progressively worse the closer they got to Taylor's house. Hopefully, Taylor wouldn't ask her what she was doing there when she walked through the door. It was definitely just an oversight and not intentional; she doubted he even knew who she was.

"Solid. You'll have a good time. I brought a flask if you want to take a sip to get loosened up. You seem a bit tight."

Ryley was always tight. It was her natural resting state. She gave a semi-laugh though and took the flask out of the cupholder, unscrewing the cap and keeping it pressed against her mouth for a couple of seconds before eventually taking a tiny sip. The liquor burned as it went down and she only barely kept the cough in her throat. She put the flask back down.

Josh kept his silence as he pulled into an open parking spot in front of Taylor's house. After parking, he paused to obviously check out a group of laughing girls who passed in front of his car in tight black dresses. Ryley looked at the girls too, liking how the dresses wrapped around their bodies like that. She should have gone for a dress instead of jeans and a blouse. At least her blouse was a pretty chiffon material even if it broadcast uptight woman rocking business casual at the office.

Josh looked over at her as she continued to look at the girls. "Are you going to get out at any point or are you going to continue checking out those girls?"

"I wasn't checking them out! I liked their dresses a bunch. I was just thinking I wish I had worn a dress."

After giving her a disbelieving glance, he said, "Okay, well, what's done is done, so let's go."

Ryley rolled her eyes and pushed open the door, refraining from asking why he too was hesitating to get out if he was so eager to go. They both walked slowly over to the house. It was a giant limestone mansion with a fountain in the front and an imposing gate left open for all the party guests to walk through.

"Makes even your house look a bit like a cottage, doesn't it?" Josh snarked, fiddling with his sleeve.

"Yeah, this place is massive." Ryley would've been intimidated even if the house was a ten-foot shack. Both started dragging their feet the closer they got to the door. Just as she was about to say something to offer comfort, he snapped, "Ryley, stop dawdling. Come on!" Feeling the nerves coming off him and adding to her own agitation, she didn't snark back and simply walked faster. She could hear the base beat pulsing outside. "Gives You Hell" again.

Josh pushed open the door—Taylor was incredibly trusting, leaving it unlocked with the gate open—and she was immediately overwhelmed by how loud and dark it was inside. The lights in the corridor were barely on, dimly flickering in ornately patterned, beautiful sconces so guests could see their feet as they first walked into the house. Beyond the corridor, the living room was dark and she could just see the silhouettes of couples making out against the wall. The furniture had been cleared away to make a dance floor of sorts, but she followed Josh closely as he walked straight through the living room and into the backyard.

There, she recognized a couple of girls from the softball team, and surprisingly, Kyle immediately shouted, "Ryley, Josh! Hi!"

Ryley gave Kyle a huge smile, feeling the strain in her cheeks as she tried to communicate her appreciation for Kyle's warm greeting.

"Hey, Kyle! How are you?"

Kyle twirled in closer to them, meeting them halfway and bringing her entourage effortlessly with her as she lightly rubbed Ryley's arm in hello and gave Josh a loose, draping hug. Josh seemed shell-shocked but immediately hugged her back. Kyle had to take a rather obvious step back before he released her.

"Ryley, going to drink at this one?" Kyle asked, and although Ryley was uncomfortable being put on the spot, she liked that Kyle had effectively intimated that Ryley had been at past parties and they'd hung out socially before. She didn't recognize most of the girls around Kyle aside from Maddie, the one other softball girl in this little circle.

"Yeah, I'm just going to nurse a beer though. I wanted to give Josh a chance to drink, so I was planning on being the designated driver." Ryley had practiced the designated driver line with her mom. She'd forgotten to run it by Josh earlier though, so she turned to him now, saying, "Good with you? I figured you'd want to drink."

"Yeah, I do want to drink, but your plan makes no sense. I live like twenty minutes away from you."

"Oh, yeah, you can crash in our guest room." Ryley had been surprised when her mom had offered to let him stay with them, but her mom had really liked the designated driver idea.

"Oh, okay. That'll be better than me making the longer drive out. Great. Thanks."

Kyle had stayed quiet as the two of them figured it out, but now said, "Okay, Josh. Let's get you wasted!"

Ryley trailed after them as Kyle poured some sort of elaborate concoction for Josh. She stuck with her proclaimed beer choice. Harrison had always told her those were easier to track. She looked around the garden. She liked how it was bracketed into parts, consisting of an off-white porcelain tile patio, an antiquated fireplace nook, and a large, well-watered, lush expanse of grass. It was a relatively nice night for February and her leather jacket was more than enough to keep her warm. Seeing someone stumble and fall in a shadowy patch of grass a little to her right, she automatically went over to help them. She was surprised to find herself helping Harrison.

"Harrison?" Ryley said, shocked. She helped Harrison over to an empty chair, located on the edge of the red brick patio. He had a cigarette in hand.

"Hey, Ryley! Good to see you here, moving on up in the world! How's it hanging?" His eyes were glazed and his words slurred as they tumbled out of his mouth. This was the drunkest she'd ever seen him. He couldn't be planning on going back home like that. There was no way their mom would be sleeping and she'd have words for him.

"Fine. I didn't know you were coming to this?" Ryley chose not to comment on his blatant drunkenness.

"I was on the beach with some friends, and they invited me along. I'm just going with the flow. I'm glad you're experiencing this as a sophomore. I was too serious before this year," he said, shaking his head and chuckling to himself.

"Yes, okay."

"Ryley, breathe! Your shoulders are all the way up to your ears. Breathe." He swayed toward her, even as he demonstrated how to breathe.

"I'm good. Do you want me to drop you home at the end of the night?"

"Nah, it's cool. I'm probably going to go over to Matt's to sleep. Don't want to face Mom like this. Don't tell her. I know you can't keep anything to yourself when it comes to her, but please keep this to yourself."

"Yes. Sure." It would be a toss-up. Ryley would probably cave if directly pressed.

"So, having fun? How's it hanging?" He cocked his head to the side, a dopey grin still on his face.

"It's good. Okay, I'm going to go." She didn't know how to talk to him when he was like this and it made her feel out of sorts. He was too pliable, too childlike, and she wanted her big brother back.

"Okay. Josh brought you, yeah?"

"Yeah. How'd you know that?" She stopped stepping away, her attention back on him.

"Just a guess," he said, attempting to wink. He didn't actually wink because he was too drunk; instead, his eyes were spasming.

Before she could say anything more, his new friends were shouting at him and gesturing for him to join. "Come on, we're going to teach you how to actually drink!" She wished they wouldn't patronize him so. She wished he wouldn't let them.

Ryley went back to join Kyle and Josh, who was still gazing at Kyle with big heart eyes; Kyle was telling a story about getting so drunk that she decided to go streaking across her neighbor's lawn. As Kyle continued the story, holding eye contact with Ryley for crucial segments of the story, Ryley found herself looking at Kyle with that same sort of admiration. Kyle's gold hair was glinting in the patio light, and her face was attractively flushed. She was so cool. Ryley wanted to be like that; able to command an audience at will with that same effortless confidence. However, when Taylor walked by them, heading toward the drinks table, Kyle immediately began wrapping up her story, cutting right to the chase in a way that felt artificial before quickly saying, "I'm out. I'm going to get another drink." Ryley would bet there was at least four gulps' worth left in Kyle's red solo cup.

After Kyle left, Josh just stood there, staring sadly down at his cup. No one even tried to take Kyle's place and the others in the circle quickly drifted away, leaving Josh and Ryley standing there alone. Ryley was sure Josh would ditch her to go hang out with the baseball guys, so she started scouting the backyard to see if she could locate anyone else she knew.

She, unsurprisingly, only had acquaintances here. All the people were "cool" and white but for a couple of spots of color; the minority quotient had been diluted even further. Josh, however, stayed stationary beside her; perhaps he too didn't feel close to anyone. After at least two more minutes of the two of them just standing there, she asked, "You good?" That seemed to wake him up and then he was moving away. "Yeah, I'm fine. I'm going to do some shots."

She looked over to where Kyle and Taylor were leading a round of shots and sighed, turning her feet to head in the opposite direction. She decided she'd pay a visit to the bathroom, perhaps, try to find Harrison again. Or Carly. Carly had somewhat tired of acting like her self-appointed older sister, but she was still infallibly kind, always offering to take Ryley in her car to get to the softball field. Carly hadn't invited her to this though, likely predicting Ryley would feel incredibly out of place.

Ryley passed by four more couples making out as she traversed the hallway leading to the bathroom. Upon seeing the line, she plonked herself down on the floor. It looked like it would be a wait. She made eye contact with the guy standing in front of her who then immediately looked away and down at his phone. Soon, two girls—the blondes she'd noticed earlier in the little black dresses—joined the line behind her, and

Ryley saw the boy immediately swivel his head back around at the sound of their higher-pitched, light-hearted voices.

He stared at them for a couple of minutes before telling Ryley, "Hey, let's switch. You can go ahead of me."

Ryley looked at him, considered saying no out of spite, but inevitably nodded and tried to block out the sound of them flirting behind her. She heard the girls say they knew no one there and the boy promise to show them around. She looked down at her hands and finally, when she got into the bathroom, just stared at herself in the mirror. She doubted the guy outside was in any rush to use it.

Staring at her skin, her face, and her hair, she wished again that she could have been born with the white skin and blond hair that seemed to make boys drop everything. That would make her a leading lady and not a dorky side character who was too frequently written out of scenes or relegated to the outskirts. She was tired of being looked through and being the odd one out automatically and tired of seeing that reflected in movies and in real life, where the only minorities who fit were white in everything but skin, or were being patronized, like they were doing to Harrison. It had been stupid to come.

She sat heavily down on the toilet seat and pondered walking home. She didn't want to see Josh fawn over Kyle all night. Eventually, someone pounded on the door, asking if she was "taking a dump." Embarrassed, she quickly exited, keeping her eyes averted as she walked rapidly away. She made her way back outside and decided she couldn't just ditch Josh but would ask him if he was okay to leave. Maybe he wasn't having too good a time of it either.

She scanned the crowd, trying to locate him, and found him hovering on the side of the circle containing Taylor and

Kyle. She went over, pulled on his sleeve, and said in a low voice, "Hey, any chance you want to go?"

"No! We just got here!" he exclaimed. Of course, the rest of the circle immediately turned to look at them, and Ryley blushed under their scrutiny.

"What, you're not having fun?" Taylor asked, eyeballing her.

"No, I am. Just tired. It was a long day."

He stared at her for a moment longer as if to consider heckling her, but Kyle pulled on his sleeve and continued her story. Ryley felt another rush of gratitude to the girl.

Josh turned to face away from Ryley, signaling the end of the conversation, but another boy on the baseball team looked over at the two of them.

"Asked her for help studying yet?" he queried.

Ryley waited for Josh to respond, already dreading what was coming.

Josh looked mortified as he stood there, frozen. "Um, no. No."

Ryley waited two seconds longer to see if Josh would give any further justification and realizing he had none, gave a dry laugh and walked away. Luckily, at least the other boy had spoken in something of an undertone and Kyle had only increased the volume of her monologue, so Ryley was spared any looks of pity from the rest of the circle.

Ryley had just reached the outer gates to the house when she heard someone run up to her and then a hand was on her shoulder, yanking her to a stop.

"I'm sorry. He twisted it. I said I liked you as a friend and then when Kyle started asking me if I was sure and asked why I was spending so much time with you, I said I also wanted your help studying because I didn't want her to think I wasn't interested." He was speaking very loudly, his words sloppily jumbling together.

Ryley looked at Josh in silence. She didn't think that was the whole story. "Why did you suddenly start being so nice to me?"

"Because I like you." He took a step closer.

"Were you going to ask me for help with studying?" She took a couple of steps back.

"Maybe, but that's not the only reason I was hanging out with you. I like you. You're nice."

"But you decided to drop me off at my house and invite me to the party all in one weekend. What's going on?" Ryley decided to remove the wool from her own eyes.

"Honestly, I just like you." He didn't take another step forward but lifted his hand slightly, reaching for her. Ryley let the pause linger and stayed where she was.

He let out a heavy breath and continued. "Harrison said if I helped you adjust and helped you fit in and belong, he'd put in a good word with the jazz director so I could get a solo at the showcase."

Ryley supposed she should feel more shocked. So much for Harrison saying she was "wonderful the way she was." Of course, Harrison thought she was a weirdo and needed help to be normal and get along with people. He'd judged her at Homecoming and he'd judged her when he overheard her talking to her mom about how alone she felt. Seeing that she refused to follow in his footsteps and accept the mantle of Queen of the Nerds, he'd conscripted someone into helping her, thinking she was doomed on her own. It was humiliating.

"But this is not like a *Ten Things I Hate About You* thing. I'm not Heath Ledger here. Harrison knew we were already kind of friends and just told me I should try to get to know you better and give you a chance. He said he could see us actually being friends. And he was right."

She stayed silent, so he continued speaking in an even louder tone. "Ryley, we're just starting to be close. Come on, don't be mad. You know I have your back. I didn't even do anything wrong except say that one line about studying."

"Right, so you have my back except when it comes to Kyle. Why are you so obsessed with her?" Ryley didn't know who she was madder at: Josh, for going along with the charade; Harrison, for making it clear to her that she wasn't fine the way she was; or herself for thinking she'd been at least semi-successful at blending in. She was a charity case.

Josh's mouth was still moving, so Ryley made an effort to listen. "Kyle makes me feel good and important. I don't normally feel like that. Usually, I just feel like I'm drifting along and doing what everyone else is doing."

Ryley found herself hard-pressed to summon up feelings of sympathy. She nodded, wanting the conversation to be over.

He perked up immediately upon seeing her nod, though he was tentative when he asked, "Are you still okay if I crash in your guest room?"

She sighed and said, "I'm still pretty upset at you, man. But yeah, I'm not going to ditch you. Come on."

They walked to the car in silence, drove back in silence, and entered her house in silence. Ryley proceeded to get the guest bedroom set up for him in silence. Her mom had done most of the heavy lifting, fitting the bed with new sheets and stocking the bathroom with towels and toiletries. Indians were nothing if not good hosts. In fact, her mom had stayed up for them, but at Ryley's insistence, she'd left the two of them alone. She knew Ryley would be giving her a play-by-play tomorrow.

Ryley gave him a pair of Harrison's pajamas and turned to leave but stopped when he grabbed her arm.

"What?" she asked semi-irritably.

"Do you like me?" He was looking her at with wide, innocent eyes.

"What?" She hoped the shock in her tone would convey enough. *What an idiot.*

"I was just thinking—do you like me, like me? Because I feel like you got jealous of Kyle earlier. Rather than talking about any of the other stuff, you asked me why I was so obsessed with her. And you seem to study her a lot, and I was thinking that maybe you were trying to copy her so you could be more like her. To impress me." Someone in the room had an inflated sense of their own importance and it wasn't Ryley.

After taking one calming breath in, she said, "Honestly, I don't know what I feel. I think you're a catch, but I don't know if I *like* you. I do think you give her too much importance, but I mean, at the end of the day, I can see why—I think she's interesting. I'd like to have that sway."

Josh stayed quiet and after a couple of seconds of silence, said, "Do you want to make-out?"

"How drunk are you?" Ryley asked, taken aback at how quickly this had escalated and slightly scared.

"Pretty drunk. But I don't know. I want to do something."

Ryley knew it wasn't about her. He was just frustrated, but she'd also never been kissed and was sixteen years old, and here he was offering. She supposed if he was using her, she was using him. She'd show Harrison he shouldn't make her his charity case; he'd be horrified.

So she leaned forward and lightly pressed her lips against his, and at first, she liked how soft he was, how tentative. As he started applying more pressure, she let herself be guided onto the bed, thinking of how grown-up she felt; however, when she felt him reach for her pants, she seized up, frightened.

"Wait, hold up," she said breathlessly.

And he immediately stopped, looking at her carefully. They stared at each other, breathing rapidly, and Ryley could not decide what to do. She could get it over with, stop feeling so weird and know she was right on track, perhaps even ahead of schedule, but she was scared. As she lay frozen against the headboard, he lightly pushed another kiss onto her, soothing her by running his hand up and down her arm. She wanted to run out of the room.

She stayed.

CHAPTER 17

FEBRUARY 2019

Nursing a slight hangover from the latest event (she hadn't eaten anything even while downing three glasses of wine), Ryley plopped herself down on the seat with a huff. She was going to take a step back from networking. All the recruiting events took place in one of a select few restaurants on rotation in Harvard Square, the New England cheery red-brick vibe invariably at odds with the visiting attorneys' formal intensity. Although she had been taken aback by how many suits there were at first, any sort of intimidation factor was fast belied by way of hands waving just a bit too much and words coming out just a bit too loud.

At every event, attorneys and students alike clearly took advantage of the open bar. She inevitably did the same but found herself saddened by the fact that many of the practicing attorneys seemed to be rather unhappy, speaking lightly with an undertone of bitterness that set her teeth on edge; her rampant wine consumption most definitely contributed to her down mood.

In that vein, one of the biggest drawbacks of attending so many recruiting events was that she was beginning to see how much alcohol affected her. She'd always been so proud that she had never blurted out a secret crush or gone on a crying jag when drunk and had thought the high she got was worth any sort of emotional fallout. However, recently, Ryley had begun to dread the after-moments, where drunk Ryley found herself trapped on her couch, completely unable to escape from a mental loop of her own making.

Had Mark meant to cut her off when she had been speaking to a partner at the firm? Was David purposefully avoiding her? Was Cassidy? Cassidy always seemed to be in deep conversation with some attorney or another at the opposite side of the room for all the recruiting events. And David and she hadn't much spoken at all over the last week; he hadn't come to any of the recruiting events and when Ryley wasn't networking, she was studying. She'd yet to reach out to Cassidy, Mark, or David to see if she could rejoin their study group. She needed to find her own voice first.

At least Winter Formal was tonight. She just needed to get through the last class of the day.

"Hey, only recognized you by your bag. You are completely bundled up," Olivia said as she sat down next to Ryley. They had been put into the same smaller twenty-person section for the Negotiation Workshop and had easily fallen into the habit of sitting together over the last couple of weeks.

"Yeah, I was going to take off my beanie and my coat, but then I got too tired. I decided I'd let myself overheat instead," Ryley said.

Olivia laughed. "Feeling okay?"

"Yeah. Still two more months of this awful weather and three more months of feeling like I should be doing more and just being better."

Ryley froze as she heard words tumbling out of her mouth that she only ever said to her mom. Although they'd gotten off to a rocky enough start—Ryley was still resentful that Olivia had told David Ryley wasn't interested—she realized Olivia was easily one of the best listeners she'd ever come across. Olivia made her feel comfortable in a way no one else at the school did—not even Mark. Olivia's whole body seemed to involuntarily lean into Ryley, communicating how intent she was on listening to and better understanding Ryley. Even if Olivia sometimes offered Ryley her unsolicited opinion in an effort to push her toward enlightenment she didn't necessary want, Ryley found herself telling Olivia things she didn't tell anyone else at the school, letting herself ramble rather than censoring herself.

Olivia opened her mouth, closed it, and then opened it again to say, "Want to get on a plane to Bora Bora and ditch for the rest of the semester?"

Ryley gave a half-hearted laugh, and Olivia looked at her with a soft smile before squeezing her wrist lightly and saying, "Well, at least we like this class, right?"

"Yes, at least we like this class." Ryley shot Olivia a full, beaming smile, enormously thankful that her display of vulnerability hadn't been met with pity. She'd liked how Olivia grouped them together in a way that felt true and showed that Olivia noticed how Ryley tended to perk up and how she actively volunteered in the class.

Professor Poomin started speaking, breaking the girls out of their bubble, as she launched the class into the newest exercise. Professor Poomin was the only female professor Ryley'd had all year, almost unbelievably nurturing and feelings-oriented when contrasted against Ryley's eight male professors, six of whom were older and white.

These male professors had emphasized logic and coherence within the Court's opinion, kind enough but fundamentally Academics at their core. One took the law so fully out of context that he argued a case that greenlit lynching was considered justifiable because it ostensibly preserved the larger public's trust in the Court. It was consequently jarring to come to the Negotiation Workshop and have context matter, have identity matter, and have feelings and intention matter.

In fact, Ryley had stayed up late last night finishing one of the books (of which they'd only been assigned a chapter), undeniably drawn to any book that encouraged understanding of self. Back in the day, her college friends had used to joke that Ryley would most definitely write a self-help book someday. She couldn't see it.

After a quick overview, Professor Poomin gave them their assigned pairings. Ryley walked with her partner, Zeke, to an isolated conference room for the negotiation. Although she tended to sit with Olivia in class, she liked Zeke well enough; they both simply recognized they needed the larger group to successfully hang out together.

By the end of the mock negotiation, she liked him less. He'd made her work for everything and forced her to walk out with something barely above her bottom line so as to come to some sort of deal before they ran out of time.

She was sullen on the walk back and sullen during the debrief, staying quiet in the class in a way she normally didn't. Professor Poomin glanced at her more than a couple of times, and when she finally wrapped up the class, she looked at Ryley when she said, "Let me know if anyone has questions or wants to talk through anything."

Ryley packed her bag rapidly, not wanting to linger and wanting to begin pre-gaming; she'd almost lost her calm and simply walked out during the negotiation. She was never anything but in control and the anger she'd felt startled her.

Over the last month, her sense of self had begun to feel increasingly fragile as everything about her began to feel like a lie. The assigned reading had caused even more cracks to form. The book asked her to explicitly think about her identity, think about what made her Ryley, and she, who had become so used to submerging anything other, anything foreign to the narrative she wished to spin, found emotions and thoughts welling up that she was used to pushing down. Taking herself as she was as given, rather than telling herself that she didn't quite fit the mold just yet, she'd felt angry when she saw the presumption with which Zeke interacted throughout the negotiation. He'd made it clear he expected her to come to him, listening to her without listening at all.

The sprint down the stairs regulated her somewhat, and when she exited the stairwell and saw Olivia exiting the elevator, she felt slight remorse. Over the last few weeks, they'd fallen into a pattern of walking out together, but Ryley had been too focused on getting alone time to wait. First semester, when she'd convinced herself she didn't need or like her alone time, was a distant memory.

Olivia paused when they made eye contact but only gave her a simple nod and a "See you later?" Ryley could have hugged her.

"Yep, see you later."

"Okay. Bye, Rye."

Ryley didn't know how she felt about the nickname itself, but she liked the sense of closeness it conveyed.

* * *

Ryley looked down at her outfits once more. She wondered how many hours in total she had spent taking clothes from her closet, laying them on her bed, trying them on, and hanging them back up. She would be meeting David, Mark, Cassidy, and a couple of others on the edge of campus in ten minutes to walk over to the pregame.

She decided to go with a black jumpsuit; unfortunately, she wouldn't even get the benefit of not having to shave. She was pretty sure she'd be having sex with David tonight. She felt bad for waiting so long; she had just wanted the connection to click and for the stress to leave her whenever they got too intimate. At this stage in the relationship, though, they'd made out and done everything but have sex. Although he never explicitly pressured her, he hadn't been able to hide his frustration the last time she'd slept over, muttering to himself after he thought she'd fallen asleep. He knew she'd had sex before, that it wasn't like she was a virgin. In fact, he'd explicitly asked to exchange relationship histories on their fourth date. He had been with the same girl all through college and had just dated casually in the three years since. She had said she dated around in high school and college and left it at that. She didn't discuss the litany of failed dates or talk about how she'd instinctively shoved multiple past partners away when they had kissed her neck.

After applying her makeup and shrugging on the jumpsuit, she went on to Instagram to kill some time. Cassidy had posted a picture of her and her med school boyfriend with a simple heart under the photo. They must be back together again. Ryley knew she'd hear about it tonight. Ryley was glad for her friend but quite frankly in awe of the way everything seemed to be working out for her. Cassidy had good grades, a solid boyfriend, and was obviously objectively attractive based on the fifty comments already compiled under her photo reading something along the lines of "girl, you are gorgeous." Ryley added her own comment, replete with fire emojis, and then went over to the kitchen and threw back a couple of vodka shots chased by lime. How very hardcore of her. She knew the buzz would kick in once she was at the party, which suited her fine. She wanted to be happy and light and put on a good show for Genie.

Ryley met up with her assorted friends at eight on the dot and arrived at Harrison's place shortly thereafter. It was still too cold. She'd put on her thickest marshmallow coat again, prompting Mark to say, "If it isn't my favorite roly-poly" when she rolled up. Ryley hadn't bothered with a response, too busy seizing up every time a cold gust hit her under the ears.

As she waited for Harrison to buzz them in, Ryley glanced around at her friends. Everyone was dressed crisply with the men wearing pressed suits and the women in formal black dresses of varying length. Mark and Cassidy were keeping themselves busy with a rapid back and forth about *A Star Is Born*, but David was on the quieter end, flipping his phone from hand to hand.

Finally, the buzzer sounded out, and they were stalking up the staircase to the fourth floor of the four-story walkup. This building was no different than any of the others she'd been to in Cambridge. The carpet was old and a faded dusk gray with beat up off-white walls. As they reached the fourth floor, Genie theatrically swung the door open, holding one arm up in welcome. Genie was rather ordinary-looking in her oversized sweater and black leggings now—nothing like the glamorized photos of her Instagram.

Ryley immediately stepped forward, stretching out her hand as she said, "Hey, I'm Ryley."

Genie gave her a wide grin and instead wrapped her arms around Ryley in a bear hug. Ryley only barely prevented herself from flinching away; she would've appreciated some warm-up icebreaker first. As Genie exchanged greetings with the rest of them, Ryley stepped farther into the apartment, looking around at Harrison's vinyl record player in the corner, the lovingly arranged posters of street art, and the carefully curated coffee books on what was clearly an expensive glass coffee table. Harrison had laid out appetizers on said table: a plate of crackers with cheese, grapes, and prosciutto.

"Wow, Ryley, looks like Harrison is the host of the family," Mark said, laughing. Ryley gave a shrug of indifference. She didn't know when her brother had transformed into such a gentleman, but she couldn't deny the truth of Mark's words.

Harrison exited the kitchen then, shouting out a happy "thanks" to Mark, while pointing everyone to the glass bar cart. Harrison had truly become a fully functioning adult. As Ryley admired the bar cart, Olivia came out of the bathroom. She looked beautiful, wearing a tight, black backless dress, with her hair twisted into a bun. She'd exaggerated her eyes with wingtips and her lips were painted a delicate pink. She usually never had makeup on and Ryley was shocked by her transformation. One of those eyes winked at Ryley now as Olivia caught her staring.

Ryley blushed, looked away, and then hung back, watching all the introductions take place. Harrison stopped to size David up, but nothing else of note happened, if that could even be counted; David was unperturbed, speaking in the slightly heightened, self-assured way he'd adopted since grades came out. As Genie hugged everyone, Harrison shook everyone's hand, and Olivia gave everyone a nod and a smile, Ryley realized she was the only person who knew everyone there. She didn't give herself enough credit; she was a real Mark Zuckerberg.

When Harrison finally got to Ryley, he said, "Hey, Ryley, glad you could make it! You and your crew are the first ones here."

Ryley noted Harrison didn't count Olivia as a guest. Olivia gave her a small smile when they made eye contact again but made no move to come closer, staying by Harrison's side. A small part of Ryley's brain had thought they had a special connection, that Olivia might even prefer Ryley to Harrison; she was bothered that Olivia remained at Harrison's side and was bothered that it bothered her. Ryley kept her bothersome feelings to herself before looking over to Genie to see if she had any reaction to Harrison's proclamation or to Olivia's hovering. Genie did not, too busy looking down at her phone.

However, as the group settled into a large semi-circle of sorts, Harrison ended up next to Genie. Harrison easily and skillfully guided the conversation through weather before making Genie the next natural topic of conversation. Genie was someone new and different, existing outside the law school bubble to remind them that a whole other world still existed. They were all eager to spice up their dialogue beyond law and their now irrelevant lives before the law, and Genie knew how to tell a story, throwing in a self-deprecating joke here and there to offset the way in which she so easily dominated the conversation. So others, even Cassidy, were more than happy to stay on the topic of Genie and her glamorous life in New York, though Cassidy managed to bring up her boyfriend who worked at New York-Presbyterian, their three-year relation-ship, and how he'd begged for her to get back together.

At one point, Harrison wrapped his arm around Genie's waist like a man in a 1950s suburban couple, turning to look at her to whisper something when she yawned a couple of times in rapid succession mid-story. He kept his gaze intensely, potentially lovingly, trained on Genie as she muttered something back, and Ryley found herself uncomfortable with the sheer intimacy of the moment. She couldn't imagine ever being so lost in someone as to gaze at them like that; absence must have made Harrison's heart grow disproportionately fond.

Ryley fidgeted, shifted her feet to the right to rest her left foot slightly against David's, looked down at her phone, and then looked up to see how Olivia was coping with Harrison and Genie's display of intimacy. Yes, she'd promised to move on from wondering if there was something more going on between Olivia and Harrison, but she promised herself a lot of things. Surprisingly, Olivia was looking at Ryley's feet, with her brow slightly furrowed; Ryley shifted her foot away from David's. Irritated for being so impressionable, she glared at Olivia when Olivia looked up at her though Olivia just smirked in response. Fortunately, by the time Ryley and Olivia were done playing out their little skit, Genie and Harrison had come to a resolution.

Taking a step back, Genie said, "Sorry, guys, I had to get up at five a.m. for a marketing disaster that occurred at the agency, and then my train got delayed, so I literally got here five minutes before you all did and haven't had the chance to regroup or change. So, I might do that now, but before I go, Ryley, come with me into the kitchen."

Ryley disliked being ordered around by someone she barely knew, but Genie was already walking away and Ryley would look needlessly difficult if she didn't follow, especially when Genie had delivered the command with such a nice smile.

Once in the kitchen, Genie didn't keep her waiting. "Tell me about you! Harrison has obviously mentioned how close the two of you were growing up, so I'm so happy to finally meet you!" Ryley kept the snort inside; she would buy into this pretense too. Besides, it was a fundamentally different Ryley who had had such a big fallout with Harrison, and she supposed they had been close enough before everything with Josh happened.

Giving Genie a light, polite smile, Ryley said, "Not much to tell. I'm at the law school now with Harrison but finishing up my first year. I like it. I like how much everyone cares though it's definitely competitive."

"Oh, I'm sure everyone at this place is so studious. I've had a couple of friends who were law students and they were so serious. You must barely go out what with being a first-year law school student." Genie delivered the statement soothingly.

"It is serious, but I go out. Good stress relief," Ryley answered, disagreeing with the girl only so she could align them more. She didn't want Genie to draw a contrast between her fun New York City life and Ryley's study-filled law school one; Ryley was fun. Ryley accordingly expanded with, "I like music. And running."

Genie merely looked at her, silently asking her to do better.

"And I'm seeing someone here. David." She hated how quickly she went to David as if she didn't have enough to offer on her own, but at last Genie's eyes lit up.

"Oh, look at you finding yourself a nice Harvard boy. He seems like a darling."

"Yeah, he is a da—he's a good one. We're in the same section." There was absolutely no way Ryley could pull off saying *darling*.

"Well done, girl." Genie gave her a gentle nudge with her arm.

Ryley genuinely smiled, appreciating Genie's validation. Feeling charitable, she asked, "Aren't you tired? It's impressive you have so much energy after the day you've had."

"Yeah, but I'm going to rally. I have such little time with Harrison that I want to push through it. I'll change into a dress now to look a bit more formal." Genie took a step back before calling over her shoulder, "I'm going to make you take shots with me in ten, so be ready! Harrison said you've become quite the little party animal, so let's bring that out tonight."

If Harrison had said Ryley was a party animal, it was interesting Genie had implied Ryley didn't go out not two minutes ago, but Ryley didn't call her out on it and just gave a large smile in response. Breaking the nerd typecast was her bread and butter.

CHAPTER 18

FEBRUARY 2019

—

Ryley decided to make herself a mixed drink. Ten minutes would be a bit of a wait and she wanted to get drunk tonight. Not for Genie's sake but for her own. She painstakingly poured one and a half shots of Harrison's surprisingly nice choice of Grey Goose and mixed in club soda alongside grapefruit juice, stopping every so often to taste the bitterness with a care she wouldn't normally have. She may also have been using the time to take a break from the conversation.

She heard the steps of someone coming toward her and looked up over the white kitchen counter divider to see David standing there, smirking.

"Hiding out in here?" he asked playfully.

"No. Just making myself the perfect mixed drink."

"Great. Want to make one for me too?" David asked, stepping around the divider to enter the kitchen and lightly wrapping an arm around her in a side-hug.

Ryley smiled, appreciating his open display of affection if only because such displays had become increasingly rare. "Sure."

Olivia popped her head in over the divider next and said, "Rye Bread, make one for me too." Ryley saw David flick Olivia an irritated glance. Olivia looked coolly back at him as she said, "Yes?" Most people would have let it go.

"Nothing, nothing. Just feel like I haven't gotten to spend a lot of alone time with Ryley," he responded flatly.

Before the two of them could say anything more, Ryley interjected, "Wait, Olivia, I thought you didn't drink?"

"I don't drink a ton, but when I'm feeling it, I'll have a glass or two." Ryley nodded, appeased. Olivia seemed too efficient to drink much.

David continued in an undertone. "I miss you, Ryley. I feel like you've been distant." Ryley looked up to see if his softer tone had cued Olivia to leave, but she stayed put and winked at her as if they were in on an inside joke together. Ryley quickly looked away and focused once more on David.

"Oh, I haven't meant to be. I've just had a lot on my mind." If she were the arguing sort, she'd say both had contributed to missing dates, but Ryley wanted them to be happy and light tonight. Ryley didn't particularly try to lower her voice as she spoke though, a part of her liking how shameless Olivia was.

"I know you've had a lot on your mind, but I hope you know that when it comes to you, I always want to hear about it. Sometimes I feel like you're in your own little world, locked away from the rest of us," he said, earnest in his delivery in a way only David could be as he kept his eyes focused on hers. Ryley felt his disappointment and wished she could be more open and comfortable talking with him about all the pressures and the feelings of wishing she could be more, for him as much as for everyone else. Ryley opened her mouth and closed it.

Finally, she said, "Of course, I know that. I'm good, I am. And I'll try to open up."

As she turned back to make the drink, David reached out to place his hand on hers. The touch felt forced and commanding, and she shook it off under the guise of reaching for the handle of vodka.

Olivia jumped in then, interrupting whatever David was about to say and telling him that Harrison needed his input about something having to do with the Red Sox. David didn't believe her obvious fib but walked away regardless. He could never resist talking about the Red Sox.

"You good?" Olivia asked.

"Yeah. I don't need your protection. He's my boyfriend." The back of Ryley's neck felt hot and her cheeks too flushed.

"I know. I wasn't trying to invade your privacy. Boys can just be oblivious sometimes, and I felt like you were getting stressed."

"Sure, okay. Thanks." Ryley poured the grapefruit juice and reached for the club soda.

"You can talk to me. You know that right?"

"Yes. Jesus. I know I can talk to everyone," she huffed out before suddenly stepping closer to the divider. "Wait, you know what? There is something I've been meaning to talk to you about." Ryley's tone sounded vaguely threatening and she liked it.

"What?" Although she spoke nonchalantly enough, Olivia took a step away from the kitchen bar, planting both feet firmly on the floor instead.

Ryley let the pause linger for dramatic effect and then sternly whispered, "Why'd you tell David not to date me?" Ryley's heart was thudding and her hands were slightly trembling. Luckily she'd already placed her glass on the counter. She casually crossed her arms, tucking her hands behind the crooks of her elbows.

Olivia sighed and leaned forward against the kitchen counter once again. Ryley gave her time to gather her thoughts though she would've liked to snap at Olivia and command her to start speaking before someone interrupted them. Finally, Olivia said, "I don't want to say something as cliché as I didn't think he was good enough for you."

Ryley interjected, "Then don't."

"But I *did* think that, and look, I never saw it working out. I'm sorry." Olivia had some nerve, pronouncing a relationship dead that was still very much ongoing.

Ryley looked quickly over at David; he was enthralled by something Harrison was saying. "Okay, that's incredibly rude. One, we're still dating. Two, no matter what you thought, you had no business telling David that when you didn't even know me." She took a step back and lifted the glasses to taste the drinks as she waited for a proper apology. One was slightly bitter and the other perfect.

Based on the obstinate look on Olivia's face, an apology was not to be forthcoming anytime soon. "I think we'll have to agree to disagree. Harrison had talked enough about you that I did feel like I knew you, and you're a square peg trying to fit in David's round hole! Or vice versa to make the analogy work better."

Ryley didn't smile. She did resolve to ask Harrison just what nonsense he was promulgating about her though.

Olivia continued, "But all this is a moot point. I've never had a problem admitting when I'm wrong, and I'll never argue with you about this again if you actually are happy with him."

Ryley fought back the instinct to respond immediately in the affirmative and paused to meaningfully think about it to show Olivia she was listening. "Look, I don't know if I am happy right now, but I think we can be. He's nice, smart, and motivated—all the groundwork for us to fit is there. We just need to adjust to each other. I don't think it's worth throwing in the towel."

She handed Olivia one of the drinks and moved away from her after that, going to stand next to David. She gave him the second, slightly bitter cocktail. He shot her a beaming grin and almost immediately included her in the conversation. He was trying.

The rest of the pregame passed in a blur as the effects of the drinks she'd been steadily consuming started to hit her. She continued drinking. Indeed, to Genie's enormous pleasure, Ryley led the group in doing a round of shots. Olivia, who was standing next to her as she poured out the vodka, refused to do the shots and looked at her significantly, as if cueing her. Ryley ignored her and led the group to do a second round of shots shortly after the first. Harrison started to eye her with slight concern at that point too. She ignored him as well.

They left for the formal shortly thereafter, and everything got hazy in a way Ryley rarely let it, exhilarating her as much as it terrified her. She danced with Cassidy, with Olivia, and with David, making out obviously with him. At one point, she announced she had to use the bathroom; either Cassidy or Olivia offered to accompany her, but she didn't pause to confirm who, and just meandered away from the strobe light illuminated dance floor. When she got her bearings again and realized she was, in fact, standing successfully in the bathroom line, she looked over to see Olivia staring at her, concerned.

"I got you some water." Olivia pushed a glass into Ryley's hand and stared at her commandingly, gesturing for her to drink it.

Ryley obediently drank. The water didn't go down well and made her feel nauseous, but Ryley took slow, measured gulps.

When Ryley had her fill, Olivia took the glass from her surprisingly gently. "Harrison told me he's never seen you this drunk."

"Well, Harrison and I rarely go out together, so that doesn't mean anything. Anyway, I wanted a break, and both Genie and David wanted me to drink. It's good. I'll show some emotion, be more fun. David and I are finally doing it tonight."

Ryley was looking at the floor to ground herself, so she missed whatever reaction Olivia had to that piece of news, but she seemed to have stunned the girl into blessed silence.

Olivia broke it by saying, "You know I don't drink all that much."

"Yes."

"I don't think it makes me any less fun."

"Cool," Ryley said in a flat tone. Olivia said nothing after that, silently standing in line with her. Eventually, she started talking—flirting?—with a girl in line behind them. Olivia was making a point of doing it in front of her, leaning forward to touch the other girl's arm, laughing too loudly right in Ryley's ear. If Olivia would move even a foot away, that would be nice.

Ryley was also more than a tad confused; she'd automatically assumed Olivia was into boys and hadn't thought to question it. Keeping to herself, Ryley let them do their thing and only when she came out of the bathroom and saw that Olivia still hadn't moved did she say, a tad impatiently, "Should I go ahead without you or do you want me to wait?"

Olivia just shot her a calm smile. "Chill. I don't have to use the bathroom. I came along because I didn't want you wandering off by yourself." She then said goodbye to the other girl rather quickly. Too quickly. Olivia was likely just being friendly and Ryley had misread it.

As they walked back to the dance floor in slightly tense silence, Ryley felt bad for her earlier curtness. "Sorry, didn't mean to snap. She seemed nice." The slight slur to her words helped her disclaim any prior malicious intent.

Olivia immediately shot her a reassuring smile, scooting closer so that their arms brushed. "All good. Yeah, she's sweet. She's in one of my classes." A slight hesitation and then, "We've been flirting for the last couple of weeks. She's cute, right?"

"Yeah, I guess," Ryley said slowly, unsure of what she should say, unsure of what she was feeling. She liked having Olivia as a friend and how connected she felt to her. She was starting to prefer hanging out with her over David. She didn't want that closeness to go away if Olivia found a partner. She only ever felt pressured to do more, to be more, when she was around David.

"What do you mean 'you guess?' She's not your type?" Olivia asked, grabbing onto her hand and pulling Ryley to a stop before they traversed the marble arched entryway to the dance floor.

"Um, of course she's not my type. I'm with David, remember?" Ryley closed her eyes slightly as she spoke, feeling a slight wave of dizziness. She wasn't sure if it was brought on by drunkenness or Olivia annoying her.

"Yeah, I know you're with David, but I thought you were at least a little fluid if not something more. The way you check me out, the way you are around David, the way you look at girls…"

Even at her drunkest, Ryley never fully lost control of her faculties. She knew Olivia had purposefully chosen to ask her about this now, when her guard was supposedly lowered, so as to make it easier for Ryley to step out of a hypothetical closet. Although Ryley was a little resentful, she tried to focus on Olivia only ever seeming to have Ryley's back, however misguided she may be.

"No, I'm not. I'm straight," Ryley said firmly if dispassionately. She wasn't exactly shocked. She regularly checked out girls' outfits and more than a few girls had hit on her in college, asking if she was gay because of said fashion curiosity or perhaps because of her energy. She found it easier to connect emotionally with a very specific type of girl and the connection was always stronger than the one she ever felt with any man. Her relationship with Olivia versus her relationship with David was a case in point, but she'd always found romantic relationships to be an obligation. If she started dating Olivia, she was sure the easiness of their relationship would also go away.

"Have you ever thought about it?" Olivia asked, with such genuine, open curiosity that Ryley felt calmed.

"Yeah, I did. In college. I've always found girls to be so pretty, easily better-looking than boys, but I've never been able to see myself with a girl physically. I've never wanted to kiss a girl when drunk, or on a dare, and I've had plenty of chances. It just doesn't make sense with the image I have of myself."

Olivia was the first girl to ask her about her sexuality in two years and was probably just confused because of their developing intimacy. Ryley had seemed to stop projecting whatever mixed-message energy she had been previously as she became more focused on finding a husband to meet her engaged-by-thirty deadline.

Olivia stood there, seemingly fighting with herself over something, and Ryley would have been content to let her work through it (she had nothing to hide), but then Cassidy walked by.

"Oh! Hi, what's up, Ryley?" Cassidy only let her eyes linger momentarily on Ryley's hand, still clasped in Olivia's, before she turned to face Ryley.

Ryley released Olivia's hand smoothly if immediately. "Nothing. We were actually just about to go back to the dance floor." Ryley began walking over to David before Cassidy could say anything further.

One fuzzy period later, David finally dragged her off the dance floor, saying she was getting too sloppy and they needed a break. As they stood off to the corner and she fiddled with his shirt, he suddenly turned to her and asked, "Hey, want to get out of here? Go back to mine?"

She knew what he was implying as he rubbed her arm up and down, and she let herself get into the idea. She was feeling loose; they'd been dating for three months. This was about as good as it was going to get. She nodded and he eagerly pulled her along, telling her to text the group saying they were leaving because it would be too hard to find them. She could see Genie's platinum blond hair from here but she wasn't going to make a production of a goodbye.

Eventually, they reached his apartment and he was kissing her as soon as they were through the door. He pushed her into the bedroom, dropping kisses all over; each time, she maneuvered to protect her neck. Everything was blurry and she considered telling him that, but she thought the blurriness could potentially help prevent her from seizing up out of instinct. They continued along, yanking clothes off each other until there was nothing left, and suddenly he was everywhere, and it was as painful as it ever was. She needed more warning, more headspace, and more connection, but he was already going and she squeezed her eyes shut. When he was done, he flopped onto his back, offering her a small, tired smile, before asking if he could do something for her. She quickly shook her head. He didn't push. They let the silence linger as he curled up around her.

A couple of minutes later, he asked, "Do you ever feel awfully alone?"

"Hm?" Ryley made the non-committal sound in the hopes of escape; she didn't want them to engage in a joint existential evaluation of themselves, knowing she did that enough by herself, having already penciled some time in for one to occur the day after.

"Like do you feel a loneliness that you don't think anybody will be able to cure you of?" He too must still be feeling their lack of connection. It made sense he'd think to debate and intellectualize the emotion.

The rephrased question wasn't a hard one though, so she answered easily. "I feel alone a bunch, yeah. And I guess it sometimes is a type of aloneness I think will be with me my whole life." She hesitated and then added, "I don't think it has to be a bad thing, though."

She peered over her shoulder to look at him. He looked let down.

"How could that not be a bad thing? Maybe you just haven't met the right person, so you don't know any better."

Ryley wasn't sure what David wanted from her—if he wanted her to reassure him that eventually they would feel that connection or if he was asking her to have the courage to call their relationship off. She couldn't bring herself to pursue either course of action; however, she found herself desperate to lift the weight that had fallen over them and didn't want to feel the burden of his sadness in addition to her own.

"I think even with the most perfect person, I'd inevitably feel alone sometimes. And I don't think that has to be a terrible thing. I like thinking of my mind as a hidden-away best friend." She'd stumbled across the idea, beautifully phrased, in the autobiographical account of a manic-depressive (her idea of beach reading) and still thought about it even months after finishing the book. Even if Ryley couldn't offer him genuine reassurance about their relationship, maybe she could show him that aloneness wasn't that bad.

David shook his head at her words. "Ryley, I think you're deluding yourself into thinking that you like being alone. It's sad you have to think of yourself as your own best friend."

She supposed he could be right, but she was too tired to continue this strain of conversation, so she let her eyes close softly instead. She did know she felt much emptier with him cuddled around her than she had ever felt by herself.

PART IV

APRIL

———

CHAPTER 19

APRIL 2009

———

Ryley sat in the car with her headphones blasting Adele at full volume. Not that Harrison had looked over at her even once in the last ten minutes. He thought her, depending on his mood that day, ungrateful or insane. At least, that's what she could gather from his not-at-all subtle mutters during the rare moments when they occupied the same air space and she didn't have her headphones in.

She had yelled at Harrison the morning after The Night with Josh, and when he had muttered about being too hungover to be shouted at, she had yelled at how he shouldn't have drunk so much then.

Their mom had come in to see what all the ruckus was about and had immediately put two and two together, seeing Harrison clutching his head as he lay in bed, having only just slunk back into the house at ten that morning.

Harrison accused Ryley of sabotaging him. She'd not bothered to respond and had instead stormed off, leaving him to his demise; however, she had fully expected their morning ride to school the next day to consist of him apologizing profusely. Instead, when Ryley had gotten into the car the next morning, Harrison had launched immediately into a lecture, accusing her of ruining his senior year. Supposedly, their mom was requiring him to be the designated driver for all parties going forward and had forbidden him from sleeping over at anyone else's house for the rest of the year.

She'd not bothered to defend herself and had tuned him out instead, making no effort to engage with him. In fact, she'd interacted with everyone in the same semi-aloof manner over the last couple of months, still ashamed of what she'd done. She felt violated and not like she was ahead of the curve. Josh had been out of it enough—she'd decided to give him the benefit of the doubt here—that he hadn't noticed she hadn't gotten the same satisfaction as he had; after he'd finished, he'd immediately closed his eyes and had thrown an arm around her. Ryley had not wanted to cuddle, so she had quickly ran upstairs.

In a turn of events that she still can't believe she had the audacity to be surprised by, her mom had popped in not five minutes after she'd climbed into bed. Ryley had then immediately started to cry, possibly out of shock and possibly because she was overwhelmed. Likely because Ryley had only ever cried a handful of times in her life, her mom had decided to save the lecturing for another time and had been her cuddle buddy for the night instead. Though they hadn't actually cuddled, seeing as Ryley had twisted away from her mom's grasp and kept firmly to her side of the bed instead, feeling ashamed.

Her mother had tried to talk about what had happened the next day, but Ryley had changed the subject, and surprisingly, her mom had not pushed. March had passed in a blur with Ryley withdrawing from everyone, but she had started to hope she could just pretend like it never happened in April. Even when her mom had slightly prodded at Ryley, she had uncharacteristically kept to herself. A part of her was convinced her mother knew what had occurred but was letting Ryley come to her in her own time. She doubted Harrison knew anything though; Josh had snuck out of the house early in the morning after folding all the sheets and leaving a note on the bed thanking her for "her hospitality."

As they pulled into the parking lot now, on what was a suitably glum morning, Harrison started up again, insisting on some type of interaction.

"I still can't believe you. I was just trying to look out for you, and god, you're so ungrateful. Stop giving me the silent treatment."

"Excuse me?" Ryley packed as much indignation as she could into the two words, leaving a healthy pause between the *excuse* and the *me*. For whatever reason, she finally felt like engaging. "How is it ungrateful if I'm upset my brother bribed someone to hang out with me to make me 'more normal?'" She shoved the air quotes she was making in front of his face.

"You have nothing to be upset about! Instead of keeping your head down and being happy with the fact that you're smart and get good grades, you tried to get in with white kids who don't get you. So, I try to help you out by having someone who I know likes you look out for you, and you have the nerve to come after me."

"It's because you made a charity case out of me! You pushed me to do something I didn't want to." Her voice cracked, forcing her to look down at her lap out of embarrassment.

"Ryley, you set yourself up as a charity case! You were trying to bat way out of your league, and I was just trying to give you a goddamn helmet so you wouldn't fall flat on your face." Softening his tone as he parked the car, he asked, "And what did I push you to do?"

"Nothing, never mind." She was mortified to hear the audible tremble in her voice.

Hesitantly, Harrison asked, "Did something happen with Josh? I know he slept over. I thought he just got too drunk to drive home."

"Nope, nothing happened." Harrison would be horrified.

"Okay. Look, Ryley, you just have to stay in your lane for now and stop trying to take up space that isn't yours. I'm not trying to be mean. I don't know how to get it into your head that it's not your time now, but it will be. We're not the sort of people they cast in the teenage underdog movies; we're the dorky side characters."

"Neha is cool." She'd be much better off if she learned how to keep her mouth shut.

"Neha is basically white. She says our last name wrong, like they do. Also, guys are always talking about how eager she is to go down on them. So, unless you see yourself doing all that, be patient." He said Neha's name dismissively, as if Ryley could never be in league with a girl like that.

Before Ryley knew what she was doing, she said, "Well, maybe me and Neha aren't so different after all."

She sprinted away from the car after that, not pausing to give him any time to respond. As she scooted down the familiar path, scurrying past the trees and the high school science building, she kept her head tucked down. The sun was shining too brightly and the birds chirping too happily. Trotting as she was, needing to keep moving, she reached the quad with its comfortingly boring beige cafeteria tables in no time.

Feeling someone's eyes on her, she looked up slightly and to the right, making sudden, jarring eye contact with Kyle, who was sitting on Josh's lap, surrounded by some of her theater friends. Ryley looked away immediately. Josh would be late for class, not that he much cared at this point. Ryley didn't know if he was capable of any rational thought beyond Kyle; they'd started dating two weeks ago.

Ryley bounded up the winding staircase leading to her history class, lightly touching her hand along the tall concrete wall to keep balance. Although normally she was no longer as winded when she reached the top, today, her heart was pounding as much as it had at even her worst physical fitness. She hadn't liked how Kyle had looked at her. That being said, she doubted Josh had told anyone about their night. Indeed, he'd probably blacked it out of his mind, so he could believe his love for Kyle had never wavered.

Although she had pulled away from Josh at first, she and Josh had gradually returned to semi-normal. They kept their topics deliberately superficial though, talking about dumb things like the weather and their homework. Josh hadn't invited her to any more parties, or asked to study with her, and she didn't know if it was because Josh felt awkward about the sex, if it was because Josh was trying to respect her space, or because Harrison had already recommended him for the solo. It was all a great big mess.

Ryley didn't look up when she heard the classroom door open or turn to face him when she felt Josh slip into the seat next to her though she could feel him gazing at the side of her face. Instead, she stared at her notes and Mr. Weber with a focus she'd only developed in the last month; at least Mr. Weber appreciated it, thought she was finally coming into her own, if the large smiles he shot her were any indication. The class passed in its usual fashion, i.e., so slowly she thought the clock might be broken, until Mr. Weber began his wrap-up and she wondered where the time had gone.

As people started to file out of the classroom, Josh fidgeted more than usual. She automatically tensed up, already dreading whatever words were going to come out of his mouth. She fished around her pocket for her black iPod, hoping to plug the headphones into her ears before he mustered up the courage to spit out whatever it was he wanted to say.

Upon seeing her successfully procure her iPod, he abruptly asked, "Do you want to get lunch with me and Kyle?" He didn't even try to warm her up first.

Ryley let herself scoff. "Why?"

"What do you mean, why? I told you before that I consider you a friend."

"Yes, but why today? Why not yesterday? Or the day before? Or the day before that?" She would have continued listing alternative days he could have invited her, but he looked ready to snap.

"Okay, geez, Ryley, you don't have to come. Stop with the Spanish Inquisition."

Ryley heaved an exaggerated sigh of irritation but decided she should just get whatever this was over with. "Okay, Josh, thank you for the invite. I'd love to come." She made sure to exaggerate the politeness of her tone, letting the fake enthusiasm lift her voice to a higher pitch.

"Awesome." Shooting her a pleased smile, he said, "Kyle saw you galloping up the stairs and mentioned it would be cool if we all got lunch together."

Before she could say anything in response, Mr. Weber interrupted, calling her over.

She nodded bye to Josh and then walked over to Mr. Weber, coming to a halt in front of him. "Yes?"

Mr. Weber took his time responding, filing his lecture notes into his folder. "Would you be interested in doing some research for me?"

"Oh. Thanks, that sounds cool." Taking a deep breath in, she made sure to sound more transparently, apparently grateful. "Seriously, thank you. What would I be researching?" She already knew she'd have to say yes; she couldn't possibly justify turning down an opportunity like this that would make her college application even more competitive.

"World War One. I'm writing a book and could use your help over the summer."

"Got it, very cool. I'd love to help you out! Thanks again." Ryley had already lined up a summer job identifying chromosomes in a UCLA lab—she had no idea what she'd actually be doing—but simultaneously being a research assistant for a history professor would be good. The research position would show colleges that even a quite young Ryley was drawn to academia and sophisticated logical theories of cause and effect. She could cater her resume to be a good candidate for pre-med or pre-law. Her parents would be thrilled. They never much pressured her, but their large smiles when she brought back straight-A report cards and extended herself across extracurriculars was proof enough. She wanted to show them she'd got their work ethic to succeed even if she didn't feel like any sort of success now. She knew adult life would be different though; everything would make sense in ten years.

Mr. Weber gave her a happy smile upon hearing her response. "Wonderful. Too few people give history its due. Studying the past gives us a unique window into the problems of the present."

CHAPTER 20

APRIL 2019

———

"So, Ryley. Fuck, marry, kill: Chris Pine, Chris Evans, Chris Hemsworth."

Ryley cracked one eye open. She was lying outside on some grass and nursing a buzz that had blanked out her mind and made her pleasantly blissed out as she soaked in the sun.

Ryley turned slightly to face Cassidy. "Hm. Marry Chris Pine, fuck Chris Evans, and kill Chris Hemsworth." She got the expected gasps of outrage because god forbid she kill Thor, but she comforted herself with the thought that at least she could be a maverick in small ways if not the big ones.

Olivia, sitting beside her, kicked her lightly in the shin before letting her foot rest against Ryley's leg once more. Ryley didn't mind the contact, liked it even, and let her foot stay there.

Ryley had woken up to texts from Olivia, Harrison, Mark, and Cassidy asking where she'd gone after she left Winter Formal without telling anyone. She'd sent them all quick copy-paste apology texts in response, saying she'd just left with David in a spur-of-the-moment decision. With the exception of Olivia, everyone had responded—Mark with especially crude emojis.

Ryley had spent an embarrassingly long amount of time deciding if she should send a follow-up text to Olivia before defaulting to doing nothing. Accordingly, when Olivia had happened to swing by Ryley's usual study spot on the Saturday following Formal, Ryley had immediately handed Olivia one of her Beats as a tentative peace offering, explaining that she'd "stumbled" upon an angsty queer pop ballad that had in reality taken her a couple of hours that morning to find. Olivia had accepted her olive branch with a gratified smile, and they'd spent almost every Saturday since doing their readings together.

This Saturday though, they were gathered on a stretch of grass near the river. Ryley, Cassidy, Mark, David, Zeke, and Sophie had made the original plan to go down to the river on what was a bizarrely nice day, soaking in the early-April sun before they'd once again hit the books for finals crunch time. Ryley had automatically extended the invite to Olivia, used to spending time with her on the weekends, and Genie and Harrison rounded out their small river crew of the day. Genie had been back in town visiting Harrison, had seen Ryley's Instagram Story, and promptly made Harrison ditch their more cultured plans to see the Isabella Stewart Gardner Museum; the two had shown up half an hour later. Genie had been a caricature of herself, wearing something that could have come out of a *Free People* catalog, with her hair tied up in a bandana and a flowing white shirt tucked into daisy duke shorts. The rest of them had been dressed rather boringly; even Olivia was just wearing a gray sweater over black jeans.

Olivia offered up a prompt for the next round. "Okay, let's do Jennifer Lopez, Olivia Wilde, and Janelle Monaé."

David answered first. Ryley considered calling him out on the rapidity with which he said he'd marry Olivia Wilde, but their relationship had only gotten more strained since Formal. She would not have been able to deliver the joke with an appropriate amount of light-heartedness.

Cassidy echoed, "Yeah, easily marry Olivia."

Olivia answered, "Oh, I'm flattered," shooting Cassidy a wink. Cassidy gave her an indulgent, slightly forced smile. Ryley always backpedaled when Cassidy looked at her like that, but Olivia just shrugged in response and leaned back onto her elbows, turning her face up to the sun.

Genie and Sophie echoed Cassidy in choosing Olivia Wilde and Ryley tried not to read into all of them choosing the only white person. It was an unfair judgment; they all just likely admired Olivia Wilde's cheekbones. Ryley certainly did.

Nonetheless, Ryley found herself chiming in out of turn. "Janelle Monáe."

Mark said, "Oh, look who's eager," giving Ryley a wide grin. He continued, "Her *Dirty Computer* album is wonderful."

Olivia responded, "Oh, yeah, I listen to it all the time. It's good that women are speaking up more and normalizing being attracted to other girls."

Ryley hoped this little speech wasn't for her benefit. Cassidy fidgeted slightly but said nothing. David, Zeke, and Sophie were checked out. Genie was on her phone, though Harrison, ever agreeable, nodded along.

"Yeah, though queer women staying alive on TV is still pretty bad. At least we have *Will & Grace*, *Queer Eye*, and so on," Mark said, loosely grabbing onto one of Olivia's hands.

"I mean I will say it's gotten slightly better for women recently. The coming-out scene in *Supergirl* was unexpected." Olivia was too careful to not look over at Ryley as she spoke. "I think it should have gotten more publicity than it did. It could help a lot of people who are confused."

As the two continued their back-and-forth, Ryley found herself focusing on David, Cassidy, and Genie, all staying silent and all very clearly bored and disengaged. Ryley felt pressured to change the topic for their sake and bring them back in. Besides, Olivia had gone on long enough.

So, in the next natural pause, Ryley not-so-naturally said, "Great. Also, I just remembered that the application to be a BSA is due. Are any of you applying?" The Board of Student Advisors (BSA) was one of the three prestigious organizations at the law school; the Law Review and the Legal Aid Bureau were the other two. She knew Cassidy would immediately chime in, and although Olivia shot Ryley a slightly startled glance at the rather abrupt topic change, she kept her peace.

Cassidy gave Ryley a huge smile before proudly proclaiming, "I'm one hundred percent going to apply for Law Review and BSA."

"No Legal Aid for you?" Olivia asked, slightly smirking. The Legal Aid Bureau was the only one of the three organizations with a non-profit bent.

"No. And remind me, which of the three are you part of?" Cassidy snarked.

Olivia laughed. "Okay, no need to get all riled up. I was just asking."

David interrupted before they could continue their bickering, speaking with a slightly self-satisfied air. "I'm going to apply to all three." He'd never voiced any interest in non-profit work, but the prestige of the organization was most definitely the only incentive he needed. Eventually, after all the other One-Ls had shared which organizations they were applying to, it was Ryley's turn.

Ryley's answer was anticlimactic. "I don't know if I'm going to apply to any of them. Maybe the Board of Student

Advisors. I'm not sure though."

"Why not?" Olivia asked, turning to look at her so that if Ryley turned her head too, their noses would only be inches apart. Ryley knew this play. Olivia had decided there were fewer things more enjoyable than messing with Cassidy and had caught on to how Cassidy would pin-ball her eyes between Ryley and Olivia whenever they got too close. Olivia only ever got like this in front of Cassidy, thought it was great fun if her smirk was any indication.

"I just don't know if I'm interested in legal writing. I like corporate stuff better. I don't know," Ryley answered, keeping her head straight though she tilted in Olivia's general direction so it didn't look like she was stiffing her. Ryley would prefer it if Olivia didn't play with Cassidy like that. She was still trying to figure out how to salvage her relationship with David, get her grades up, and maintain her friendships, all while maintaining an aura of composure; she didn't need Olivia messing up group dynamics.

In response to her answer, the rest of the circle nodded in a generic way. The way everyone bobbled their heads without making eye contact showed just how much they got it.

Harrison finally interrupted his bobbling to say, "Could be worth it to apply anyway; this sort of opportunity only comes along once in a lifetime, and you could always say no."

Ryley shrugged, hoping to avoid a strain of conversation that could only be stressful. She took a couple of rapid sips of her beer.

Cassidy spoke into the silence. "Look, let's move on. I'm sure there are certain reasons why she doesn't want to apply. No need to make a big deal." Cassidy shot her a supportive, all-too-knowing smile as she said this and Ryley felt herself freeze up.

Ryley had talked with David about her grades on their last date, feeling like the distance between them was becoming insurmountable; quite frankly, she had thought it worth it to try to manufacture closeness through vulnerability. David had been shocked but had assured her it was just a stumble and she would get all honors this semester. The way in which Cassidy was looking at her now convinced Ryley that David had unfortunately told her about Ryley's grades, but Cassidy seemed to have Ryley's back. She'd make small jabs, little insinuations here and there, but she wouldn't out Ryley. She kept herself calm and gave Cassidy a small smile as Cassidy maintained eye contact with her.

Ryley took a couple more sips of beer, trying to think of another topic in earnest.

Genie broke the silence. "You should hear Harrison talk about Ryley though. He won't shut up about how smart she is." That was not the topic change Ryley wanted.

Olivia said, "Oh, I've heard," with a laugh.

Ryley looked down at the brown patch of grass underneath her, feeling like a fraud and hoping people would just take it as modesty. The silence lingered as none of her friends, no one in her Section, voiced their agreement. Eventually, she looked up to see Mark tentatively nodding his head. David and Cassidy's too-knowing gaze pierced her more than any words could've.

Ryley eventually asked Genie questions about the sports agency for which she worked. Ryley thankfully settled into a topic that had nothing to do with law, relationships, or anything else that would make Ryley think about herself and the ways in which she was coming up short. The others chimed in too with questions, Genie's life still removed enough from theirs to be uniquely interesting, and allowing them to take a break from thinking about themselves and from comparing themselves to one another.

Olivia seemed to finally have enough when they started talking about Genie's childhood and said, "Anyway, moving on, let's go back to Fuck Marry Kill, except with Professor Kilmer, Professor Gold, and Professor Rake."

Mark started howling with laughter and even Cassidy cracked a smile. Ryley stayed for two more rounds before saying, "Hey, I'm pretty beat. Day drinking really takes it out of me, so I'm going to head back early. Great seeing everyone though!"

Ryley gave them all a cartoonish, overdone smile and then swiveled her body in a circle, waving goodbye to everyone before finally starting to walk away. Ryley took up a brisk pace, trying to wake up her too-drowsy, sunbaked body and run away from all the *do differentlys* already floating around in her head. She should have looked at David once more before leaving; she could have asked if he wanted to walk back with her, but he had only given her a quick wave goodbye before immediately turning back to Zeke, *so* enraptured by their stimulating talk about professors. Ryley knew they needed to have another talk, but she didn't want to lose her boyfriend.

When Genie had first sat down to join them, she had squeezed Ryley's arm and said, "Harvard should put you all on the brochure; show that you come to Harvard and get it all."

Cassidy had given Genie a beaming smile and Mark had gotten up and given Genie a sloppy kiss on the cheek, exclaiming about how much he'd missed her, but David and Ryley had just looked at each other and given each other soft, tentative smiles. Both were at least somewhat aware they were perpetuating a lie, but it was a comfortable lie. She didn't think David wanted to end it either. He too had avoided talking to her about anything directly, seeing if they couldn't push through. Maybe he still held out hope that she'd open up in the way that he wanted, come through with her second-semester grades, and live up to the image he had in his mind. She, in turn, was waiting on tenterhooks for their connection to click, wanting to feel it every day, and pointing it out to herself every time he did something nice.

As Ryley turned onto JFK Street—Bostonians' patriotism was unparalleled—she felt an arm loop through hers, and a rather loud, "Hi, will you *please* slow down? You're not a horse, you know." There went her thinking time.

CHAPTER 21

APRIL 2019

"Hey, what's up?" Ryley asked, inching her arm slightly away so they were not pressed as tightly together. Ryley had not expected Harrison, especially a Harrison who was feeling very cuddly toward her.

"Nothing. I was getting tired, and Genie said she wanted to stay out a bit more. Besides, I wanted to check in on you."

"I'm good. How's it going with Genie?"

"Ryley, don't be—just talk to me. You looked, for lack of a better word, beat-up when Olivia and Genie were joking around about how smart you are. You never used to look like that in high school. Sure, you'd be tight-lipped about your grades even then, but there was always a sense of superiority about you." He paused and then said, "That air of yours used to drive me absolutely nuts, by the way. That's why I can tell it's gone."

Ryley weighed the pros and cons of confiding in him; her earlier efforts with David hadn't exactly panned out. Finally, she said, "I thought I'd do better."

"Have you talked about it with anyone? Met a professor? I'm sure it's something that can be fixed."

Ryley wished she could shove him away; of course, he jumped right into big-brother problem-solving mode. Olivia would have just listened—or switched the topic to focus on Ryley's sexuality in a not-at-all subtle way.

Ryley responded, "Yes, I've met with a professor and I'm studying more now. I've also started to look at more sample exam answers online to try to figure out what they're looking for."

"Got it. Have you talked with any of your friends about this? I'm sure at least some of them didn't do as well as they would've liked."

"Cassidy and David know." Ryley veered slightly to the right, creating a bit of distance between the two of them, trailing her fingers along the black cast-iron gate that formed the perimeter to Harvard's undergraduate campus. Only ten minutes until she was home and could tuck herself into bed.

"Oh. What did they say?" Harrison didn't try to shift closer, instead keeping to his side of the curb.

"Well, David said he was sure I'd get all Hs this semester. And I didn't actually speak to Cassidy about my grades. I know David told her based on how she was looking at me though."

Harrison said nothing for a couple of steps. "Are you going to ask him if he told her?"

"I don't know." Ryley sighed. It was one more thing to add to the list, and in a twisted way, it gave her leverage. David had done something wrong and he'd be making up for it without either of them having to say a thing.

"Why on earth wouldn't you bring it up? That's a violation of your trust."

"Yeah, I know. There's a lot we need to talk about. We just need to get through this rough patch."

"It's a rough meadow, not a rough patch." That jab coming from Harrison was startling. He'd only ever seen them interact two times.

"What? Has Olivia been talking to you?"

"No. I just thought you didn't look all that comfortable around him at Winter Formal or by the river today, and when I talked about it with Genie, she agreed."

"Oh, because if Genie, who has only ever met me twice in her life, says so, it's true. Harrison, every relationship is different. We're comfortable not having to perform and show everyone how in love we are." *The way you do* went unsaid.

"Okay, that was uncalled for. All I've ever done is try to look out for you and every time I somehow end up the bad guy." He was whisper-shouting. Both had given up the pretense of walking and were currently facing off in a truck-staging area. Ryley wouldn't mind if a truck happened to pull in while they were arguing and ran Harrison over.

"Because you *are* the bad guy! You're always trying to shape me and fix me! You did it in high school and you're doing it now. Can you ever turn it off?" Ryley would let him get one more response in and would then sprint away.

"I was never trying to fix you. Ryley, I told you repeatedly how much I loved you and how wonderful I thought you were. You were so set on fitting to a certain type of image though that I just tried to help you. And I'm sorry you thought I was pushing you to be something other than what you were."

He paused to see if she had anything to say. She didn't, shifting her weight onto her back foot as she prepared to pivot. Of course it was still her fault.

He grabbed onto her arm loosely, predicting her normal flee pattern and stopping her before she could do anything. "Ryley, honestly, I'm sorry. I was horrified; I couldn't deal and

I still can't deal with the idea that I might at all have been involved in making you feel like you had to do that with Josh, so I let the distance build between us. I never spoke to Josh again after you told me what happened, by the way. I told the jazz director not to give him the solo."

Ryley hadn't known that, but she didn't want the easy reconciliation right now. She wanted to blame Harrison; she'd gotten by on blaming Harrison for betraying her and pushing her to fit in and she needed that. If he started taking some of the blame, she would have to acknowledge how much of it was her own fault, and she wasn't ready for that.

"Thanks for telling me that. I need a bit of time," she mumbled and began to walk away.

He called out, "Ryley, you don't have to keep performing for them, for an audience you can no longer even see. You can be yourself."

But it wasn't an invisible audience—she could see them. Kyle had been reincarnated as Cassidy, Josh as David, and her other high school brethren found in the faces of her Section. Ryley was on the inside this time, and she wasn't going to give up her place, no matter how fake she felt.

* * *

Ryley sat on her couch in her usual post-drinking mental loop, unable to escape her compulsive pattern of dissecting and replaying every interaction one by one; looking for a distraction, she decided to pull up the *Supergirl* clip Olivia had mentioned. Ryley didn't think it would have too large an impact. She had watched queer TV before, seen the traumatic coming-out scene in a repressive home environment, and had felt fortunate. Her family was liberal, she grew up in California, and being homophobic was a huge faux pas in any social circle she frequented, so if she'd had any queer tendencies, she was sure they would have blossomed by now. There must have been some significance to the clip though, likely to Ryley; Olivia was never anything but intentional with her words.

Ryley played it, curled up comfortably underneath her plush, dusky blue, elephant-patterned blanket. However, as the dialogue on-screen continued, she started to straighten, her shoulders locking up, even as her heart began to pound. The girl wasn't her and hadn't had her bad luck with dating guys that ended up only being good on paper.

But.

The emphasis on just wanting to be perfect and not liking dating nor intimacy with men made her dizzy and feel like she was on the verge of passing out. There were still questions and still some attraction to certain men, but seeing a woman in her thirties say lines she'd thought verbatim confused her. The words rang too true for her lived experience thus far— for her experience with David, with Josh, and with the three other men she'd been intimate with in the intervening years.

Just like Alex Danvers in *Supergirl*, she'd never thought of girls as an option. Indeed, she'd only ever shied away from an errant hand resting on her thigh, thinking her consistent desire to be around certain girls like Olivia was nothing more than wanting the ultimate Timon to her Pumbaa. Olivia must have done it on purpose to push her over the edge, sensing that Ryley was frail and vulnerable, and trying to force Ryley to see that everything about her was tainted with pretend in a manner even more far-reaching than she'd thought previously. She was furious.

Ryley could no longer breathe; her chest was too tight. She put on Jeff Buckley to try to calm herself, but as he reached his crescendo chorus of "Hallelujahs," her heartbeat ratcheted up in tandem. She tried to force more air into her lungs, taking deep inhales through her nose as she stumbled her way up and walked unsteadily over to the kitchen, drowning a paper towel under the faucet and slapping the wet cloth onto her arms.

She settled back into her couch again only to be overcome by a wave of disorientation with the walls feeling too far and all too close at once. She felt as if she would topple sideways onto the couch at any moment and experienced a turn of nausea within her stomach as her eyes couldn't focus on anything. Her body seemed to be trying to will itself to unconsciousness, and her mind struggled against the slippery pressure of the black encroaching on her vision even as she fought against succumbing to the feeling. And yet her thoughts fragmented even as she tried to form complete sentences in her head, tracking through the lyrics of an old Hindi mantra to ground herself. Her mom used to sing it to her every night when she was young and she thought she'd forgotten the words, but she whispered the chant to herself now, mumbling the starting line of *Jai Shri Krishna Jai Shreeman Narayan*.

As she repeated the words again and again, she felt pressure pushing down against her eyes and her forehead, causing her to feel ever dizzier; she could not bring herself to focus on anything, and when she did, her eyes seemed to delude her. Why was she seeing black cracks on the previously pristine white cabinets? What was most frightening was not knowing if what she was undergoing was a panic attack or if her health had finally given out on her. With that thought in mind, that she could be dying, she reached out a shaky hand for her phone, fumbling the lock screen open to call the only person that made sense.

CHAPTER 22

APRIL 2009

———

Ryley drifted through American Literature, Calculus, and Spanish, readying herself for lunch with Kyle and Josh. She and Kyle hadn't spoken much since the party though they'd celebrated a recent string of wins together. Although Ryley was most certainly not the next Babe Ruth, she wasn't half bad. She'd caught a couple of important fly balls and prompted a raucous *yes, Ryley!* to echo through the stands on a key bunt. But perhaps their loyal fanbase of ten was only so thrilled when she did come through because there really were more than enough times she didn't. She'd given Carly an inadvertent black eye last game by throwing the ball at her during warm-ups when she thought Carly had been ready for it. Carly had not been. Ryley had been so mortified that Carly had started laughing after she finished cursing Ryley out.

Ryley had her softball gear with her now as she slid her tray onto the table, settling in across from Josh and next to Kyle. They would be leaving for a game as soon as their lunch period was over.

"Ryley!" Kyle shot her a beaming smile; she was positively glowing with health. Kyle's skin had a nice bronze sheen to it and her dark blond hair was full of highlights. Ryley would appreciate it if she could keep her general sense of well-being to herself. At least Josh's skin was still a ghostly pale color.

Ryley gave her a smile of hello but busied herself arranging her food on the tray, waiting to see what Kyle wanted before she risked running her mouth.

"So, excited for summer? What are you doing?" Kyle asked.

"I guess I'm excited. I can't believe it's almost the end of the year. I'm going to work at a lab during the day and then I decided to join a swim club for fun."

"Oh, that's great! It'll keep you in shape for softball next year!"

Ryley didn't know if she planned on rejoining the team. She'd not quite gotten the family she'd been promised. She was not one to make hasty decisions, though, so she kept her thoughts of quitting to herself and simply said, "Yeah, I guess it'll be good." With her thick black hair, the amount of upkeep swimming would require was mind-numbing. Ryley also intensely disliked individual competition sports, mainly because she was bad at them. Her mom had, however, "lovingly" badgered her into signing up, citing endorphins and Ryley's unrelenting moodiness.

"What about you both?" Ryley asked.

"Oh, I'm helping out at a softball camp," Kyle said. That sounded much more normal and fun than Ryley's summer.

"I'm working at my dad's company. I want to get some business experience on my resume," Josh added.

Ryley nodded, even as Kyle elbowed Josh in the side and said, "How very prep school of you."

Josh gave a half-hearted chuckle and then pushed the spotlight back onto Ryley. "Why did Mr. Weber hold you back?"

"Nothing important." Ryley knew how competitive everyone was, no matter that Kyle acted light-hearted right now; she wouldn't be surprised if the softball camp was for recovering drug addicts.

"Look at Ryley playing coy! Who would've thought you had it in you." Although Kyle's tone was light and airy, her lips were pulled into a smile that effectively bared her teeth.

Ryley moved the topic right along. "So, any fun plans for the weekend?"

"Taylor's throwing another party, so we're probably going to go to that." Kyle looped an arm around Josh as she spoke; Josh beamed. Ryley tugged her sweater to be wrapped more snugly around her body. Kyle continued, "Anyway, Ryley, I'm sad I haven't seen you around more. Josh said the two of you were friends, so I wanted us to get lunch together instead of always making him hang with my friends."

"Got it."

"Actually, I also wanted to ask you something. I saw you talking with Ankur yesterday. You two would make a cute couple." Kyle smiled winningly.

Ryley gave her a strained smile in return. "No, we're just friends." Even that was a stretch; he was just a friend of her brother's that she had spoken to in passing, but she wouldn't parse words. The distinction would be lost on her audience.

Josh chimed in. "I think you both truly have a connection though."

Ryley felt a wave of bone-deep tiredness wash over her. Josh, she, and Ankur had never been in the same room together. She already knew Josh would come to class tomorrow, explaining that he'd been lost in trying to impress Kyle. He loved painting himself as the underdog, the nerdy boy in the high school movies, with Kyle the ultimate prize, the popular cheerleading girl that justified why he could make a fool of himself and by extension, Ryley. Ryley, however, didn't care about his Hollywood ending and was tired of having no role in the narrative her fellow students were spinning. Ryley would give Josh the cordial shoulder starting tomorrow but held her peace for now.

Re-routing the topic of conversation to the party, Ryley said, "The party sounds fun."

"Yeah, we'll see. What, are you interested?" Kyle asked Ryley in a casual, breezy tone though Kyle's careful, unsmiling eyes clearly provided Ryley with direction otherwise.

Ryley sat back, unperturbed. When Ryley had asked Carly why she'd skipped Taylor's party in February, Carly had shrugged and said she was over it with such casual disdain that Ryley's eyes had lit up. She'd liked the idea that Taylor's parties could be passé.

"Nope, I'm good." She'd liked that Kyle, so confident and popular, would talk with her, but she realized then how much Kyle fundamentally viewed her as the other, as someone to whom she could dictate rules, dismiss, and look through. Ryley listened with half an ear as Kyle began once more to discuss the play production they were putting on next week.

And then Ryley got up. She shot them both a fake smile, said, "I forgot I have to do something," and left. Both looked momentarily startled, but then Kyle just waved her off and Josh went back to pushing things around his plate.

Ryley would bide her time. She'd observe and wait. She'd go along with things and stop trying to force them to see her when they couldn't; they were too focused on themselves. She'd wait until the time was right, until she'd learned their language so thoroughly—how to embody confidence, how to project belonging, how to hold her ground—they'd see her and see *one of us.*

She was to blame too, she knew that. She hadn't ever made a genuine effort to assimilate for all her pretense otherwise. Her mom had let her get away with it, thinking she could protect Ryley with the right clothes, by showing her how to minimize her Indianness, but all that had done was allow Ryley to zero herself out without building a new white-oriented experience over it. She'd not internalized the culture promoted in TV shows or movies, not consumed the right entertainment news, and not followed the latest beauty trends, jealous at being excluded and not wanting to partake in the visual erasure of herself.

She'd do it all, but for now, she'd focus only on moving from periphery friend to core friend in her old extended friend group, who'd excluded her because they must have sensed in part that she was in a no-man's land. She'd been unwilling to accept the protection of being slotted simply as a nerd, which she could've done (probably should've done), had it not been for her desire to show she had choices and her place in the social ladder was not predestined; had it not been for seeing her mother so effortlessly mingle with other prep school moms and feel sad that she'd been too slow to learn. For all the proclamations celebrating difference, everyone wanted the same, and others, minorities and white people alike, had been much faster at delivering.

Ryley spent the rest of the day thinking and thinking—so not all that unusual of a day—and when Carly finally dropped her home after the softball game, she slowly and dramatically dropped herself onto the chair across the table from her mom. "I'm done. I'll actually do it this time, keep my head down, and really just learn and observe. I finally see I can't be both me and be white, so I'm going to be white instead."

Her mom stayed silent, sighed, and then asked, "What happened?"

"Nothing. I finally realized how much of a no-man's land I was in, where I didn't stick out but didn't fit in. Instead of living two lives, I lived one. Unsuccessfully."

Her mom had tried so hard. She'd taught Ryley how to pretend to drink at parties, had dressed her according to rules linked up with seemingly arbitrary fashion trends, and had made pasta or a sandwich in the mornings instead of just letting her pack leftover Indian food from dinner.

Ryley looked down at her hands, back up at her mom, and said, "Want to go shopping this weekend?"

"Ryley, there is room for you to be you and to be white. Keep who you are strong inside, keep your strength and your heritage strong inside. Just present the white outside until you learn their language well enough that you don't need it anymore."

"Okay, well, right now there isn't room for both. Want to go shopping this weekend?" Ryley kept her gaze focused on her hands, the color the same rich brown of the oak wood table. She liked the color on the table.

"Sure," her mom eventually said.

Ryley walked out with one thought floating around in her head. *If you can't beat them, join them.*

CHAPTER 23

APRIL 2019

———

"Hello?"

Ryley breathed in, breathed out, and breathed in again. She pressed the phone closer to her ear, as if to mimic the feeling of her mom wrapping her arms around her when Ryley would bury her head in her mom's stomach.

"Ryley?"

She let another breath out, took another one in, and forced herself to speak. "Hi, sorry. I couldn't catch my breath."

Ryley heard her mom settle back into the couch and a part of her felt enormously guilty. They always fell back so quickly and smoothly into the pattern they had perfected years ago. She was constantly the little bird with the broken wing that her mom would nurse back to health only for the dumb little bird to hop out of the nest and try to fly again before it was ready.

"You're okay," her mom crooned. She kept repeating it until Ryley did finally start to calm. "Okay, walk me through it."

Ryley couldn't bring herself to talk about what had immediately precipitated the panic attack, so she decided to go to the very beginning. "I don't know. I think everything just got to be too much. I feel like I've been on the verge of a panic attack for the last three months and it finally happened. Getting those grades wrecked me. You know that academics is the one thing I always had, where I could be myself, even if I was just fitting in everywhere else. And honestly, I'm so tired of pretending and doing everything I can to belong when it all feels fake. I'm faking with my grades, my relationship, my friendships." Ryley was slightly breathless by the time she finished.

"Okay, then maybe you should take a step back. Figure out what you actually like and what *you* want so things can feel real." Her mom's tone was appeasing; pacifying.

Ryley fell back against the couch, shocked into silence, and then she felt her head begin to pound with rage, taken aback as she was by her mother's audacity. She tried once again to breathe in and breathe out but could not calm herself this time.

"You're the one who taught me how to live for others! To always be so focused on blending, on belonging. You wanted me to perfect that double life, keep the Indianness inside, keep everything 'other' about me inside. And I couldn't do it so I gave up the 'other,' I gave up *me*. And now you're going to tell me I should think about what I actually want?" She was talking loudly, any ability to control her volume thrown out the window. "How dare you?" Her fist was clenched, her jaw was clenched, her entire being drawn taut as a violin string.

"That's not fair." Her mom was talking loudly too now; Ryley could hear her get up and begin to pace. "Yes, I did want you to learn white people ways and white people talk, but I never wanted you to internalize it. I just wanted you to feel assimilated, feel like you belonged, because you felt so alone. I never wanted you to lose sight of who you were inside! You know how much I love you. How could I ever want you to be ashamed of who you fundamentally are?"

"Well, great intentions but awful execution. I should go." She knew she was being unfair now and had been unfair to Harrison as well by pushing blame onto everyone but herself.

"Ryley, stop. Talk to me. Don't run away. Just talk."

"Look, I don't even know. I don't know who I am anymore, and I don't think I like what I'm left with if I'm not pretending. When I was down by the river, and Genie had looked at me, saw me with a boyfriend, surrounded by white friends, and at Harvard Law, she said I had it all. I liked how I felt when she said that." Ryley looked down at the paper towel still clenched in her hands and at the water she'd spilled all over the wooden coffee table when she'd yanked herself up to run over to the refrigerator. "I'm scared of letting that go. I'm scared of being nothing when at least after years of work, I hypothetically belong."

"Ryley, you'll still belong without that. You know what Genie was reacting to? She was reacting to your belief that you are somebody. Harvard, David, your friends—it all helped you to finally see that, but it was about you, Ryley, interacting with the presumption that you belong in a way you didn't before. You, Ryley, are just enough as you are." Her mom took a deep breath and continued. "I'm sorry if I ever made you feel like you weren't good enough, but I don't regret teaching you how to assimilate. Now you've lived the mirage and you've realized you don't like it. You can give up the pretense without always wondering what it's like on the inside."

Ryley got up and went to her room to pick up her stuffed turtle; he'd always been there for her unquestionably. She needed his support now.

Squeezing him, she said, "Stop making it seem like I have a choice. I didn't get the grades, my relationship sucks, and who knows what will happen to my friendships if I just be me. I failed out of the 'mirage' as you put it. Stop making it sound so romantic."

"Fine, you failed out. But it wasn't like you were happy when things were supposedly going your way and you were so focused on belonging and doing everything right."

Ryley opened her mouth to interject, but her mother was not done.

"You know why I never had that hard of a time? I wasn't asking anyone to let me belong. I knew my roots were in India—that India would always be my home. That made it easy for me to learn their game and learn their rules because my identity stayed strong inside. No one could ever touch me at my core. No one could take my sense that I was somebody away from me."

"Good for you." Ryley's voice was decidedly sullen. Her stuffed turtle looked up at her in disappointment.

"Ryley, all I'm trying to say is that once you know who *you* are, nothing else matters. No one can make you feel on the outside if you don't let them. We both know you'll end up doing well in law school, if not this semester, then the one after that; you care about learning too much to give up. And you already have so many people batting in your corner who would love to know the real you. So, take this year and see it for the gift it was."

Ryley needed to digest and think through everything, so that's what she said. The farewell tone in her voice was soft as she said she just needed time. Her mom let her go, only slipping in a quick *I love you* before hanging up.

Ryley didn't let herself think about her mother's words immediately. Instead, she picked up the breadcrumbs on the table and cleaned the stack of dishes in the sink. Looking around, she decided it looked presentable enough and skipped the dusting; she doubted anyone would be running their finger along her bookcase in the near future. Ryley definitely wouldn't.

She should reward her cleaning effort somehow, though. She considered texting Olivia or David, but both would be too draining for her to deal with now. Before she had to ponder the matter any further, she got a text from Mark. He was asking what she was up to and if she wanted to watch something together. She responded immediately, inviting him up. Mark must have been walking by her apartment right when he texted her because he was buzzing up only moments later.

She welcomed him in and soon they were settling onto her couch. She hadn't hooked up the TV, a relic from her old apartment, yet. She was usually fine to just use her laptop to watch whatever had temporarily caught her fancy.

"Oh, what did you think?" Mark asked, pointing to the *Supergirl* scene still open on her computer.

"Different than I expected." Ryley closed out of the window and navigated to Netflix. Mark side-eyed her very obviously but kept his mouth shut. They watched a couple of episodes of *Parks and Recreation* in silence but for the occasional chuckle and lazy back-and-forth every so often. They did this occasionally, one going to the other's apartment at the end of a long day of drinking, but it had been a while.

After they'd gotten an order of Indian food delivered— Mark had wanted something spicy and Ryley felt homesick— Mark slowly began collecting his belongings. He looked as if he were moving through molasses as he inched over to pick up his phone from where it was charging, slowly put on his sweater, and carefully slipped on his shoes.

Eventually, Ryley asked, "What?" Sloths moved faster.

"Nothing. I was thinking of study plans for tomorrow."

Ryley nodded before turning her attention back to her phone to give him time to gather himself.

Finally, he said, "I didn't do so hot first semester."

"Oh." Ryley wondered if Cassidy had told Mark about Ryley's performance or if today was just her day to have heart-to-hearts with every person imaginable.

"Yeah. I felt like shit about it and still haven't told my parents. They think of me as the next Pete Buttigieg and can't see beyond it." Mark had shown Ryley the twenty texts that had streamed in from his parents the day Pete Buttigieg had announced his candidacy. He continued, "And I don't know, I always thought you'd be someone safe to talk to, so when you said you didn't even know if you wanted to apply to Law Review today, that felt like a sign."

"Got it. I mean, I said that because I didn't like sub-citing for a journal all that much, and Law Review would be that times ten." Ryley couldn't bring herself to talk about her grades—not after how she'd felt under Cassidy's gaze earlier.

He looked down, tied a shoelace that didn't need tying, and then gave her a soft, "Got it, bye," before making his way to her front door. She felt Mark's palpable disappointment and felt disappointed in herself. She thought about her mom's words.

"Look, wait. I didn't do so hot either." Her voice slightly wavered and she looked down at her feet. When she looked up, Mark's big, blue eyes were full of such fondness and care that Ryley felt warm all over. She pushed on.

"And it really got to me, so I met with Professor Kilmer. He said I needed to find my voice and I needed to learn how to communicate and cogently advocate for something." She threw in an SAT word in case Mark thought she was dumb now. She was psychotic.

Mark responded, "Well, I'd love to study with you. If you'll have me. Or do you and David do your own thing? I've been skipping most of the study groups Cassidy sets up, so I don't know what's up there."

"Oh, we don't study together. I think we're going to break up." Ryley couldn't help the way her hands slightly, automatically clenched, as if already missing the presence of a security blanket, but otherwise, her body remained lax.

Mark lifted one shoulder up, put it down. "I mean, I can't say I'm surprised. You both barely talked today. I was going to ask about David earlier but didn't want you to feel like I was putting you on the spot."

"Yeah, I guess it's been a long time coming." Seeing Mark beaming at her now, she continued, "Why are you smiling like that?" She would've appreciated a bit of sympathy for her impending breakup.

"I'm just happy. I'm glad you're finally sharing real things with me beyond your favorite song of the day," Mark said.

Ryley felt herself reaching emotional capacity. She needed to lie down and sleep for a good twelve hours.

As he reached for the door handle, he rushed out, "I may regret asking this, but because you seem to be unusually open right now, can I ask if the *Supergirl* clip has anything to do with you wanting to break up?"

"Nope. Olivia had mentioned it and I was curious," Ryley said flatly.

"Okay, cool," Mark said, immediately crossing the threshold as if to physically show that he was not trying to step over any lines. "I figured that was the case. I'm going to leave now." Then, giving her a cheery wave goodbye, he pulled the door shut behind him.

Ryley felt incredibly drained but proud of herself. Mark had respected her boundaries and respected her. He hadn't looked at her like she was a failure or said he was sorry she was breaking up with David. He'd known not to push her about *Supergirl*. She felt free and powerful. She couldn't be relegated to the status of outsider if she didn't let someone else define the boundaries of the house.

CHAPTER 24

APRIL 2019

A couple of weeks after Ryley's come-to-Jesus—or, more accurately, come-to-Krishna—moment, Ryley and David met at one of the tables outside the library. Even though it was late April, the grass was brown and dead...like their relationship.

They chatted about nothing, even as Ryley tried to muster up the courage to open Pandora's Box.

When another lull of silence settled too heavily between them, David decided to take the reins. "This isn't working. We both know it isn't."

"Yeah, not for awhile now." Ryley tapped her foot restlessly against the side of the table.

"What went wrong? We were so good for the first few months and then I felt like we kept missing. We stopped getting each other." He ran a hand through his mop of brown hair; it was getting shaggy, falling into his eyes and exaggerating his youth. He seemed more innocent and vulnerable.

"Hm. Honestly, I don't know if we ever got each other. I think I had a large part to play in that though."

As Ryley opened her mouth to expand, David interjected, "What do you mean?" She finally let herself acknowledge how much he'd always liked to guide and control their conversations.

Ryley took a deep breath and continued, "Well, I was just about to tell you. I think I was so busy living for everyone else that I lost sight of who I was."

"I can see that."

"And how exactly can you see that?" Ryley echoed the words Olivia had said to her so long ago in response to just such a phrase.

"Well, you never opened up. I had a deeper relationship with my kindergarten girlfriend!"

Ryley didn't laugh. "Okay, David. I don't know if you ever actually tried to understand me, though. You were always trying to get me to match up to the ideal relationship you had in your head."

He sighed. "Maybe, I don't know. I guess we fundamentally weren't right for each other at the end of the day." Ryley swung one leg over the chipped green bench. David reached his hand out to rest lightly on hers, momentarily stilling her. "But wait. If you're going to say I never even tried to understand you, then who are you?"

"I'm still figuring that out day by day, but it's not who I've been. It's not being the safest and most palatable option. It's not always feeling like I should be the slightest bit more normal, more assimilated, just the slightest bit better."

Swinging her other leg over the bench, she said, "We all contain multitudes, and I'm tired of pretending that's not the case." She couldn't believe she had paraphrased Walt Whitman as her mic drop line.

In response, David simply said, "I'll see you around." He'd see her sooner than later, them being in the same friend group and all, but perhaps it was time for her to meet new people. She'd keep Mark and inevitably Harrison as well. She hadn't offered Harrison an apology for storming off, but she had texted him a link to some street art prints last week. He'd responded instantly and had also seen fit to update their mother, who had immediately followed up on his message with a heart emoji, a turtle, and a shooting star. Again, Ryley would have preferred being equated to another animal, like a bald eagle or a phoenix, but she'd make do.

* * *

Ryley walked rapidly to the last negotiation class of the year. The conversation with David had taken longer than she had expected and she was running late.

She didn't particularly mind that she wouldn't have time to chit-chat with Olivia beforehand; over the last two weeks, both had earnestly kept to topics as mundane as how they liked to drink their tea. Ryley didn't think they were in a fight, but she was taking the space to process things and Olivia seemed content to keep her emotional distance.

Ryley quickly dropped into the open seat next to Olivia just as Professor Poomin started speaking. Olivia's posture remained stiff with her back unnaturally straight. Ryley whispered a slightly out-of-breath "Hi."

Olivia merely looked over at her and gave her a small smile of acknowledgment.

Ryley asked, "Wait for me after class?"

Olivia kept the same placid smile on her face before murmuring, "Yeah, course I will."

Ryley turned her attention back to the professor just as she partnered them up for their newest negotiation exercise. Ryley was annoyed to see she'd been partnered with Zeke once more. However, this time around, she found herself only slightly ruffled when he badgered her. Zeke was reckless and over-confident. Observing him now, she stayed calm and told herself that she didn't need to reach a deal and said she was going to walk away. He was surprised. She was surprised. She'd become known as being very conciliatory. As she began to actually walk away from him, he finally called her back, realizing he could move to her and it wasn't solely her responsibility to move to him. When they exited the conference hall and walked back into the classroom, she found she was finally free of the slight resentment she normally nursed; indeed, for the first time, both she and Zeke looked at each other with genuine respect. When they shared the results in class, the wink Professor Poomin gave her was all she needed. Ryley was thrilled.

As Ryley waited for Olivia to finish packing, she couldn't stop shifting her weight from one foot to the other.

Finally, Olivia came to stand near Ryley. "So, what's up? Glad to almost be done with One-L?"

"Yeah, it ended up flying by."

"I'm sure. Are you nervous for exams?"

Ryley couldn't help the slight twitch of her shoulder. The conversation felt stilted and generic.

"Yes, but at the end of the day, either I'll do well or I won't. And either way, I'll still be standing and have two more years to learn what they want. Like you said at the Harvard-Yale game: there are so many ways to do things to make something of myself." Ryley looked over at Olivia as she finished her little monologue and was heartened to finally see a genuine smile though Olivia kept her gaze facing forward.

"Well, look at you being all zen," Olivia said but offered no further follow-up, content to let the sound of their feet pounding down the gray marble stairs be the only thing breaking the silence. Soon they'd be separating. Ryley clenched her fist, unclenched it, and then when they reached the bottom, before they'd swing open the double doors to brave the no longer terrible cold, Ryley said, "Wait. I broke up with David."

Olivia nodded, unsurprised, though she stopped walking, sitting down on the bench offset to the side instead. She was stiff with her arms crossed in front of her.

"What, you have nothing to say? Why are you being so weird?" Ryley settled down to sit next to her.

"I'm not being weird. I think I've been a bit too pushy lately and you seemed like you wanted space, so I wanted to give it to you." Olivia finally turned to look at her, her dark chocolate eyes contrite and her lips slightly downturned.

Ryley hurried to assure her, reaching out her hand to lightly squeeze Olivia's wrist. Olivia looked at her visibly surprised; Ryley never initiated contact.

"No, you were fine. You were right about David and me all along. I was just staying with him for the sake of feeling like I was doing life right; like I was walking the same successful path as everyone else."

Olivia nodded, but she was still sitting too straight, as if on a marionette string.

Before Ryley could say anything else, Cassidy exited the elevator directly across from the bench on which they were perched. Upon seeing the two of them sitting there, she paused and asked, "Ryley, are you coming to David's pregame tonight?"

"Nope, I'm going to sit this one out." She was tired of the games. Cassidy knew Ryley and David were giving each other space in the immediate aftermath of their breakup.

Cassidy hesitated and tucked a chunk of her hair behind her ear before saying, "Okay, if you're sure. I feel like this is going to be one of those nights that define One-L."

Ryley simply gave her a nod and a wave in response. Cassidy began walking away, and then, when she'd almost reached the door to exit the building, she suddenly stopped.

Swiveling her body back around, she said, "If you're not feeling like tonight is in the cards, I'd love to get coffee with you tomorrow. If you're up for it. I want to make sure I'm up-to-date with *all* my friends."

Ryley shot her a much more genuine, warm smile as she said, "Sure, I'd like that." She had no doubts that their relationship would continue to have its ups and downs, but so long as they remained equals, she'd be there for all of them.

After Cassidy walked away, Ryley would have been happy to spend the next ten minutes basking in quiet, contented self-admiration.

Olivia, however, had other ideas, so she broke the silence. "What are you going to do tonight if David's is not an option?"

"Nothing." The glee with which she said the word made Olivia flinch in surprise before a slow, steady smile unfurled on Olivia's face.

"Sounds like a good Thursday night."

"Yeah. Look, I want to thank you. Although your methods could really use some work, that *Supergirl* clip finally pushed me over the edge and I had the panic attack I've been on the verge of having for the last three months. I feel clearer now."

"Oh. Well, I'm sorry you had a panic attack, but it's good to hear that you feel clear?"

"Clearer. I'm still in the process of figuring out who I am, but there was at least some truth to what you said at Formal. I'll just have to figure out how much."

Olivia gave her a kind smile and lightly squeezed her arm before stepping back. "Take your time. There's no rush for any of this."

Ryley nodded in response, and through unspoken accord, the two girls decided to get up and make their way over to the door.

As they stepped outside into the only slightly windy night, Olivia turned to Ryley and asked, "But you're happy now?"

For the first time, without having to think about it and without having to compare her life to all the grand dreams she'd had for herself, Ryley said, "Yeah, I am." She was finally just living day to day—living for herself.

ACKNOWLEDGMENTS

————

There are so many people who have been essential to shaping me into the person I am today and I am eternally grateful for their mentorship and love. For the purposes of keeping this page relatively concise, I will focus on thanking people who directly contributed to making this book possible.

Thank you to Eric Koester for giving me the opportunity to join the Creator's Institute Program and to my editors, Karina Agbisit and Joanna Hatzikazakis, who were so crucial in helping me to shape this story. I am also incredibly grateful to Brian Bies, Kristy Carter, and the rest of the wonderful team at New Degree Press for making this manuscript a reality.

Thank you to Anna Goldberg, Anna Sarin, Bennett Levine, Colette Gilner, Connor Bernstein, Dana Bulik, Fergal Seiferth, Lakshmi Kumar, Lauren Li, and Morgan Franklin who were amazing and gave me their in-depth thoughts on my manuscript when I gave them an incredibly tight turnaround time.

And thank you foremost to my family: my twin brother, my older sister, my father, and my mother. They were incredibly patient and giving of their time, reading numerous drafts and spit-balling ideas with me. They also consistently provided me with support and encouragement, even when I was at my moodiest. So, although there were numerous times they wanted to kill me (they told me so), my being alive today to write this page is a testament to their self-restraint and love.

Lastly, I am immeasurably grateful to all the law school friends who talked with me about their experiences at Harvard, the high school friends who talked with me about their experiences at Harvard-Westlake, and all the friends who ever talked with me about their feelings of being the "other." All those late-night two a.m. conversations contributed to making this book possible; thank you from the bottom of my heart.

CPSIA information can be obtained
at www.ICGtesting.com
Printed in the USA
BVHW090629190521
607645BV00002B/236